NO PORT IN A STORM

ANNA BOWMAN THRILLERS
BOOK FOUR

Westley Enterprises Publishing
Helena, Montana
www.westleyenterprises.com

ISBN 979-8-9916308-3-2 (Paperback)
ISBN 979-8-9916308-4-9 (eBook)

For Linow and Duo, for teaching me how to write, how to drink whiskey, and how to stop caring so much what other people think.

ALSO BY AK WELLER

Enemy Closer

House on Fire

Bigger Fish

No Port in a Storm

The Lost Portrait

CONTENTS

NOTE ON THE 2ND EDITIONS

If you've already read the first editions of *Enemy Closer*, *House on Fire*, and *Bigger Fish*, along with their companion prequels *2.15.2020*, *Friday the 14th*, and *A Last Time for Everything*, you may be wondering whether you need to go back and read the second editions to pick the story up with *No Port in a Storm*.

You don't. Happy reading!

NO PORT IN A STORM

CAST

MOSTLY HEROES

Richard Beauchamp
*Upper management at the FBI;
Jim and Anna's boss;
It's pronounced "Beecham"*

Anna Bowman
*FBI Analyst from Texas;
Speaks several languages;
Kicks butt with Krav Maga;
Loves Dude, Jim, and guns*

Bruce & Evelyn Bowman
*Anna's dad and mom;
Live in Manchester, Texas*

Dude Bowman
Anna's German Shepherd

Emily Bowman
*Anna's older sister who just got
out of prison in Texas for drug-
related offenses*

Emma & Ellie Bowman
*Anna's nieces;
Emily's daughters*

James (Jim) Camposanto
*Anna's boss, paramour,
worst enemy, and favorite
person in the world; A rich,
arrogant jerkwad*

Dominique (Dom) Danes
*Anna's coworker, friend,
and neighbor; Jim's co-
conspirator and rising FBI star*

Luke Jackson
*Assassin; Anna's other
paramour; Used to work for
Marcel Marchand; Killed
Francisco Lira and
Fernando Serna*

MOSTLY VILLAINS

Paolo Barbato
*Jim's uncle; lives in hiding
somewhere in Italy;
Ordered the deaths of many
family members*

Thomas (Tommy) Holladay
*Anna's former partner,
presumed dead in Houston in
February 2020; Deserved it*

Philip Levin
*Anna's former boss who was
working for the Tres Islas
Cartel and went to prison
for trying to kill her*

Francisco Lira
*Tres Islas Cartel big wig killed
by Luke Jackson in Houston;
Son of Regina Lira*

Regina Lira
*Paolo's aunt; Lives in hiding
somewhere in Colombia; Head
of the Tres Islas Cartel*

David Marchand
*Youngest brother of Marcel
Marchand; Murdered in London
by culprits unknown*

Giles Marchand
*Middle brother of Marcel and
David; Terrible human being*

Marcel Marchand
*French crime boss; Luke
Jackon's former employer; Loves
no one but his dog*

Penelope Marchand
His dog

Fernando & Marisol Serna
*Brother and sister living in
hiding in Argentina until
Luke Jackson found and
killed Fernando*

Prologue
Anna's Story So Far

It all started in 2019, when James Camposanto ruined my life.

I wanted to be an FBI agent ever since I was a little girl, coming of age in rural Texas on a steady diet of X-Files, true crime TV shows, and history's most infamous unsolved art heists. I worked my butt off, learned multiple languages, graduated college twice, and landed an internship on the FBI's Art Crime Team. After nailing every test between me and agent, I scrubbed out and soon learned why: James Camposanto (Jim to me) had hand-picked me for a different operation, childhood dreams be darned.

That was New Year's Day, 2020. Two and a half months later, I nearly lost my life in Houston when my undercover operation with the Tres Islas Cartel was blown. My partner, Tommy, didn't make it out. Jim sent me to Colorado that summer to find and question an assassin who'd been in Houston that night, someone Jim claimed could help me get to the bottom of what

1

happened. By the end of 2020, I'd chased my assassin, Luke Jackson, all the way to London, only to discover he didn't have the information I needed.

As Jim had hoped all along, my entanglement with Luke got me sucked into Luke's world, a world where Jim had been pulling the strings since before I ever got to Washington, DC. I wrapped up 2020 in Berlin helping the German BKA out with a little side operation, then got on a plane to return home at long last. Instead of flying me home, Jim flew me to Argentina to meet his cousin, Fernando.

Fernando had something Jim wanted: *Portrait of a Young Man* by Raphael. Believe it or not, the Renaissance masterpiece stolen by Nazi looters in World War II was hanging in Fernando's house, and Jim was one of very few people who knew about it. The whole charade was supposed to end in me recovering the painting without Fernando knowing Jim put me up to it, and Luke Jackson was there to give Fernando a reason to hand it over. Not so unfortunately, Jim's psychotic cousin ended up dead at Luke's hands, and Fernando's sister, Marisol, was left on her own to clean up the mess.

Luke worked for a Frenchman named Marcel Marchand, and Marcel had recently partnered with an Italian named Paolo Barbato. At Paolo's request, Marcel had sent Luke to Houston, then to Argentina, to kill people who turned out to be related to one another, to Paolo, and even to Jim.

A picture is worth a thousand words:

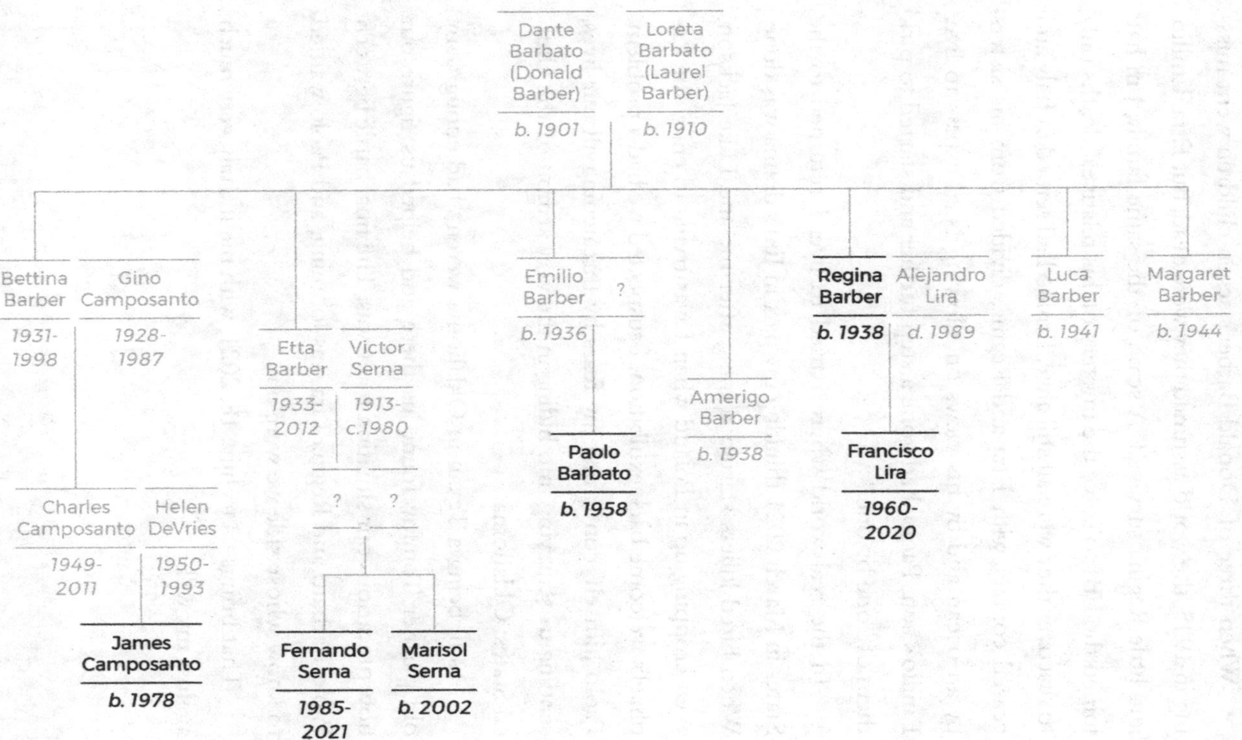

Dante Barbato (Donald Barber) b. 1901
Loreta Barbato (Laurel Barber) b. 1910
Bettina Barber 1931-1998
Gino Camposanto 1928-1987
Etta Barber 1933-2012
Victor Serna 1913-c.1980
Emilio Barber b. 1936
?
Amerigo Barber b. 1938
Regina Barber b. 1938
Alejandro Lira d. 1989
Luca Barber b. 1941
Margaret Barber b. 1944
Charles Camposanto 1949-2011
Helen DeVries 1950-1993
?
?
Paolo Barbato b. 1958
Francisco Lira 1960-2020
James Camposanto b. 1978
Fernando Serna 1985-2021
Marisol Serna b. 2002

When three of Donald Barber's seven children went missing in 1945, the world assumed they were dead; but Etta, Emilio, and little Regina survived. A scion of the same family, Jim had joined the FBI to solve the mystery of his relatives' deaths only to discover they were all still alive. Emilio had settled in Italy and ceased contact with Etta and Regina, divided from his sisters by an ocean and by his views on allowing Nazi expats to live. Emilio's son, Paolo, had gone a step further and started to pick them off one by one.

In the real world where I tried to live, I returned to the States in March 2021 thinking my part in Jim's drama was done. When hired killers started coming after me and Luke Jackson, even cropping up in Poland when I was trying to enjoy the Raphael's welcome back exhibition, I suspected we had a problem. Paolo himself confirmed my fears by threatening all our lives, sending us scurrying into hiding in the very armpit of the United States: Oklahoma.

As if being a Texan in Oklahoma weren't bad enough, my old partner Tommy found us there and helped us figure out how precarious our situation really was. The final battle between Paolo Barbato and Regina Lira was looming, and Paolo wanted to know whose side we were on.

That brings us to June 18, 2021, with me in Italy very much against my will.

1

Friday, June 18 to
Saturday, June 19, 2021

There is no rest for the wicked. My body was starved for sleep, my heart aching for a few hours of numbness, but my brain hummed and snapped like a bug zapper on a Louisiana summer night. *You can't close your eyes!* it sang. *You're in Florence. You speak Italian. Your window is open. Everyone else is asleep. You're only on the second floor. Climb out.*

Run.

"Well that's idiotic on its face," I whispered to the dark ceiling above where I lay.

An answer floated under my door in sotto voce Italian.

"Ho fame. Non ho mangiato tutto il giorno. C'è del cibo in casa?"

Translation: One of the men outside my door was hungry.

"Perché me lo chiedi? Non lo so. Vai in cucina e scoprilo. E portami del vino."

The other man wanted wine.

At least two other people weren't asleep, then—the two most likely to take umbrage to me climbing out my window and disappearing into the sultry Mediterranean night. I listened to the two men bickering, smiling to myself at the banality of their argument. After a minute or so, one set of feet clumped down the stairs in search of food and wine. Silence reigned until my inner voice chimed back in.

You love wine. Don't you want some wine right now? And some cheese? Cheese, Anna!

My brain had it right that time. I could most definitely go for some wine and cheese. My empty stomach was gurgling, and if I couldn't pass into dreamworld, I could at least numb my senses with alcohol. The problem remained what it had always been: the wickedness.

I climbed out of bed, disturbing no one. My travel companions, Tommy and Jim, had been taken to different rooms. I supposed Tommy was locked in like I was, and that was for the best. No one here trusted him, and God only knew what he'd do if left to his own recognizance. Jim, on the other hand, would be considered trustworthy enough to avoid the indignation of a locked door. All Paolo Barbato had to do was make the demand, and Jim had whisked Tommy and me from Texas to Florence to meet him.

Paolo Barbato and Jim. PB&J. It was worthy of being carved into a tree with a heart around it.

Tiptoeing to the window, I eased it open as far as it would go and leaned out over Via Riscoli. Though midnight approached, people were still out and about, mostly tourists by the look of them. Directly below me, a leggy blonde was sitting on the hood of a black Maserati, posing for a cameraman across the street. She kept shaking back her luxurious mane of curls, annoyed at the tourists wandering fecklessly between her and the camera.

I watched her for a while, then looked up over the city toward the Basilica di San Lorenzo. The floodlights illuminating its façade had been shut off, and I could barely make it out. Disappointed, I propped my elbow on the windowsill and rested my chin in my hand, not realizing what a poignant pose I'd struck until a waspy voice below caught my attention.

"Do you want to join us, lady?"

I peered down again at the Maserati model and saw her upturned face scowling at me. Her offer appeared to be sarcastic. The camera across the street was pointing up at me, which explained her verbal attack.

"Scusa," I mumbled.

I leaned back and shut the window, drowning out the woman's angry chattering as she berated her wayward cameraman. Glancing down at myself, I confirmed I was mostly decent in a silk camisole and pajama shorts. Another overpriced item I'd bought for this trip, to torture and punish Jim.

Thinking of Jim and why I was torturing him unleashed a wave of anger that cut right through me, heating me. A surprise vacation to Italy was far from the worst thing Jim had done to me, but I didn't want to be here. Not like this, not when we were so close to the finish line. How could he not see that?

I stalked to the door and rapped smartly on it.

From outside, a wary, "Sí?"

"Enzo?" I guessed. I'd known Enzo and Aldo all of an hour, so I was still learning to tell them apart.

"Sí."

In his native Italian, I asked, "Can you let me out? I'm hungry. I'm starving."

I felt his hesitation, which ended in a click as the door unlocked but didn't open. I did the honors, cracking the door to smile out at Enzo. Aldo was still downstairs.

"I heard you two talking," I confessed. "I could really use a glass of wine right now, you know?"

He smiled, revealing a row of straight, white teeth. I took a moment to study him more closely: dark eyes, nearly black to match his short-cropped hair that was beginning to curl at the ends, a straight, Roman nose, full lips, clean-shaven. He wasn't attractive per se, but individually his features were quite becoming.

A nasty little gremlin which had recently taken up residence where my soul used to be suggested an efficient and fun way to punish Jim. I smiled back.

"I won't cause any trouble," I whispered.

"Paolo told me to watch out for you. He said you're dangerous."

Paolo Barbato thought *I* was dangerous? That was high praise, coming from the mysterious mafioso whose Hatfield-and-McCoy-style vendetta had set all this in motion.

"Do I look dangerous to you?" I asked, opening the door all the way so he could make a proper risk assessment. The insubstantial pajamas, the long, red hair, the toned limbs, the breasts that weren't quite as perky as they were ten years ago but still held up thank you very much, all were supposed to be driving Jim crazy with hopeless longing. I wasn't above using them in a more roundabout way.

Enzo took his time studying me from head to toe before concluding, "Yes."

"What do you think I'll do? Try to leave? I want to meet Paolo."

Relenting with a sigh, he waved me out of the room. "Come downstairs. I'm sure we can find something to eat, if Aldo has left us anything."

I followed him down the stairs and through the darkened house to a kitchen at the back. Aldo was indeed within, standing by the island at the center of a small, homey kitchen and stacking together slices of tomato, mozzarella, and bread. He wasn't alone.

Leaning against the stove was James Camposanto, the very Jim I wished to torment. Tall and thin with salt-and-pepper hair and serious gray eyes that ordinarily drove me bananas with longing, the sight of him was currently a source of bitter irritation. He was sipping at a large glass of red wine and watching Aldo with detached interest, at least until Enzo and I appeared in the doorway.

"What are you doing up?" Jim asked me.

Neither Enzo nor Aldo understood his English question, but neither could mistake his hostility. They shared a glance, and Aldo forced a laugh.

Switching to English and a decidedly less seductive tone, I shot back, "What do you care?"

"Make me one of those," Enzo said before Jim could reply, gesturing at the massive sandwich Aldo was about to shove into his mouth. With a good natured grumble, Aldo complied. I sidled up next to him and stole a slice each of mozzarella and tomato, then sat down at a stool on the other side of the island to enjoy them.

The Florentine cocina wasn't so different from an ordinary kitchen back home in the States, but one feature kept me firmly grounded in reality: the heat. In Texas, my parents' AC would be cranking out cold air in June, even at night. Here a warm, sticky atmosphere pervaded indoors and out. One could catch a stray breeze outside, but the windowless kitchen was stuffy. I risked a quick glance at Jim to make sure he was wearing the long-sleeved t-shirt and flannel pajama pants I'd picked up especially for him. He was, and his forehead was glistening with sweat.

I smiled sweetly at him when he met my eyes. "Hot in here?"

He shook his head but didn't answer, giving his full attention back to his wine glass. Enzo sat down next to me and asked, "Can you ask him to share?"

He nodded toward the wine bottle at Jim's elbow. I hopped off my seat and fetched three more wine glasses from the cabinet next to Jim's head, ignoring him while I emptied the rest of his Chianti into the first glass, opened a second bottle from the rack behind him, and tipped a healthy measure into the other two glasses. These I took to Enzo and Aldo before returning for my glass.

"Why don't you put some clothes on?" Jim murmured, barely looking at me.

My answer was to return to my stool, facing Enzo with my back to Jim, and proceed to act as though Jim didn't exist.

It wasn't so much that Jim was angry at me. That was nothing new. I did things to make him angry all the time, most recently by leaving him, along with our friend Luke Jackson, my sister Emily, and my dog Dude, in the middle of a tornado in Oklahoma to climb into the trunk of a car and let Tommy unwittingly drive me to the Dallas-Fort Worth airport. It was an impulse, and Jim was quite accustomed to me following those.

If that wasn't the source of his rudeness, my second best guess was that Jim was mirroring my bad attitude, but that hardly made sense. Jim took pride in being the foil to my petty reactiveness, acting like he had ice in his veins, Mister Cool as a Cucumber.

Cucumber. Hng. I let my thoughts wander for a moment, then reeled them back in.

His rank hypocrisy was keeping my vindictiveness alive. Jim had put me through hell, almost two solid years of it, starting with ruining my dream of becoming an FBI agent in July 2019. A few months ago, he'd capped off months of lies and manipulation by tossing me between his cousins and an assassin's bullets, all so I could save his cousins by offering up a priceless, lost Renaissance masterpiece for their lives.

The whole tale is a little more complicated, but the point was simply that, after hearing Jim's full confession, I'd forgiven him. I'd come to a conscious decision, dismissing logic and evidence, to trust him. To *love* him. And there the smug puppet master sat, treating me like a wayward child, some kind of burdensome baggage, when it was his idea to drag me to Italy without even asking if I wanted to come.

"He really doesn't speak Italian?" Enzo asked.

I sensed his disbelief and shrugged. "He doesn't even know what 'Camposanto' means," I said, provoking a laugh from both men.

Jim was far too genteel to let us get to him, giving no sign he'd heard his own name.

Enzo cast a hooded glance at Jim and asked me, "Can you tell him we don't mean any offense? I don't think we're making a great first impression on our cousin."

"Cousin?" I echoed, ignoring the rest.

"Aldo is my brother—well, half-brother—and Paolo is our father. So that would make James a… second cousin? Something like that."

"But you'd never met him until today?"

"Nope."

"Don't waste any time worrying about his feelings," I said. "He doesn't have any."

"Why did you come here with him, if you hate him so much?"

I thought hate was a bit strong, but rather than correcting him, I repeated my earlier lie. "I told you, I want to meet Paolo. Why isn't he coming until tomorrow?"

"He's a little paranoid. Don't worry. He's eager to meet you, too."

That may have been true, but it wasn't the reason Paolo was coming. Neither was Jim. The third member of our party, who was hopefully still locked in his room upstairs, was the real reason Paolo was emerging from wherever he'd been hiding from his family, why he'd ordered Jim to Florence. That would be Tommy Holladay, who'd entered my life two years ago a fresh-faced, eager trainee at the FBI's Organized Crime Unit and left it a violent, angry casualty of an undercover operation in Houston that went pear-shaped in the blink of an eye.

At least I thought he'd left my life. Tommy had turned up last month, alive and not-so well, seeking safe harbor. He'd claimed he was living in fear of Philip Levin, our former boss who'd personally betrayed and sent us to our deaths in Houston. That claim turned out not to be super duper true. Tommy was, in fact, now working for a woman named Regina Lira. Paolo had ordered Regina's son, Francisco, killed that same night in Houston.

Paolo had accepted Tommy as a peace offering from Jim, and here we were to deliver him on a silver platter. I assumed Tommy was lying awake this very moment, wondering if he knew enough about Regina to make himself useful to Paolo, and what would happen if he didn't.

2

Saturday, June 19, 2021

"Are you still hungry?" Enzo asked, drawing me out of my grim thoughts.

"Not really. I am bored, though. You'd think I'd be tired after the trip, but I'm wired."

"Wired?"

"Lots of energy. Too much." He studied me, curious, and I added, "Will you and Aldo stay here tonight, too? To guard us?"

"Do you need to be guarded?"

"Oh yeah." I grinned. "I'm a handful, Enzo. You better keep a close eye on me."

I caught a familiar gleam in his dark gaze. It was jarring, seeing those eyes from Argentina to Italy, in the face of every member of this family I'd met so far. Jim, Fernando and Marisol Serna, even Francisco Lira, they'd all at one time or another subjected me to that unnerving glimpse into a roiling soul either fighting or embracing something dark, something they all shared.

Maybe it had something to do with the violent and tragic way their progenitors had been flung to their own corners of the globe. Over 75 years ago, a house fire had supposedly claimed the lives of three of Italian expat Donald Barber's seven children. Etta, Emilio, and little Regina. I'd remember their names 'til my dying day.

From Etta sprang the Serna family of Argentina, of whom 19-year-old Marisol was the sole surviving member. Little Marisol had Paolo to thank for it. He'd employed none other than my friend Luke Jackson to finish off the last two Sernas, and Luke had half succeeded.

Emilio was Paolo's father, the grandfather of Enzo and Aldo. He held the honor of igniting this feud by turning on Etta and Regina, then passing the torch to his only son, Paolo. No one knew where Emilio was, if he still lived. The Barbato clan had gone to ground somewhere in their native Italy.

And Regina Lira… She'd be in her early 80s now, but the years hadn't cooled her blood one degree. After Paolo ordered the murder of her only child, the gloves formally came off. Whyever she and Paolo's side of the family had split, she was as determined to punish Paolo as Paolo was to find and kill her. Like Paolo, her exact whereabouts were unknown, but no one believed she'd left Colombia since finding herself there in the 1950s.

There were other Barbers scattered around the United States, descendants of the four children who'd officially survived the fire. Jim was one of them, his grandmother, Bettina, being the eldest of the Barber children. So far as I had any reason to believe, Jim was the only member of his family who knew

Etta, Emilio, and Regina had survived, let alone that a war raged among their offspring.

And there I sat, mixed up in it because Jim had seen fit to impress me into his service. What a lucky girl I am. My family back in Texas, to include Luke, was probably in a fair amount of jeopardy too, but there was nothing I could do about that except what I was doing, namely trying to bring all this to a conclusion. Luke would have to deal with the there-and-now in Texas, and I knew he was good for it even if my sister Emily could occasionally be a handful and a half.

If Enzo noticed my thoughts wandering again, he didn't mention it. He continued to scrutinize me with frank curiosity while I savored my Chianti and mentally rampaged through the pages of Barber family history.

"Pedal faster, brother," Aldo mumbled, a smile in his voice.

"It's a children's game," Enzo argued.

"Your eyes are bigger than your stomach," Aldo shot back.

For once I knew how Jim felt as the brothers started a rapid-fire volley of idiomatic expressions in Italian, each more nonsensical than the last. They were being deliberately cryptic at my expense, or I was misinterpreting the occasional taunting grin thrown my way.

Having taken the trouble to learn Spanish, Italian, French, German, and even a bit of Portuguese *and* Polish, I was unaccustomed to being shut out of a conversation. I didn't like it.

I stood, interrupting Aldo in the middle of something about green mice. "Well, I'm going to be a bad sport and go to bed. Good night."

Someone followed me out of the kitchen, and though I hoped it was Enzo, intuition told me he was too smart to let himself be a pawn in whatever miserable game Jim and I were playing. Sure enough, when I reached my room and turned around at the door, I found Jim looking down at me.

He slipped the half-full wine glass out of my hand, tipped it back in one swallow, and wished me the most sarcastic good night I'd ever heard. I shut the door with gusto and flipped him off through the wood. Alone in my room again, I consoled myself with the knowledge that I had introduced sufficient booze and food into my system to lull me to sleep at last.

While the alcohol and calories did their thing, I did my best to convince myself I was excited, not afraid. Not a month ago I'd been certain Paolo wanted Jim and me dead. He had taken such exception to our combined efforts to save Jim's young cousin, Marisol, from Paolo's chopping block. We'd been so certain Jim was on Paolo's kill list that we'd gone into hiding in Oklahoma, of all Godforsaken places. Even if Paolo didn't care to whack me too, someone did. A string of attacks from Albuquerque to Kraków had me convinced on that score.

Logic was my ultimate refuge and the lullaby that sang me to sleep at last: Paolo didn't need to be in Florence to kill us, and we didn't need to be here to die.

▼

My sleep was short but heavy, leaving me wide awake in the predawn hours of Saturday morning. I planted myself in front of the window again, gazing at a sliver of the Basilica di San Lorenzo and recalling my last trip to Florence. It compared quite favorably to the current visit.

I had peeled away from my tour group and stumbled into the cool, deserted basement of San Lorenzo. Alone and ignored, I'd spent an hour rhapsodizing over the sculpted marble figures in the Medici Chapel. I couldn't believe I was standing a few feet away from the work of Michelangelo's own two hands, completely unsupervised just a stone's throw from the sea of tourists in the street above. I'd never been ambushed by art before. That was why I fell in love with Florence.

In the dismal present, I stared at the basilica until weariness lured me back to bed, and I fell asleep and woke up almost in the same instant. The room was still dark, but it had changed.

Someone was sitting on the edge of my bed. More than half asleep, I mumbled, "Jim?"

His familiar silhouette excited me, urging me to reach for his tall, angular body and pull it down onto mine, until I remembered we were mad at each other.

"I would appreciate you exercising restraint while you're punishing me."

Fewer than half his words made it through the haze of sleep that was trying to drag me back under, but his disdainful tone did the rest. I sat up, switched on my bedside lamp, and held my watch three inches from my nose to see its face.

"It's four a.m.," I whined.

"Did you hear what I said?"

"Not really."

"I get that you have to punish me for bringing you here, even if I don't know why. I'm asking you to draw the line at screwing my cousin just to get back at me."

Rage pulled at me again. Why couldn't he just *ask* me why I was mad?

"Nobody's screwing anybody's cousin," I grumbled. "Get out of my room. Go away." When he didn't immediately comply, I gave him a couple half-hearted shoves. "You're the one punishing me. You won't even let me sleep. Do you have any idea how daggum tired I am?"

Unmoved, he pressed, "Tell me you'll leave Enzo alone."

"I'll do what I want." After one final shove, he took me by the shoulders and held me at arms' length. Savagely, seeking to wound, I breathed, "Thanks for letting me know it bothers you."

"You're too old to act like this," he fired back. He let go of me, stood, and snarled, "Grow up."

Stung into silence, I watched him leave and twitched in surprise as he slammed the door shut. Why did he have to cut right to the bone like that? Switching back to anger, which was safer, I got up and left the room right behind Jim. He was already at his door, freezing as I passed him on my way to the stairs. I could feel his eyes on my back as I made a beeline for the front door, but at the last second I turned left and let myself into the empty sitting room off the foyer.

I curled up in a leather armchair, dragged a quilt over me, and stared out the window. There I sat, waiting for the city to wake up, come to life, and give me something to think about other than how mad I was.

Ever eager to help, my brain reminded me that I was also terrified. It took me back to Jim's kitchen three weeks ago, where I'd seen the message from Paolo that had sent us scurrying into hiding. Paolo had received a letter from Marisol, a cutesy card and a note letting him know that she was thinking of him. With the card was an old photo of Etta and Regina, a too-subtle hint which Tommy himself had helped us interpret: Marisol and Regina were together now, and hell had no fury to match theirs. Paolo had killed Marisol's mother, father, and brother; and he'd done the same for Regina's son.

Marisol had almost certainly figured out Jim and I were in cahoots with Paolo through his hired killer, Luke Jackson. Now Regina knew, too. But Marisol had sent her message to Paolo, and it was Paolo who had forwarded it to Jim. Marisol would be out of the picture if it weren't for me, and I wanted to know exactly how Paolo felt about that.

I didn't remember nodding off, but when I woke up, the room was bright and warm, the window was cracked, and Paolo Barbato was sitting in the armchair next to me.

3

Saturday, June 19, 2021

"Good morning, Anna," Paolo said, giving me a tight smile.

He nodded at a small table between us, where two perfect little cups of espresso sat steaming in the fresh sunlight.

"You look like you could use a double serving."

Struck dumb, I smoothed back my tangled hair and rubbed my face, trying to wake up. While I sorted myself out, Paolo added two cubes of sugar to his espresso. He offered me the bowl of sugar cubes.

I shook my head, cleared my throat, and said, "No, thank you. Where's Jim?"

"Still asleep, along with everyone else in the house. A lazy generation, the lot of you," he concluded, frowning into his beverage.

I couldn't think of a defense for that, so I picked up my espresso and sipped at it while taking the measure of this man who'd played such a crucial role in my life.

An image flashed through my head of a black-and-white poster hanging in Jim's office in DC. Donald Barber had it made following the disappearance of three of his children in 1945. Emilio Barber, aged nine at the time, was by far the best looking of the children with his heavy, stern brow, strong chin, and straight nose. I recalled thinking he looked like an old soul.

Paolo, his son, bore all the same defining features, though his thick crown of hair had faded to a steely gray. Seated, I pegged him at 5'10" tops. Now in his 60s, Paolo's physical age had caught up with the dark, solemn eyes he'd inherited from his father. Paolo studied me right back, a slow smile revealing unexpected laugh lines.

"So, we meet at last. James has told me little enough about you."

"Likewise," I whispered.

"Now that you're here, will you accept my apologies for that business with the card from Marisol? I fear I may have misdirected my anger." He waited for a response, continuing when none came, "I should have known the little Serna girl would provoke your compassion. She was Jackson's to kill, and so it is his fault she's still alive."

"Maybe you should have left them alone," I suggested.

"Perhaps you're right," he sighed, then shook his head as though to fling away an irksome fly. "How it rankled me, their fortune built on Nazi plunder. It wasn't their fault. They were born into it."

"At least the Raphael is back where it belongs," I allowed.

Paolo nodded. I was tempted to ask him how and when he'd

learned of the painting's existence, but by then it was a moot point. Everyone in the world—at least everyone who watched the news—knew about it, and about Jim's and my connection to it. If Paolo wasn't among the few who knew Fernando Serna had been hiding it in Argentina, I'd just rung that bell for good.

Instead I asked, "How did Marisol know where to send the card?"

"And why send a card instead of a bag of anthrax?" he asked, rounding out my thought.

"Well… yeah."

"Occasionally my aunt and I exchange addresses," he said casually, as though this weren't the most confusing answer imaginable. He caught my expression and added, "Post office boxes, of course. She can't resist taunting me… I admit, I fall to the same impulse from time to time."

"Haven't you ever tried to track her back to where she's living when someone picks up her mail?" I asked.

"Of course. She has tried as well. Unsuccessfully, but why else should we bother mailing anything?" He shifted in his seat, frowning again. "You ask as many questions as Jim. It's impolite."

"Sorry."

I knocked back the rest of my espresso in one gulp, begging the bitter bean juice to do its good work before I thought of another question.

"I was there," I said. "When Luke came to kill Fernando and Marisol. You know that already, though. No matter what, I would have stopped him from killing her. You shouldn't blame Luke."

Paolo granted me a philosophical smile and muttered, "You

will both come to regret letting her live. I no longer believe it's my responsibility."

"So… you won't do anything to hurt Luke?"

"You care for him?"

"Yes. Very much."

"Then consider him forgiven. I have much more substantial problems now, as do you."

"I… I do?"

Rather than clarifying, he took the empty cup from my hands, stood, and asked, "Another?"

"Oh, um. Yes, please. Thank you."

He carried both cups away, leaving me bewildered while the concentrated caffeine set my heart racing. I can't say being waited on by an Italian crime boss while clad only in my pajamas was pleasant, but it was certainly novel.

I took in the view through the street-facing window until I heard what I thought was Paolo returning. Turning, I saw Jim standing in the doorway, regarding me with an unreadable expression.

He'd already gotten dressed and, I realized, was doing the exact same thing to me that I'd been doing to him. In a tailored black suit, black tie, and black shirt, he looked dapper as all get out and too expensive to touch. I'd never appreciated until that moment how intensely Italian he was, likely because his grey eyes, above-average height, and ignorance of the language set him so far apart from his countrymen. Also, he wasn't all that hairy. A real winner of the genetic lottery, this man.

Favoring me with a brief smirk, he asked almost pleasantly,

"How do I look?"

"Dreadful."

"Good, that's what I was going for. I thought I heard Paolo."

"He went to the kitchen. You just missed him."

Jim walked away without another word. Now that he'd forced me to feel like a stray cat that had wandered across his path, I dashed upstairs to take a shower.

▼

Once I'd showered, dried my hair, brushed my teeth, and thrown on a white cotton dress, I didn't feel quite so feral. I made the mistake of leaving the bathroom door open while I braided my hair, leaving Tommy free to duck inside to brush his teeth while both my hands were fully occupied.

"Wow, just make yourself at home," I muttered.

Around his toothbrush, he asked, "What? You want me to leave?"

"Ugh. Whatever, I don't care."

For about a minute we saw to our individual tasks with laser focus, then Tommy rinsed out his mouth and said, "We could address the resident pachyderm if you want to."

I was down to the last few inches of hair, my arms aching from the prolonged effort. The pachyderm to which he presumably referred, namely the violent sexual assault I'd endured at Tommy's hands last year, was the very last thing I wished to address.

Moodily, I spat, "I do not want to."

"Ever?"

I finished, tied off the end, flipped the braid behind my back, and snarled, "I don't even want to *think* about it, let alone talk about it, let alone with *you*. How could that not be self-evident?"

Pausing to judge the effect of my words, I noticed two things at once. Tommy actually looked stricken and saddened by my diatribe, and he was blocking the bathroom door, the only exit. If not for the first fact, the second would've launched me straight into fight-or-flight.

"Yeah, well," he mumbled, tossing his toothbrush into the sink and slouching away. I refused to feel pity, recoiling at the very suggestion of it. The nerve of him, cornering me and trying to make me talk about *that*. I took one last, evaluating look in the mirror, rearranged my snarl into a Mona Lisa smile, and started to follow Tommy downstairs.

I was arrested at the top of the stairs by the sight of Enzo standing in the open doorway to my room, beckoning silently to me with his finger. I changed course, started to ask what he wanted, and clamped my mouth shut as he pressed a demonstrative finger to his lips.

I waited until he'd shut the door softly behind us to ask, "What in the world do you want?"

He gestured to the bed and said, "Sit down, please. Don't worry, it's a good surprise."

"Okay…" I did as instructed, a nervous laugh bursting out of me as he knelt in front of me and reached for something underneath the bed. Baffled into silence, I watched him pull out a shoebox that wasn't there when I'd gone to bed last night.

Flashing me a grin, he pulled out a pair of plain, black stilettos and held them up for me to see.

"I went down the street and bought these while you were in the shower. Sorry, but I had to look through your luggage to make sure I had the right size. What do you think?"

I studied the six-inch, razor thin heel, supple-looking leather, and violently crimson soles and concluded, "I am very confused right now."

"Let me explain." He untied my left sandal, slipped it off, and slid his hand up my leg to grasp me by the back of the knee while he slid the stiletto onto my foot.

Until that moment, I'd have bet every penny in Jim's bank account that putting on a shoe couldn't feel naughty. Another nervous laugh slipped out of me, followed by a barely audible, "Wow."

"Do they fit okay?"

"Uh huh. Why did you buy me shoes? Not that I'm ungrateful."

While he repeated the process for my right foot, he explained, "I have nothing against my cousin, but it seems to me he's treating you very badly. And Aldo was good enough to point out last night after we were so unkind to you, that a man only lives once."

"I'm not following."

In answer, he lifted my right foot off the ground, pressed his lips to my ankle, and began kissing a path up my leg.

My mouth formed the word, "Oh," but no sound came out. Had the preceding conversation not taken place in Italian, I wasn't sure I'd have allowed him to continue, but there's something about a romance language.

Once his lips reached my inner thigh, I gave up and flopped backward onto the bed. Not only was that how Jim found us one second later, but I was sure beyond a reasonable doubt that Enzo meant for it to happen that way. I was so near catatonia by then, I didn't even bother to sit up.

"Go away, we're busy," Enzo said into my skin.

Jim crossed the room in two strides, lifted Enzo by the back of his shirt, and threw him bodily from the room. He slammed the door shut and rounded on me.

"Seriously, Anna?"

"He came at me like a tiger," I sighed, totally unrepentant. "I had no defense. Besides," I added, rising to my elbows to glower at him. "It's not like he was invading anyone's turf."

Jim's eyes burned into mine, convincing me he was moments from picking up right where Enzo left off; but his gaze faded back into calm disdain, his voice turning to steel. "I'm not letting you do this to me. Understand?"

"No."

"Paolo is waiting for us downstairs. Let's go." When I collapsed back onto the bed, he grabbed me by the arm and hauled me to my feet, gritting out, "Stop it, Anna. Do you have no shame at all?"

I pushed his hand off my arm. "Why would you even ask me that? You know I don't."

"Yeah, I know."

Still a little punch drunk, I trailed him to the door and held him back, asking, "Wait, wait. What are we doing?"

"What do you mean?"

I shook my head to clear it. "With Paolo. Now. What are we…?"

"We're getting out of here, if we can. We brought Tommy. That was the deal."

"We're just leaving him here?"

"Is that a problem?" he asked.

"I… I don't know. It sounds a little heartless, even for you."

"Does it?" he asked, not caring. "How about you just keep your mouth shut down there?"

My mood turned on a dime, and before I knew what I was doing, I'd slapped him across the face and hissed, "Stop being so mean to me. Just *stop.*"

Jim rubbed a hand across his cheek, more surprised than hurt, and favored me with an evaluating look before he leaned in close to whisper, "You first."

He stalked away. I knew my cheeks were flushed, my ears glowing red, when I slid into a seat at the table in the courtyard where Paolo, Tommy, and Jim were waiting. There was nothing I could do about the blood rushing to my cheeks, so I stared holes into the tablecloth and tried to compose myself while Paolo got down to business.

"So, young man. You've been working for my aunt."

Tommy replied, "She didn't give me much choice, but yeah."

"Regina Lira is a very powerful woman," Paolo agreed. "Did you tell her I was behind the assassination of her loathsome son?"

"No."

"What did you do for her exactly?"

"I was tracking the guy who killed her son. From a distance."

Before Tommy could blunder on, Jim cut in. "Regina has been tracking Luke all this time, since Houston, with the help of Tommy and their boss, Philip Levin. Levin dropped out of the picture. She must have made the connection to Anna and me when we were all in New Mexico earlier this year."

Paolo asked, "How did she know you were in Mexico?"

"*New* Mexico," Jim corrected. "I don't know, but she must have figured it out. She sent someone to kill Anna there."

"Did she?" Paolo asked. I glanced up and realized the question was directed at me.

"I think so," I said.

"But why you?"

I started to answer, found I couldn't, and looked unwillingly at Jim. He replied for me, "I used the GPS tracker in Anna's dog to lead Luke to Fernando and Marisol in Argentina. Anna knew nothing about it, but Regina can't possibly know that. There's no reason Regina would hold Anna any more blameless than Luke, or you. Or me, for that matter."

"Has she sent assassins after you?" Paolo asked Jim.

"Well… no."

Jim turned to Tommy, who hurried to add, "I didn't know about anyone trying to kill Anna or Jackson. Regina doesn't tell me everything."

Paolo cut to the heart of the matter by asking, "What does she tell you?"

<h1 style="text-align:center">4</h1>

Saturday, June 19, 2021

I hated to admit it, even to myself, but Tommy's reply was pretty stinking brave.

"Regina tells me a lot, and I'll tell you anything you want to know. But I need to know you'll keep me safe from her. Once she knows I've betrayed her, I'll move up to second place right under Jackson."

"Rest assured, young Mister Holladay, Regina will never get her hands on you after this."

Tommy paled, hearing the would-be assurance for what it was. Ever the white knight, Jim took the opportunity to ask, "And us, Paolo?"

"I would like you to stay," the old man said gravely.

"What can we do, now that we're here?" Jim asked. I wasn't sure if this was an offer of assistance or an argument.

Readily, Paolo answered, "You can represent the might of the Federal Bureau of Investigation at a meeting among Marchand, my Sardinian associates, and myself. We must dismantle Regina's Tres Islas Cartel to the benefit of all parties."

Tommy and I were suitably impressed by the gravity with which Paolo delivered this pronouncement, but Jim shook his head and countered, "I can't help you there. I assumed you knew: Anna and I don't represent the FBI anymore. Not that Anna ever really did," he added spitefully, throwing me a loaded glance. I glared at him but otherwise held my tongue.

"Don't patronize me," Paolo warned. "I know why you were supposedly placed on leave, and I know what will happen when you return to Washington. You fled your home because of my threat, and leaving the FBI was merely part of a story you wished to tell to anyone who would listen."

Rather than arguing the point, Jim shrugged it off. "Be that as it may, the FBI exists to enforce U.S. laws in the United States. You'll want to go to the CIA for help this time. This is an entirely international matter."

"Is it? Regina has her tendrils in the United States through the Port of Houston, Texas. Marcel has his operation in Atlanta, and now he has partnered with my family here in Italy with their reprehensible trade in human beings. I would think an FBI man of your caliber would be quick to see the implications for domestic law enforcement."

Jim frowned but didn't respond.

"I know you've been playing both sides, James," Paolo went on, "and I don't blame you at all. It's your job. Ridding the world of my criminal relations is a passion of mine, but why should you make a distinction between them and me?"

"What about Marcel?" I challenged, reminding Paolo of his French middleman. "He's Luke's boss. He's a criminal, him and his disgusting brother. He just gets to swoop in and operate at his leisure once all the Barbers are out of the way?"

"That is up to the FBI," he dismissed. "I seem to recall the American government displaying a preference for keeping their enemies close."

No one had an answer to that, least of all me. I met Tommy's eyes, reading in them a question I couldn't quite discern. He looked away before I could figure it out.

"What about Anna, then?" Jim asked. "We don't need her here. Send her home."

I stared at Jim and tried to guess whether he'd just changed his mind or was deploying reverse psychology on Paolo. His studiously blank expression was unhelpful.

Paolo asked, "With Regina flinging assassins at her right and left? I'm shocked at your lack of concern, James."

"Of course I'm concerned," Jim sighed. "But you're talking about a meeting that includes Marcel and Giles Marchand. I'm not sure what they'll do if they see her again. For all we know, they blame her for David's death."

I interjected, "I don't care, I'm not afraid of them. I don't want to go home."

Had Jim used reverse psychology on *me?*

"Anna—" Jim started, only to be cut off by a wave of Paolo's hand.

He said, "You heard her, James. Didn't you tell me yourself not so long ago that it's easiest to give the lady what she wants?"

I glared at Jim again, taking this as an insult no matter how Jim had meant it. He avoided my gaze and offered no further argument about me staying.

"Good," Paolo smiled. "As to the rest of it?"

"It can't hurt to meet with them," Jim relented.

"Unless they kill us," Tommy pointed out. No one had an answer for that, either.

▼

By the end of lunch, Tommy had not yet been forced to part with any information about Regina. We had come to a consensus about this all-important meeting: Paolo would contact the relevant parties, Jim would find a suitable location, and Tommy and I would stay out of their way.

After his brief display of testicular fortitude, Tommy reverted to the nervousness he'd exhibited since I'd ambushed him at DFW Airport and wrestled the truth about Regina from him. He was only too happy to be ignored by Paolo, as happy as I was to avoid Jim. Tommy elected to pass his free time in his room doing who knew what, but I wasn't about to ogle Florence from my window all day.

I dug through my suitcases and put together the most Italian outfit I'd been able to assemble from among the offerings in DFW malls—black shorts, a loose, white cotton shirt, and my strappy gladiator sandals. I knew I looked like a tourist trying not to look like a tourist, but I was fine with it.

Enzo and Aldo, easily located in the kitchen again, seemed fine with it, too. The latter flashed an unsolicited thumbs up from behind another massive sandwich, while the former poured me a glass of sparkling water and handed it to me with a wink.

"You look warm," he said.

I downed half the glass before replying, "I am. Hasn't air conditioning technology made it to Italy yet?"

"You could go to an American hotel," Aldo suggested.

Forcing back a burp, I asked eagerly, "I can?"

"Well, no," Enzo said. "But it's cooler outside in the breeze. Paolo said I could show you around the city, if you promise not to ditch me."

I missed neither the sharp look Aldo shot his brother nor the impish gleam in Enzo's eyes, but I chose to ignore the obvious meaning. An escape, a day of fun, and an unrepentant return was exactly the sort of stress I felt honor-bound to inflict on Jim. Enzo's company was hardly a concession, as I wasn't at all opposed to more attention from my silver-tongued young Italian.

Paolo and Jim needed time to set up this grand meeting Paolo envisioned, so Enzo and I had all day to kill. We slipped quietly through the front door, leaving Aldo behind to make our apologies and excuses, and stopped first at a trattoria for espresso and breakfast. After dragging Enzo to San Lorenzo to spend a little more time with Michelangelo's Medici Chapel sculptures, I gave him the reins and followed him around to his heart's content. We ate lunch, then dinner, burning through pasta, pizza, and gelato with a multi-mile foot tour of the entire old city on both sides of the Arno. Feet aching, we stopped last at the Piazzale Michelangelo to watch the sun set behind the duomo.

I sat on the steps next to Enzo and leaned back on my arms, savoring the ache in my muscles and the glow on my skin. We watched the distant duomo change colors in the setting sun, a young couple furiously canoodling a few feet in front of us. A photographer in a long, flowing skirt occasionally obstructed our view of the city center as she moved back and forth in search of the perfect shot. Her movements were oddly mesmerizing, exaggerated by the swish and twirl of her skirt.

"Is this the weirdest day of my life?" I mused in English.

"What?" Enzo asked.

"Nothing. We should go back soon, right? I don't want you to be in too much trouble."

"Who's in trouble? I said Paolo was okay with it."

"But you were lying," I reminded him. He grinned.

We took a cab back to the house, where the recriminations unfolded a bit less dramatically than anticipated. Paolo was waiting for us in the front room, but he looked more tired than angry.

"Finally," he said, not looking at us as he rose from his seat and stomped toward the back of the house. Enzo followed him, mumbling halfhearted apologies, and I marched upstairs to send myself to bed in the absence of anyone else bothering to do it.

Cranky that my latest tantrum hadn't provoked the response I wanted, I shut my door too hard and sat down on the floor to yank off my sandals. On top of everything, sadness was creeping up on me from one too many days without Dude. Just when

I thought I was done ruining his life, there I was on another dogless adventure. He would have loved the tour of Florence.

A couple bumps from the room next door were all the warning I got before Jim let himself into my room without so much as a perfunctory knock.

I leaned back on my arms, one sandal half off, to gaze up at him and ask, "What?"

Without a word, he shut the door, knelt down in front of me, and started taking off my left sandal. I shrugged and finished with the right one, and then Jim stood and offered me his hand.

Though I took it and allowed him to haul me to my feet, I asked, "Cat got your tongue?"

"No."

When I tried to take a step back, he pulled me forward by the shirt and held me there. With his lips brushing my temple, I caught a delicate whiff of something—whiskey, or bourbon. Maybe scotch. His hand twisted into my braid and tightened, forcing my face up toward his, and I tasted it on his tongue. Definitely scotch.

He was still wearing the black shirt I'd seen him in this morning, but the tie was gone. Since he probably hadn't even left the house, I wanted to ask why he'd bothered getting so dressed up. My mouth was busy though, and something told me Jim wasn't in a talking mood, so I worked the first few buttons on his shirt free.

No sooner had I started kissing his chest than I spotted another distraction: a bruise about the size of a kiwi to the left of his sternum. It was fresh but healing, deep purple and ringed by a larger circle of yellow. I ran my fingers over the spot, not wanting to ask what happened. It didn't take a genius to work it out, since I had a couple similar (though smaller) dings from flying debris. For all I knew, he had other injuries. I hadn't touched him, had hardly looked at him for days.

"You're mad at me for getting in Tommy's car," I suggested. "And for leaving you behind, right? You're trying to get me to apologize, aren't you?"

"Try it out," he said, not caring.

"You expect me to fall all over myself apologizing for that one thing after I forgave you for what you put me through in Argentina, and did you ever apologize for that?"

Jim tried to shut me up with a kiss, but I twisted away, far from finished.

"No, you didn't, and if you want to argue the point, I'm happy to walk you through each and every thing you *did* apologize for that *wasn't* literally the worst—the *third* worst thing anyone has ever done to me. So you want an apology? Here's your apology: If I hadn't done it, Tommy'd be in Colombia with Regina right now, and we'd still be up crap crick in Bumblescum, Oklahoma waiting around for someone or something to try to kill us, and I'm *sorry* you fail to see that!"

He leapt into action the moment I ran out of steam, switching from cold detachment to impassioned self-defense so quickly I actually twitched in surprise.

"You just made it perfectly clear that you haven't even come close to forgiving me for Argentina. So go right ahead and be mad about that, and I'll be mad about Oklahoma, and we'll both *die mad.*"

He backed me toward the bed and pushed me onto it, then without a word he turned and stalked back to the door. Leaving in the middle of an argument—That was novel. I sprang back to my feet and followed him to the door.

"So you forfeit," I said, causing him to pause with his hand on the doorknob.

He turned back to me, grabbed me by the hair again, and said against my lips, "We'll talk about this later."

Then he was gone, leaving me and our argument half finished. I crawled into bed and fought sleep while I waited for him to come back, but I couldn't keep my eyes open. I fell asleep alone, and I woke up alone.

5

Sunday, June 20, 2021

"Enzo told me he lied to you. Is this true?"

I tore my gaze from my plate and unwillingly met Paolo's eyes. Having eaten most of my breakfast in silence, joined only by Paolo at the little table in the kitchen, I'd been hoping to get through it without conversing.

I nodded. "Don't come down on him too hard. I knew he was lying."

"Did you speak to anyone while you were out? Did you call anyone?"

"No," I sighed. "Enzo was very careful. He didn't let me out of his sight. He wouldn't even let me have a cappuccino after noon."

Though he started to smile, a scowl won out. "Leave them alone. Both of them." He stirred sugar into his third cup of espresso, then pointed at me with the spoon. "They're young and stupid. They think you're just a pretty girl. I can't convince them to be smart, so you will be smart for them. Am I clear?"

I held the old man's gaze, my mind racing. He'd just told me so much. He thought I *wasn't* just a pretty girl, and he thought I was smart. Or at least that I could act smart. I had to know more. The misleadingly direct approach seemed best.

"Why do you even want me here?" I asked.

He stirred his espresso a couple more times before answering. I wondered if he was loading up the spoon to fling espresso at me, but he let it fall against the side of the cup with a delicate *tink*.

"I did not expect James to bring you, but now that you're here, I do want you to stay."

I love it when people answer the wrong question. I took a drink of my own espresso to hide a smile. So this was all Jim's idea.

Paolo went on, "He seems to think you'll be useful, and I have to agree. You speak several languages, and you can fight. Who knows… Depending on how this meeting goes tonight, James may prove prescient."

"Wouldn't be the first time," I agreed.

"You and I will have no quarrel if you leave Enzo and Aldo alone. Yes?"

It was probably for the best. The stab of disappointment precipitated by Paolo's words was a sign I'd already allowed myself to become too attached to Enzo.

"Yes. I will."

"Good. We will leave in a few hours. Please be ready."

Paolo and Jim spent the beginning of the day the same way they'd spent yesterday, shuttered in Paolo's study, making phone calls, and negotiating arrangements for the meeting that would take place tonight.

Marcel and Giles Marchand were the first to be cajoled into joining us, as they had the farthest to travel. The Marchands had insisted on meeting in neutral Switzerland, and Paolo had agreed. He had to convince his Sardinian partners to do the same, then help Jim find a place where all of us would fit and the utmost privacy could be upheld. Travel arrangements had to be made as well, safety and secrecy governing each part of the process. I didn't envy Paolo the logistics, but it was all his idea anyway.

After an early lunch, we packed up our latest round of temporary possessions and bundled into a pair of spacious Alfa Romeo Stelvios for the eight-hour journey to a remote ski lodge near Silvaplana, Switzerland.

Silvaplana was a small resort town nestled in the Alps, just across the Swiss/Italian border from Lombardy. When we reached the city limits around eight o'clock, few lights and no people appeared to great us. The deeper shadows hid melting snow drifts, but nothing else hinted at the bustling, crowded ski mecca Silvaplana must have been only a month or so ago. After passing through the town, we climbed partway up one of the surrounding mountains and found our way to the ski lodge east of town. Though the building was surrounded by other lodges, none—including the one we walked into—appeared occupied.

Since money was no object, Jim had booked the entire lodge for two nights, thereby excluding pesky non-combatants and allowing the attendees several rooms with a lot of empty space between. Most of the staff were gently encouraged to take the days off, helped along by generous remuneration, and a skeleton crew awaited us to serve dinner and turn away walk-in guests. I got the feeling this wasn't Paolo's first barbecue.

The room to which Paolo and Jim had consigned me was on the top floor of the rustic, four-story lodge, and the implication was clear. I noticed two things missing from the room that went a long way toward deepening my already foul mood: There was no attached bathroom, and the room phone was conspicuously missing from the nightstand.

Jim, who'd shadowed me upstairs under the guise of helping me with my luggage, announced, "You don't have to come to dinner. You must be tired."

He didn't come right out and say I wasn't welcome, instead leaving it to me to decide if I cared to impose my unwanted company on the other guests. Since I only had enough energy for a brief snit, I kept my response simple and to the point.

"Stop trying to make me feel like baggage, you clown. I know it was your idea to drag me here."

He'd been hefting a rather heavy piece of actual baggage into the room as I said this, and he let it fall with a thump before turning to me. To my disappointment, he hadn't risen to the bait and was perfectly calm.

"That's not what I'm trying to do. I just don't want you to put yourself in unnecessary danger because you're curious—"

"If Paolo didn't want me here, I wouldn't be here."

"Paolo wants to keep you under his thumb."

My response faded as we both heard a low rumble approaching. It grew so loud, I knew long before I looked down through the dormer window that Marcel and Giles had arrived in Marcel's Dodge Challenger Demon. They must have left London the very minute the meeting was confirmed, refining their course as they went.

I pictured myself behind the wheel of Marcel's Demon, freshly stolen from under his haughty, French nose. Jim in the passenger seat, reaching toward me with those long, nimble fingers of his. Racing toward freedom on 808 horses. Something about Panama.

Jim and I were silent until the engine cut off, and then I continued as though there had been no interruption.

"You know, now that I'm here, I don't mind being under his thumb. He seems to like me, and I like Italy. Maybe I'll stay there once this is all over."

Perceptive as ever, Jim asked, "So that's it? You really didn't want to come."

"I was finally home! Why wouldn't I have wanted to stay there?"

Quietly, he answered, "Because I'm here. I thought you…" He fell silent, then moved toward the door, muttering, "Dinner's at nine."

"Hold on." I sidestepped, blocking his retreat. "You can't pull that Uno Reverse card and make me feel bad for hurting your feelings." He frowned down at me, making no attempt to get around me. I pressed, "If you had *asked* me, I probably would have come."

"I would've bet my right arm wild horses couldn't keep you from tagging along. And I didn't have a chance to ask you."

"So you made an assumption without asking me a simple

question. That's par for the course. At least we put on a good show."

I'd forgiven Jim for worse. I was just too smitten with him. It was a little late to draw a line in the sand. He stepped too close and I forgot what I was going to say, very nearly kissed him, and looked away toward the window. I thought I heard more cars coming, but I couldn't be sure. They weren't nearly as loud as the Demon.

Whatever Jim saw on my face must not have been entirely discouraging, because his left hand twisted into my hair again and he nuzzled at my temple in a mute request to look up at him. The moment I did, he kissed me. His right arm slid around my waist, pulling me against him and up a little so that I started to lose my footing. His lips moved down my neck, and I twisted out of his arms.

"Leave it to you to skip the best part of making up," he said wryly.

"Oh, is that what that was?" I challenged. "I missed the part where you explained any of this to me. Why's it so important for Tommy to think we're at odds, for starters?"

"For the same reason we're not mentioning Lira's watch to anyone."

"Lira's watch?" I echoed, instantly confused.

Last I'd seen, Francisco Lira's watch was still on Luke's wrist, where it had been since he'd looted it off Lira's body. Presumably the GPS transmitting, anti-theft device within was still broadcasting his location to Regina Lira, unless he'd been smart enough to wrap it in aluminum foil again.

I asked, "Not that I'm taking issue with that, but why?"

"I have a guess about how this might end. Keep it to yourself for as long as you can."

"*End* as in a season finale, or a series finale?"

He smiled at me, the first smile I'd gotten out of him in what felt like months. "Don't tell me you're getting tired of this, Bowman."

"Oh, no. It's… *so* fun."

"Good." His hands slid around my waist, pulling me into a kiss. "Because I can't do this without you being exactly you."

"I wouldn't want you to try."

I got a couple more kisses, then one hand began sneaking up the back of my shirt before he stopped himself and said, "I better go. If someone comes to get you for dinner, come down. If not, see if you can figure out how hard it'll be to steal one of those Alfa Romeos. And try to find Paolo's room and see where he's keeping our passports and phones. Don't take them, just file it away for future reference."

"He has our passports?"

He nodded gravely. "Friday night, before you found us in the kitchen, Aldo made me hand over our passports, phones, cash, everything. He was nice about it, but it wasn't a request."

"I'm sure I could convince Enzo to find them and give them back," I taunted.

"I'm sure you could."

"Am I supposed to go without dinner?"

"If you're not there, I'll bring you a plate."

He kissed me again, told me to be careful, and left. As soon as the door closed behind him, I tried to do the natural thing and lock it. Unfortunately, there was no lock.

"That's just great," I snarled at the doorknob.

With an hour to kill before dinner, I gathered up a few essentials and found a bathroom one floor down to take a shower. I borrowed the hair dryer—which I could safely assume no one else would need—and took it back to my room.

Rain was pattering against the windows, mocking the Texas thunderstorms I missed so much. The hair dryer easily drowned it out, but after a few minutes I heard a low rumble of thunder. The rain picked up, and I closed my eyes and imagined I was home. I was sipping wine on the porch with my mom and sister. Dude was curled up at my feet. My dad was inside, showing the girls how to make John Wayne casserole. It was hard to fit Luke into the scene, but eventually I put him in the upstairs bathroom taking one of his marathon showers and using up all the hot water. The minutes slid by as the drumbeat intensified and the fantasy took shape.

My hair was nearly dry when my door flew open, startling me so much that I overhanded the hair dryer at the intruder before my brain caught up. It was only Enzo. He stepped backward in automatic self-defense, but he didn't need to. The appliance sailed about a foot through the air before the cord caught and it snapped to the floor, still whining as it spewed warm air onto the carpet. I dragged it back to me by the cord, not sure whether to laugh or berate him.

"I didn't mean to scare you," he said once I'd switched off the hair dryer. He still had to raise his voice to be heard over the downpour. "You must not have heard me knocking."

"I was pretending I was back home," I blurted. I was also starting to replay the highlights from last night, wondering when I'd get more alone time with Jim, but Enzo didn't need to know that. Shaking my head to snap out of it, I asked, "What do you want?"

He reached down to grab something behind the door frame and held it up for me to see.

"Little heater," he said in Italian. A space heater. "It will get cold tonight, so when I found out you were up here…"

"All alone in a room without a lock," I finished, grinning.

He raised his eyebrows. "No lock?"

I shook my head.

"Well." He set the space heater down just inside the door. "At least you'll be warm. If you want to be safe *and* warm to-night, I'm in room two fourteen."

He left without closing the door, forcing me to cross the room and shut it behind him. Either Enzo hadn't gotten the memo that Paolo wanted me to leave him alone, or he didn't care.

I finished drying my hair, letting my thoughts wander free-range. I was already shivering thinly as I did a quick, final check in the mirror, reminding me Florence was at a significantly lower elevation than Silvaplana. The summer weather I'd shopped for in Texas wouldn't be here for weeks yet, making my low-cut, sleeveless white blouse of insubstantial silk and lace a very poor choice indeed. My legs were warm enough now in loose-fitting, black cotton pants, but even the slightest breeze would cut right through the fabric.

Stubborn as ever, I abjured a jacket in favor of letting my bare skin distract whomever it would. I could move, at least, thanks to my heelless black boots. I could even run and fight if it came to that. Hoping it wouldn't, I descended the stairs to the ground floor of the deserted lodge and followed the German-language signs to the dining room. I hadn't officially received an invitation to dinner, but I was a human being who required energy in the form of calories, so I figured I'd try to get some grub anyway.

After the fashion of proper manor houses and other such fine dwellings, the dining room was completely enclosed and separated from the rest of the house by a set of double doors. To the right of these, a hallway burrowed back toward the kitchen where only employees ventured and from which enough light and sound were currently drifting to dissolve the illusion that I was wandering alone through a haunted hotel.

As I was leaning around the corner, looking down the hallway, a serving woman emerged from a side door of the dining room with several empty glasses balanced on a round tray. Not seeing me, she tottered away toward the kitchen on stilettos that looked profoundly unsuited to her employment.

I leaned back toward the doors and was about to push through them when the memory of Jim's earlier instructions made me pause. Depending on how this dinner went, I may only have this one chance to scope out the situation and possibilities re grand theft auto. I backed away, getting my bearings, and headed for the front doors and the small parking lot beyond.

6

Sunday, June 20, 2021

The outside air hit me like a bucket of ice water. It had stopped raining and wasn't objectively cold—maybe low 50s—but the contrast from the warm interior was jarring. Night had long since fallen, and the parking lot beneath its warren of tall, dark pines was illuminated by half a dozen halogen lamps strung between pine boughs.

The matching pair of jet black Alfa Romeo Stelvios that had ferried Paolo, Enzo, Aldo, Jim, Tommy, and me from Florence was parallel parked across the front of the lot, mostly blocking my view of any other cars. I walked quietly toward them, hugging myself to retain what body heat I could.

Standing between the Stelvios, which offered some protection from the wind, I surveyed the scene. My presence was noted immediately by several dark-clad, hulking gentlemen who'd apparently been left behind to either stay out of the way or guard the cars. I guessed the latter, since I was looking at many millions of dollars worth of narcissism on wheels.

Marcel's red Dodge Challenger SRT Demon was on the far right, flanked by two Land Rovers. Four men had been leaning against them, smoking, but when they saw me they stood up straight and puffed up a little, warning me off like enormous birds of prey. Compared to the rides favored by the Italian entourage, Marcel's American muscle car was, dare I say it, not all that impressive. I spotted a Bugatti, a Lamborghini, two Maseratis, and… oh, baby.

I edged toward the nearest car on the left, a pale blue and matte black creature slung low to the ground like the Lambo, but it wasn't another Lambo. I didn't know much about cars, least of all electric cars, but I thought I was looking at a Rimac—a Croatian hypercar worth more than the sum total of everything I'd ever owned.

When I was almost close enough to make out the logo on the hood, the hypercar's babysitter decided it was time to intervene.

"Stop," he barked in Italian. "That's close enough, lady."

"Is this what I think it is?" I asked, softening him a bit with my overawed tone.

"Rimac Nevera," he confirmed, as smug as though he personally owned it. "Are you familiar?"

"Not really. I saw one on TV once. Fourteen hundred horses?" I guessed, sure I was wrong but happy to be corrected.

"We don't measure things in horses. You're thinking kilowatts. One thousand, four hundred and eight, to be exact. The Dodge over there gets about six hundred."

"Bet the Dodge is a lot louder, though."

He chuckled appreciatively. "If that's what you're into."

"Can I take a peek inside?" I wheedled, sliding one quarter-step closer to both him and the car.

"Even if I had the key, the answer would be no. You should get inside, lady. It's too cold out here."

I totally agreed, scurrying back into the shelter of the lodge with one last longing glance at an array of fetish autos that looked like a poorly-attended car show. At least now I knew where the key to the Rimac wasn't.

The net result of my foray outside was warmth, like jumping out of a hot tub, into a pool, and back into the hot tub. No longer shivering, I pushed into the dining room and paused inside the doorway to take in the scene.

The five Italian (and Croatian) cars had transported seven men from Sardinia, two more than I'd encountered at Marcel's house in London six months ago. I recognized the two Anthonys, father and son, seated side by side. The father was at the head of the table, while Marcel occupied the foot (or the other head, as he probably thought of it). Giles was to Marcel's right, across from the only empty spot—next to Jim. I headed toward it before my hovering near the door became too terribly awkward.

I eased into a chair with Jim to my left, Tommy on his other side, and Paolo and his sons arranged to Giles' right. The other end of the table was given to the Sardinians. With the possible exceptions of Jim and Enzo, I couldn't think of any group of people with which I'd less enjoy a late dinner in a remote ski lodge.

As soon as I was seated, Jim's hand slid over my knee in a protective and possessive measure hidden beneath the solid mahogany table. I smiled at Marcel, ignoring Giles, whom I deeply hated.

"I was sorry to hear about David," I said in French, my sincerity halfway melting Marcel's icy expression. "I liked him."

"Thank you, Anna."

My appearance had forced a pause in whatever conversation had been underway. Embarrassed, I avoided many pairs of eyes until my gaze settled on Paolo, who was regarding me with open suspicion. I hadn't done anything to deserve that, unless he expected me not to talk to anyone. If so, he might have mentioned it.

"Thank you for joining us, Anna," he said coolly, turning to the older Anthony before I could do more than glare at him. "As I was saying," he sighed in Italian, only to be interrupted by Giles.

"English, please," he snapped.

Paolo laughed to himself, responding in English, "Ah yes, I forgot myself. My apologies. As I was saying, Regina's infrastructure in Colombia and the Port of Houston is well established and, from what I have been able to learn, quite sophisticated. We need only to replace her and those closest to her, and our operation there will practically run itself. We simply need to choose the right people for the job."

"It sounds like an enormous liability," one of the Sardinians said in Italian.

I was pretty sure his name was Ottavio, or something along those lines. He was of an age with the elder Anthony, portly and balding with dime-sized liver spots adorning his bare pate.

Though he wasn't pleasing to the eye, his voice was deep and rich.

Before Giles could complain, Paolo translated his comment into English and then snapped his fingers at Jim. He asked, "How much money did the cartel make last year?"

To his credit, Jim neither jerked in surprise nor bristled at the demeaning gesture. He did make Paolo wait an agonizing few seconds for his answer, "Between five hundred and seven hundred million. Only seventy-five million the year before. They're growing fast, branching out across the southern United States."

"Right under your nose?" Marcel asked, openly dubious.

"Yep," Jim shot back, taking a drink of wine to demonstrate that he had nothing else to say on the matter.

"I don't buy it," the Frenchman muttered.

The serving woman reappeared with a tray loaded with refills, and the discussion again lapsed into silence. Undismayed by the effect she'd caused, she passed out glasses of wine, snifters of amber liquor, and a couple of mixed drinks before the younger Anthony flagged her down. He beckoned her closer with one finger, and she had to lean down to hear something he whispered into her ear.

A pair of large, bright green eyes flicked toward me and away again, nothing discernable in the woman's deadpan expression. She leaned away, nodded, and loped around the table toward me. Since I had no reason not to focus on her, I was free to do so.

I was comfortable enough with my own good looks to know

when I was in the presence of a much more attractive woman. With thick, wavy, naturally blonde hair, flawless skin, and miles of slender leg extending from the hem of her too-short dress to the tips of her black stilettos, she was a solid eleven. I guessed she was about 25, but she could easily have been younger.

"I can bring you drink, ma'am?" she asked in halting English, a Polish accent coming through strong. I smiled blandly up at her, enjoying yet another dose of pure, dumb luck. I'd been working on my Polish.

"As long as that jerk didn't ask you to poison me," I answered in Polish, as far as I could tell.

No doubt I mixed up a conjugation or chose one or two wrong words, but she got the message. She bestowed a tiny smile on me, shaking her head once.

"How about a glass of pinot grigio? I don't want wine lips," I said.

'Wine lips' didn't seem to translate, causing a flicker of confusion to cross her face, but she nodded and retreated back through the side door to fetch my wine. I turned to the younger Anthony, letting his nonplussed expression cheer me up.

"You speak Polish?" he asked with insulting disbelief.

"I'm learning," I answered modestly. "The trip to Kraków inspired me. I really hate not being able to communicate with people."

His eyes narrowed, and I realized he was drunk. His father, however, wasn't. At least he was sober enough to realize the import of what I'd just said, and the language in which I'd said it—Italian.

Hotly, at Marcel, the older Anthony hurled the question, "You think we are not recognizing this woman? You tell us she speak only French!"

Unashamed, Marcel pushed his array of fancy forks around one-fingered and muttered to them, "I might have left a few qualifications off her résumé. Mea culpa, Signore."

Of me, Anthony demanded, "What does he talk about? What résumé?"

Jim's hand, still on my knee, tightened once. I glanced at him, caught his almost imperceptible nod, and took it as a signal to spill a few beans over the proceedings.

"Didn't you know?" I asked the elder Anthony, concern coloring my tone. "Marcel brought me to the meeting in London because he thought Paolo and I were working together. Thanks to this little ferret," I snarled, waving a dismissive hand at the younger Anthony, "he mistakenly concluded we were. I assumed you all had settled whatever disagreement was caused by the misunderstanding."

"You're trying to turn everyone against me, Camposanto," Marcel accused, not seeming all that put out about it. He had to have noticed Jim's go-ahead nod. "I wonder why? To impress Anna, or do you have a more pragmatic reason?"

"What could be more pragmatic than trying to impress a beautiful woman?" Jim answered with a benevolent smile. Marcel raised his wine glass in a sarcastic salute and let the matter go, just like that.

Anthony wasn't so forgiving. He glowered at Paolo, hissing in Italian, "You told me you didn't come because you don't trust

Marchand. Is it the other way around? Is he right not to trust you?"

"Preposterous," Paolo scoffed, also in Italian. "The idiot called to brag to me that your son tried to rescue Anna on my behalf. You know yourself this is a fiction."

While I whispered a translation into Jim's ear, Giles howled, "For heaven's sake, *English!* Anna, what did he say?"

Maybe Jim's hand on my knee was imbuing me with some of his near-supernatural strategic abilities, or maybe I was learning from him the old-fashioned way. Whatever it was, it helped me realize in about half a millisecond that exactly one other person at the table could answer Giles' question in French, English, or Italian: the younger Anthony. He was so drunk already he wasn't even paying attention to the conversation.

Anthony thought Paolo didn't trust Marchand.

Marchand didn't trust Paolo.

Paolo wasn't an FBI asset, but Marcel believed he was.

After a delay so brief it could easily be written off as irritation at taking an order from Giles, I lied smoothly in perfect, rapid French to the exclusion of everyone but the Marchand brothers, "You just heard our Sardinian friends learn that Paolo was working for Jim. For the FBI. They're not happy."

7

Sunday, June 20, 2021

Neither Frenchman was dumb enough to react to my words. While I wondered how suspicious it would be if I kept whispering in Jim's ear, Marcel asked without inflection, "How does he defend himself?"

"He said it wasn't true. I can't tell if they believe him."

Paolo slammed a fist twice on the table and shouted, "Anna, I must insist that you speak only English. To all of us. Tony, boy—What did she say to Marchand?"

The younger Anthony looked up from his empty plate, blinked at Paolo, and mumbled, "I wasn't listening. Sorry."

"I told him what you said," I argued. "You're the ones who keep switching to Italian. But you called this meeting, so I assumed you wanted to, you know, *meet.*"

Jim's brisk pat on the knee plainly stated, "That's enough, kiddo." I fell silent, my heart pounding, wondering what exactly I'd just done and whether Jim meant, somehow, for me to do it. But that was impossible, even for Jim. How could he have known the younger Anthony—Tony—would render his linguistic talents useless with too much wine?

"I apologize for the disruption," Marcel said coolly.

"What did she tell you?" Paolo pressed.

"Merely that you and the Signore had a disagreement about why you skipped our meeting in London. I asked what the disagreement was, and she declined to answer. Are you satisfied?"

Paolo huffed, signaling that he was satisfied enough. "Be that as it may. Anna. English."

"Okay, yeah. Sorry."

"As to who is working for whom," Paolo went on. He took a moment to compose himself, then looked at Jim. "Are you with me, or against me?"

I met Marcel's gaze and held it while Jim answered, "With you, as always, Paolo."

"Are you? You haven't always been helpful, in the past."

"I'm sorry you feel that way. I do have a job to do, you know. A security clearance. A boss."

"Well, now I expect you to prove your worth. You've brought me Thomas, rather than delivering him to your superiors as you were duty bound to do. The line is already crossed. Will you cross back over it?"

I couldn't believe my ears. Paolo was asking Jim, right there in front of God and the appetizers, to change his stripes, turn his coat, join the dark side, whatever you want to call it. Jim vented one short, disbelieving laugh.

"I told you, I'm on your side. If you want to make it official somehow, knock yourself out."

"I do," Paolo said, casting me a sad little smile. "I want you to prove you are my man, that I can trust you implicitly. How else can I, can we, trust you to do your part to topple Regina's empire?"

"How can I do that?" Jim asked. I wished he hadn't.

"You have given me Thomas, yes, but the boy is nothing to you. I want Anna."

The first one to react after a lengthy, breathless pause was Giles. He leaned forward, an eager, malicious gleam in his eye, but said nothing.

Finally Jim asked, somewhat less calmly than before, "Can you explain what you mean?"

"You understand me perfectly, James. When you leave here, Anna stays with me."

"Never mind that I'd never agree to that," Jim spat. "I'm sure you've noticed she does what she wants."

Almost on cue, to cut the tension enough that we could all draw a breath, the Polish woman returned with my wine and set it carefully in front of me without a word. She nodded at a few drink requests thrown her way, then left. The few people around the table who'd allowed themselves to be distracted by her returned their gazes to me. I felt like I was under a heat lamp, and Jim's hand was the only thing preventing me from fleeing the room.

"Does she?" Paolo asked. "Or does she do what *you* want?"

If, as I'd just tried to convince Marcel, Paolo had been working for the FBI all along, his request didn't amount to much. An interdepartmental transfer, really. So how would I react if that were true and I didn't want anyone but Marcel to know I knew he knew it was true? Whatever powers Jim had bequeathed me, they must have worn off. I was sitting there with a lump of coal between my ears.

Eventually I latched onto the most important, concrete fact: Paolo was giving Jim a chance to prove his loyalty, and Jim was fumbling it.

"What do you want me for?" I asked Paolo.

"Oh, I'm sure he'll think of something," Giles sneered.

"Don't mistake me for a creature of your vile appetites," Paolo snapped. "Anna has more to offer than that. I merely wish for her to remain here, in my employ, when James goes home."

"Then you should be asking her, not me," Jim concluded.

"Then what, exactly, did you claim a moment ago that you'd never agree to?"

"I said—" Jim started to argue, only to be cut across by Anthony shouting, "This is all wasting of time! Talk later. We should be speaking of Regina. Is not why we're all here?"

Mumbled assent swept down the table. Anthony resumed the Regina discussion with another question to Jim about the Tres Islas Cartel, the main course of stroganoff and rice was served, and I did the only thing I could think to do: I cleaned my plate and then stared at it, I delicately sipped my wine, and I tried to be a non-entity.

As the Polish woman was clearing away the dishes so dessert could be served, I glanced up at Paolo and gave him a shy half-smile that both he and Marcel could interpret however they wanted.

▼

By the time dinner was over, battle lines had been drawn. On one side sat those who preferred to leave the TIC alone and let Paolo deal with Regina himself; on the other, those who'd already been swayed by the promise of even greater profits. This line didn't follow any regional or familial boundary. There were proponents of both on either side of the table.

I didn't actually know where Jim stood, as he didn't say much other than to answer the odd question here and there, but I hoped he was in favor of whatever avenue allowed us to extricate ourselves from this mess.

Ultimately the question of whether those assembled would join forces against Regina Lira, Marisol Serna, and the might of the TIC wasn't decided, but a majority was leaning in favor of more money, and fewer people to share it with. We agreed to meet again the following afternoon, dispersing to our rooms for what all present assumed would be a relatively sleepless night.

As Jim hustled me away, I noticed Tony determinedly chatting up the Polish woman while Giles hovered near the foot of the stairs, watching the exchange with inordinate interest. Before I could wonder aloud what that all meant, Paolo caught up to us, his two sons flanking Tommy behind him.

"Go on," he said to Enzo and Aldo, waving them forward. Though Tommy wasn't physically restrained, it was clear the two young men were his de facto prison guards.

At the foot of the stairs, Tommy turned back to give me a look that said quite clearly, "We're in the same boat now, aren't we?" It was a disturbing thought to say the least, but he wasn't wrong.

"I'd like you to drive Tony home," Paolo was saying to me, making it a firm but polite order.

Jim went on the defense before I could respond. "Why her? Anthony's got people for that."

"Anthony's people are here to protect him. The boy didn't even tell his father of his arrangements until just before dinner. Anthony doesn't want to spare the men." He lowered his voice to add, "You can see he's a problem. A loose cannon. I need you to keep him from doing anything stupid. Anthony and I have conferred, and we agree this is the best option."

I asked, "Where's home?"

"He refused to stay here at the lodge and insisted on renting a home across the border, in Lombardy. He's obviously too drunk to get himself there safely."

"We went through a lot of trouble to make sure it was safe to meet here," Jim reminded Paolo. "And what did Tony do? Reserve an Airbnb from his phone?"

"I agree it's not ideal. He will be safer with Anna there."

Before Jim could protest further, I asked, "You want me to stay there with him?"

"If you would be so kind. Otherwise he'll have no way to get back tomorrow, as you'll have the Rimac."

"The… the Rimac?" I repeated, my voice clenching into an embarrassing squeak. Clearing my throat, I told a distraught-looking Jim, "It's fine. I can handle him. Paolo's right, he's not up to the drive. Look at him."

We all took a moment to observe Tony, who helpfully demonstrated his need for assistance by trying to take the Polish woman's hand, missing it, and falling back against the dining room door. She swallowed back a laugh, then met Giles' stony gaze before resuming the blank expression she'd worn the entire evening.

"He's kind of a mess, isn't he?" I commented.

"James?" Paolo asked, leaving it at that.

"I don't know how to make this any clearer, Paolo: I don't like it, but if Anna wants to go, she will. If she doesn't, she won't. I'm not entertaining this fantasy you've concocted in which she can be bought and traded like a racehorse. I'm not going to stop her, and you're not going to make her." He turned to me and asked, "That was crystal clear, wasn't it?"

I nodded, and Paolo sighed, "Yes, James, thank you. Ah—Anthony…"

I took the chance while Paolo was waving the elder Anthony over to whisper to Jim, "Please stop being so enlightened. You're on thin ice."

"Yeah, well, he's grinding my gears."

"He can do a lot worse than that," I reminded him.

"You just want to drive the Rimac," Jim hissed, and of course he got the last word before Anthony joined the conversation.

"You can drive the Nevera?" the old man asked me.

"Mhm," I sang. I mean, I'd watched someone drive one on television once. Sure, he'd wrecked it, nearly died, and started a fire that lasted a week, but that probably wouldn't happen twice.

Anthony nodded. "Thank you, Anna. I'll go peel my son away from that poor woman."

Left standing between Paolo and Jim, I stared at my feet, not sure what to say or whether to say anything at all. Jim didn't seem too fussed about staying on Paolo's good side at the moment, and I didn't want to do anything to make it worse. Jim didn't need my help, though.

"Let me go with them," he insisted. "I'm not crazy about Anna being alone with him."

Abandoning any pretense of solidarity, Paolo replied, "No crazier than I am about you and Anna making a break for it in the fastest car here."

Jim didn't bother replying. Paolo walked away, looking rather grim, and Jim rounded on me. "You have no idea what Tony will do," he warned.

"I think I can handle him. He's already falling down drunk."

"I don't like this."

"Yes, you've made that apparent to everyone here. If this is all some kind of test of your loyalty, you're not looking at a passing grade."

"Yeah, well. You're scoring high enough for the both of us. Are you planning to tell me what you said to Marcel and Giles, or is that your little secret?"

"Well…" I looked around, made sure no one was within hearing distance, and repeated the brief exchange that had caused so much consternation. "What do you think? Was that the right move?"

He favored me with a quick smile. "That was brilliant. How

did you know to do that?"

"I don't know. I just thought 'What would Jim do?' And obviously the answer was, don't clear up someone's convenient misperception if you can possibly avoid it."

"Clever girl." He eyeballed me for a moment, making heat rise to my cheeks; but too soon we heard Tony stumbling over to us. Jim squeezed my hand and left me with, "Don't get hurt. That's an order."

8

Sunday, June 20, 2021

I smiled blandly as Tony approached, looking unsteady but so pleased with himself I nearly fell apart laughing.

Looking after Jim's retreating figure, he said, "Don't worry, bella mia, I'll take much better care of you than that fugazi idiot." He plopped a key fob into my waiting hand.

"Are you too drunk to give me directions?" I asked, trying not to sound fed up with him already.

"I've got a nice place in Lombardy, you'll love it. Livigno. Just an hour away. Less if we don't get pulled over. Don't worry," he repeated. He made a grab for my free hand and just managed to pluck it out of the haze of double vision he was likely fighting.

Okay, that didn't really answer my question, but I was willing to go on a little faith; and I wasn't above experiencing the finer things in life, especially in pursuit of the greater goal of getting Paolo to trust me, and Jim by association. To my delight, Tony led me outside toward the very car over which I'd been drooling earlier. He released my hand and let his rest on the small of my back, where it drifted down to rest happily on my butt.

"What do you think of this?" he asked, gesturing to the Rimac as though perhaps I hadn't noticed it yet. "What do you think, huh? Is that a bella macchina or what?"

"Magnifica."

"I totally agree. Climb in, go on."

"Shouldn't I pack a bag or something?"

"Don't be silly, I've got everything we could possibly need."

He opened the passenger side door, nearly falling over as the winged panel flipped up toward him. I caught him, asking, "You're not going to throw up in it, are you?"

"Signora, I am a gentleman. In fact, actually…" He laboriously focused on my right hand and made a slow motion grab for the key fob dangling from it.

Like heck I was going to die driving off the side of a mountain in Switzerland. I skipped out of reach and purred in my very best Italian, "You don't want to start this fight, party boy."

Grinning like an idiot, he raised his palms in surrender and climbed into the passenger seat.

To the extent a chimpanzee could figure out how to drive a golf cart, I figured out how to drive the Rimac. Fortunately for me, the elder Anthony had already configured it for the winding mountain terrain, while the younger was still barely sober enough to talk me through starting it up, putting it into gear, and meandering around the smaller roads to gain the Swiss highway that would take us up and around the nearest mountain and back down into Italy.

Either Tony was too drunk to realize how likely this was to end in his fiery death, or he was just a trusting person. The excess alcohol caught up to him about halfway there, and he fell asleep in the cool, black-lit peace of the hypercar. That left me to navigate by signage to the Italian city of Livigno near the Swiss border. I got the Rimac up to 200 kilometers per hour on a straightaway, but I'm ashamed to say I was too chicken to go any faster than that.

The drive afforded me ample opportunity to mull things over. Paolo's barely-veiled accusation that Jim wanted to take me and flee, Jim's non-denial, their mutual rancor about the gauntlet Paolo had thrown at Jim's feet during dinner—none of it gave me much hope that this trip to Italy was going to end well for Jim or me.

I knew next to nothing about their relationship, but it had never seemed all that friendly. Perhaps they were always at odds, and I had no reason to fret. But if Jim were thinking about relinquishing the goal for which he'd first established contact with Paolo—a chance to talk to Emilio to learn what he could about what happened back in 1945—I privately thought he wasn't handling it all that gracefully. He would do better to let us get home to relative safety before severing ties with the cranky, capricious mafioso who held our lives in his hands.

Jim usually had something up his sleeve, though, and I had to trust that he knew what he was doing. I reminded myself that Paolo wanted something from Jim, too: the locations of Etta's and Regina's branches of the family. They'd been whittled down to two people, Regina Lira and Marisol Serna, who seemed to be together now. Maybe Paolo believed Jim would help him like he had in Houston, like he had in Argentina; but Paolo hadn't known of Jim's ulterior motives in those cases.

Neither had I, of course, until after the fact.

We arrived in Livigno around midnight, and I had to shake Tony awake so he could guide me to our final destination. Livigno was another ski town in the lull of impending summer, its dark and uninviting streets lined with ski resorts and tourist traps that were closed for the season. Tony directed me through the small town and up another winding road that climbed back into the Alps, finally stopping in front of a closed gate at the end of a short, steep driveway.

"Four two, four eight, four four," he said smugly, nodding at the keypad just outside my window.

I entered the code and the gate slid open, revealing a three-story, compact little castle of a home with modern-looking right angles, lots of glass, and no homes visible behind or to either side of it. From what little I'd seen of the town, the latter was its most enviable quality.

"I'm only renting it until we go home," he sighed, as though deeply inconvenienced. "At least we've got the place to ourselves."

"Goodie," I wheezed as I carefully maneuvered the Rimac into the empty two-car garage and turned it off.

"How did we get here so fast?" he asked, glancing at the clock on his phone. "You didn't speed, did you?"

I shook my head mutely, not trusting myself to lie when my thoughts had turned sharply toward mischief at the sight of his cell phone.

"It's a good thing you drove. I was way too drunk," he laughed, climbing out. I groaned. If he *was* way too drunk, that meant he wasn't anymore.

While he set up the Rimac's elaborate charging apparatus, I gazed around the empty, spacious garage and tried to figure out how I was going to get his phone away from him. It all depended on how assiduously he'd be guarding it. Had his father or Paolo warned him that I wasn't supposed to have access to a phone? That I couldn't be trusted?

Said phone *dinged* from Tony's pocket. He pulled it out, studied the message, and cast me a look loaded with exaggerated suspicion. I guess that was my question answered.

"What?" I asked.

"Nothing." He opened the door and led me into the house. "Come, be my bodyguard while I take a look around. I think this place has a sauna *and* a hot tub." He caught my quelling expression and said, "No, no, don't worry, I know you're Camposanto's own private plaything. My father told me about the phone call Paolo received from that frog lover, Marchand. Apparently I'm a wretched fool for somehow leading Marchand to believe Paolo is—what do you call them? Double agents?"

He met my eyes, and I shrugged, refusing the invitation to react.

We found the kitchen, and on the counter a bottle of rosé, a corkscrew, and two glasses. A welcome gift from whomever had rented the place to Tony. I felt a new twinge of apprehension as he uncorked the bottle and filled the glasses. At the hotel, thanks to Jim's efforts, I knew we were reasonably safe. At least from Regina.

"If this is you interrogating me, you're not very good at it," I said. He passed me a glass of wine, undismayed by my news.

"I'm making conversation, that's all. Just between you and me—look at that! I bet the view at sunrise is to die for—Just between you and me, I wanted to bring that delicious blonde woman home with me. No offense to present company intended, of course." His eyes twinkled as he looked me over. "The fun the three of us might have had."

"Your father nixed that idea?" I ventured.

"Well, given what happened back in December, he thought she may have been planted there by the Marchands. I thought that was ridiculous, of course. Why would they try the same trick twice in a row? They're disgusting, of course, but not stupid."

"Not a fan of the Marchands?"

He waved one hand at me, his mouth occupied with his wine glass. "None of us like them," he clarified. "But what can we do? The Marchands can get anything into the United States. Anything."

I crossed my arms, grinning, and said, "Go on."

"Ah. Let me think."

While he thought, he led me through two living rooms, a dining room, three modestly-sized bedrooms, three massive bathrooms, a workout room with a small indoor pool, an elevator, a wine cellar, a kitchen, a dry bar, and a balcony. He seemed to take great pleasure in pointing out all the home's luxuries and conveniences while I dangled in suspense.

Finally, at a sauna just off the master bedroom, he grabbed my wine glass and deposited it on a nearby table along with his own. "You and Camposanto work for the FBI."

"Is that a question? We're both probably fired by now. I think we're what you'd call 'free agents.'"

"Camposanto, he's FBI whether they're paying him or not. Even a fool like me can see that. But what about you?" He traced the line of my collar from neck to sternum, asking my breasts, "Is that unfortunate aroma of American law enforcement only skin deep?"

"Why do you ask?"

"Maybe I want to know whether you taste salty or sweet. Maybe I'd have a lot to say… but not to an FBI woman. Not to Camposanto's woman."

Ugh. I slapped his hand away. "Then your father did himself quite the favor by keeping you away from Blondie."

Undeterred, he pressed, "Give me a fun night, bella mia, and in the morning I'll tell you more than you could possibly want to know about the Marchands."

"Tempting, but I'll pass."

"Ah," he sighed, shaking his head. "Is there anything uglier than an honorable woman?"

"I can think of something," I mumbled as he walked away. Though I'd much rather have locked myself into one of the bedrooms and fallen asleep, I trailed a good distance behind Tony as he found the door to the basement and started down the stairs.

Knowing I was still obediently following him, he called,

"There's a pool table. Come, let's have a game before bed. Maybe if you win, I'll—"

I'd reached the doorway just in time to hear an odd *thwump* and a series of meaty bumps that sure sounded like someone tumbling down the stairs.

"You idiot," I chastised. "Are you okay?"

When I received no response, I descended into the basement and found Tony sprawled on the floor between the pool table and a fold-out sofa.

He lay still, face down, oblivious to my shaky, "Uh… Tony?"

As I studied him, not sure what to do, blood began to appear under his head and chest, forming a pool in which he remained motionless. At a sound behind me I whirled, finding myself face-to-chest with an enormous man dressed in black from head to toe, his face obscured by a black ski mask.

I dove with both hands toward something matte black protruding into the space between us.

9

Sunday, June 20 to
Monday, June 21, 2021

The crack of the rifle was muted, no more than a clap in the echoing, enclosed basement. I drove my palm into his face over and over, sheer, naked panic turning me into an animal as I struggled to distract him from the rifle over which we were now scuffling, to keep the business end of it away from my body at all costs. I landed a close-fisted hammer blow to the base of his skull just as he freed one hand to grab at me, the loosed hand falling limply to his side.

With two hands on the rifle, I twisted it to a perpendicular against his chest, stomped downward on his knee, and allowed myself to fall over backward as he released the rifle and me at the same time.

He recovered quickly while I was still on my backside three feet away from him. I pointed the unfamiliar weapon in the general direction of his body and squeezed the trigger, unleashing not one round but a burst of ten or twelve that stitched a line from his abdomen to his skull as the fully automatic weapon jerked upward in my hands.

I screamed as he toppled backward one step and then collapsed down onto his knees. He reached one hand toward me as he fell forward, and I sent another burst into his head and chest. That seemed to do it. Except for the first round, I hadn't heard a single shot.

Suddenly all I cared about was being on my feet. I realized I was sitting in the V formed by Tony's splayed legs, the outstretched hand of the assailant flopped down between my own. Much, much too close all around.

I slid to my side, scrambled to my feet, and pressed myself against the wall opposite the foot of the stairs. No one else was in sight. I trained the weapon on the man in black again, searching his body for signs of movement.

Hours, or maybe a few seconds later, I started intoning, "Crap, crap, crap, crap, crap." I shook my head, trying to make my senses work. I couldn't seem to hear, and the edges of my vision were dark. I shut my eyes, pleading with myself to just get through this, get some kind of help, and then I could fall apart at my leisure.

I sidestepped over to Tony and checked his pulse. He was dead. I didn't think it was smart to approach the other guy to feel for a pulse. After sucking up that many rounds, he was either dead or dying anyway.

I finally looked down at the weapon in my hands and saw an AK-47 fitted with a suppressor that was gently smoking in the icy air of the basement. I popped out the magazine and saw I had at least three rounds left, two visible in the magazine and one in the chamber. I didn't trust my shaking hands or frazzled brain to examine it any closer than that. I switched the selector bar from fully automatic to safe, looped the heavy weapon's retention strap over my shoulder, and called that good.

Gripping the rail with my left hand, I dragged myself up the stairs and found a landline phone mounted on the wall in the kitchen. I couldn't remember a single phone number except Jim's, which I knew to be in Paolo's possession. He answered on the first ring.

"Who is this?" he asked. The old man's voice, a study in serenity as he waited to see who was calling Jim near midnight on a Sunday from an unknown Italian number, brought a wave of unexcepted calm crashing down on me.

I drew in a deep breath, let it out slowly, and said, "It's Anna. I need help."

His tone sharpened. "What happened?"

"It's… it's hard to say," I rasped, my voice thinning as I forced it through the tiny opening my throat had become. "It's bad." I choked on a sob and begged, "Bring Jim with you. Please."

"What's the address?"

After giving Paolo the address, absorbing his assurances that everything would be fine if I only stayed put and waited, I hung up the phone and forced myself back down to the basement.

The dead man was like a spider to me. It wasn't enough to shoot at it and hope it died, I had to be sure. The last thing I needed was an angry, vengeful spider surprising me.

The scene in the basement hadn't changed for the better in my short absence. Neither man had moved, but both bodies had released liters and liters of blood onto the cold concrete floor. I had to circle the unhappy pair four times before I found a place where I could stand close enough on one foot, without stepping in blood, to root through the masked man's pockets.

Since he'd fallen face-down, and I couldn't have rolled his massive bulk over even if I wasn't weak with shock, I was limited to the two back pockets of his pants and a Velcro pouch on the back of his tactical vest. The former were empty, the latter yielding nothing but a well-used paper map that had been folded over to favor a small-scale map of Livigno. I assumed the red circle he'd drawn on it pinpointed this house.

I glanced at Tony, feeling pity rise like bile in my throat. Forcing my eyes away from him, and my thoughts from how I was going to explain this to his father, I looked over the assassin's body again and saw two more pockets on his pants, one on each thigh. The left I couldn't reach without getting blood on me, but the right was easily accessible. I worked the flap free, slipped my hand inside, and drew out a plastic hotel key card bearing the imminently recognizable Hilton logo and the words "Hilton Garden Inn Davos."

"Okay, that's a place to start," I whispered to the dead man. The air in the basement was so cold my breath fogged the air, and I fled upstairs in search of warmth, water, and a convenient place to vomit if my body so chose.

While I waited for whatever assistance Paolo would see fit to send, I forced down three cups of coffee and two granola bars, barfed up the lot of it, and began nursing a more suitable glass of water. I made myself reasonably comfortable on the sofa in the ground-floor living room, my looted AK-47 close at hand.

Once I was finished with the water, I carefully washed and put away every single dish I'd used, including my wine glass. I found bleach under the kitchen sink and flushed some down every sink and toilet I'd used. I wandered around for a while wiping fingerprints and footprints off things, hating myself, knowing the destruction of evidence was in vain. Eventually a crime scene tech would find a long, red hair, and part of me would be evidence. Still, I couldn't do nothing.

By the time the cavalry arrived some ninety minutes after I called Paolo, I'd already guessed he wouldn't be among them. If he'd suspected before that the last-minute rental in Livigno wasn't safe, my distress call only proved him right. He'd keep his sons away, too. I hoped he'd honor my request to send Jim, but I wasn't counting on it.

The doorbell rang, making me jump, and I carefully rose from my seat so the rush of light-headedness that followed wouldn't drop me. I grabbed the AK-47, looped the retention strap over my shoulder again, and crept to the front door. I spied three men through the peep hole, illuminated by the porch light over their heads: the man who'd shooed me away from the Rimac 400 years ago, one of the Marchands' heavies, and Jim. A representative assortment, none of whom looked pleased to be there. The first man had raised his fist to knock again when I yanked opened the door.

Had the circumstances been different, I might have laughed at all three of them twitching in perfectly synchronized surprise at the sight of me, Kalashnikov at the low ready, too strung out to know friend from foe. I could only assume I looked ghastly. Ignoring the unfamiliar men who stood closest, I looked beyond them to meet Jim's eyes.

He broke the silence to ask, "Want to tell me what happened?"

"They're in the basement."

For a moment he seemed to worry that I'd start shooting, but he muscled past that and the other two men and stepped inside. They followed, and I pointed toward the basement stairs with a jerk of the AK-47.

"What is down there?" Marcel's man asked. His halting Italian must have been the reason Marcel chose him for this all-important joint task.

"Tony and the one I killed." My ever so slight emphasis on the word 'I' caused his frown to deepen considerably. He exchanged a look with Anthony's man, who took control of the situation.

"Stay up here with her," he instructed Jim, who nodded only after I'd translated the command into English. He and the Frenchman filed down into the basement, leaving Jim and me alone by the front door.

Jim wrapped his arms around me, pinning the rifle between us, and asked, "Are you okay?"

"I'm not injured."

I had to give him props for not wasting time on softer concerns. He simply asked, "Still have the key to that Rimac?"

Feeling in my pocket to be certain, I said, "Yeah."

Voices rose up from the basement, at least one of the men expressing his consternation over the scene. He didn't sound grief-stricken as much as panicked. The elder Anthony would not be pleased. Before Jim and I could take one step toward the garage and the swift-winged freedom it held, both men returned from the basement. Blood-free clothes told me they hadn't examined the scene all that closely.

Anthony's man said only, "Give me the rifle."

"I would really rather hold onto it," I said very carefully, sounding nearly sane.

In answer, both men unholstered handguns that had been concealed on their belts. For two men who probably hadn't met before yesterday, they moved with uncanny coordination. Though both weapons remained directed at the floor, their intent to disarm me came through loud and clear.

"Hey, whoa," Jim cried, stepping between us as I took a tighter grip on the AK-47 and all three or so rounds it held. "Take it easy. Uh… calmo."

"I didn't kill Tony," I said, directing this at Anthony's representative. "I heard him fall down the stairs, went to check on him, and found him like that. The other man was there. We fought over the gun, and I took it and killed him. He had a map of Livigno, with a circle around this house. Understand?"

After a prolonged pause, the Italian holstered his weapon, followed somewhat reluctantly by the Frenchman. Seeing they weren't going to shoot me, I wormed out of the retention strap and gingerly laid the AK-47 on the floor in front of me. I stepped over it to stand next to Jim.

"What do we do?" I asked.

No one seemed in a hurry to offer a suggestion. Obviously they hadn't been forewarned of exactly what they'd find here. At length the Frenchman said, "Back to Silvaplana. Leave them here."

"There's no way we can clean this up ourselves," the Italian agreed.

I asked, "What about—the—Tony's body?"

"What can we do? We can't bury him."

"What are you saying?" Jim snapped. I summarized for him, and he eagerly agreed. "The sooner the better. Let's go."

He took my arm and moved toward the garage, but the Italian arrested us with a barked, "No! I'll go with you, Anna. Tell Camposanto to go with him."

Jim didn't need a translator for that one. We shared a commiserative look, reading one another's thoughts well enough: We can't make our escape in the Rimac without killing both of them. Let's wait for a better opportunity.

He pressed his palms to my face, kissed me on the forehead, and asked, "Are you okay? Really?"

"Andiamo," the Italian complained.

"I'm fine. I'll see you back at the lodge."

Jim left with the Frenchman through the front door, and I locked it behind them. As the Italian and I headed for the garage, he said, "Wait—take the Kalashnikov. Fingerprints."

Whether he meant mine or the killer's, I didn't ask. I grabbed the weapon and followed him into the garage, surrendering the

Rimac's key upon request. I climbed into the passenger seat, wedging the rifle into the floorboard and strapping myself in.

He unplugged the car, then adjusted the seat back so he could squeeze his substantial mass into the driver's seat and start it up. He was familiar with it, but that came as little surprise. With a flash of rage, I thought about telling Anthony he ought to have guarded his son as closely as his cars.

"Well," the man sighed. "You wanted to see the inside."

I waited to answer until we were on the road, the headlights of whatever car Jim and the Frenchman drove winking in the Rimac's mirrors.

"What's your name?" I asked.

"Benito."

"Did you search the body?"

"We didn't want to disturb the scene. I took Tony's phone, that's it."

"I went through some of the shooter's pockets. I found a keycard for a hotel in Davos."

He nodded slowly. "Are you injured?"

"No."

"There's blood on your shirt."

I glanced down, stomach clenching at the sight of high-velocity splatter I hadn't noticed when I'd washed the same off my hands and arms. It stood out like glitter under the cab's black lights. "I was really close to him when I shot him."

"How did you get the weapon away from him?"

"Can we skip the replay? I'm sure Anthony will make me go through it."

"Have you ever killed anyone before?"

"No."

"You're in shock," Captain Obvious said, his tone unexpectedly gentle and sympathetic. "Try to get some sleep. It's going to be a long night."

10

Monday, June 21, 2021

I tried to take Benito's advice, but the technicolor blood splatter on my shirt kept me awake.

Midnight was well behind us when we parked at the lodge, and my stomach had a lot to say about it. Sadly, I had time for neither a snack nor a change of clothes. When Benito and I walked into the lobby, we saw everyone, even Tommy, occupying sofas and armchairs around a cold, empty fireplace.

Everyone was subdued, except a guest who hadn't joined us for dinner who was now seated primly on the floor next to Marcel's chair: Penelope the cosseted Belgian Malinois. She wriggled with excited recognition at the sight of me, and I had to resist an impulse to sit down next to her and grab a quick, fortifying cuddle. That would put me uncomfortably close to Marcel, who was plainly furious. I wished I hadn't left the AK-47 in the Rimac at Benito's insistence.

Benito walked straight to Anthony, who'd risen to his feet at the sight of us and demanded to know where his son was. They conferred in whispers, which ended in Anthony sinking back into his chair and falling deathly silent.

I remained near the door, shivering, waiting for Jim, as too many eyes studied me. Paolo's held the least suspicion and anger, but I wasn't inclined to take a seat next to him. It was his fault I'd been there, and I sensed every single person assembled knew it.

Jim finally walked in and wrapped his arms around me from behind, sending just enough spare body heat through my clothes to remind me I was frozen to the marrow. He felt me shivering for a few seconds, then started to usher me toward the stairs.

"Where do you think you're going?" Marcel spat.

Jim ignored him. As we neared the stairs, which beckoned to me with their false promise of rest and warmth and safety, I heard several people rise to their feet. Exclamations of dissent in three languages taxed my brain to the breaking point. Only Paolo's voice made any sense to me.

"Anna, come back. We must discuss this."

Turning, I spoke only to him. "I'm so tired, Paolo. Please."

He dismissed me with a wave, staying behind to handle continued protests from the people who'd been dragged from their beds for no reason.

▼

I awoke in daylight with amorphous, quasi-memories rolling around in my skull and mixing with disjointed segments of so many meaningless dreams. I should have been tired still, but I was wide awake the moment my eyes opened.

Sitting up slowly, the better not to jostle my pounding head, I found myself alone in bed, dressed in one of Jim's t-shirts, my underwear, and nothing else. I wasn't in my fourth-floor room but in his, and I didn't even know what floor it was on. It was larger and nicer, with an en-suite bathroom and an electric fireplace, which was currently filling the room with bone-dry heat. His room phone was missing, too.

My stomach heaved at the sight of my outfit from last night lying in a heap on the floor next to the bathroom.

I'd killed a man. His corpse was right where I left it.

Longing filled my empty body, begging me to find some way to make contact with Luke. I had to ask him how I was supposed to feel about this, how long I'd be hearing echoes of the wet smack of bullets as they hit my target's flesh.

I spotted a bottle of water on the nightstand and took my time drinking it. It stayed down, but only just. I was so hungry I could barely think straight, and a little caffeine wouldn't hurt, either. The problem was, I was nearly naked and separated from my luggage by who knew how much distance. I had no idea where Jim was, and I was beginning to get annoyed that he'd left me alone.

Sensing I was at an impasse, I lay down and tried to fall back asleep. It was no good. Not only was my mind going Mach 11, but after a few minutes my bladder started chiming in. I was emerging from the bathroom, trying to stretch Jim's t-shirt into a more effective dress, when he let himself into the room. He had my luggage, which he dropped just inside the door.

With his arms around me again, I felt safe enough to let a few, scalding tears escape. They were enough. It wasn't grief that haunted me, but guilt, and apprehension about what I still needed to do.

"You were completely unresponsive last night," he breathed, crushing me. "You scared the daylights out of me. You were like a zombie."

"Sorry. I never killed anyone before. I honestly don't remember much after I saw the gun," I lied, hoping that would keep his protectiveness tamped down to a manageable level. "But I wish I hadn't killed him. We could have asked who sent him."

"Yeah, right. Too bad we're not from some kind of federal bureau that investigates things."

I forced a laugh. "Too bad."

"Anthony's been hounding me all morning. I told him what I could. He wants to talk to you."

"I know. Can I take a shower first?"

"Of course. I'll go find you something to eat, okay?"

"Thanks."

The shower was a nice surprise, a large square of slate floor enclosed in floor-to-ceiling glass, with two shower heads mounted on the wall and one on the ceiling. I didn't spend any time sitting on the shower floor letting hot water mask my tears as I hugged my knees to my chest, but I was sorely tempted. It always seemed to make people feel better in the movies.

In truth, I was in a hurry to get the formalities with Anthony over and done. I showered in a rush, threw on the first clothes I found in my suitcase, and almost rubbed toothpaste in my armpits and deodorant onto my toothbrush. Once I got myself sorted and applied the correct products to the correct body parts, I hoovered up the cheese danish and coffee Jim had brought before venturing downstairs.

Anthony was waiting for me in the lobby, at the foot of the broad staircase. He was facing away, toward the front doors, but I knew why he was there.

Stopping halfway down, I said, "Signore?"

He half turned, his profile a blank mask, and said, "Please come with me."

I trailed a few yards behind him all the way to a hallway on the north side of the lodge, where the doors were spaced much farther apart than those in Jim's third-floor corridor. He disappeared into a room midway down the hall, leaving the door propped open behind him. I stepped inside, looked around, and decided I did not care for the arrangement.

Benito, along with three other men of similar size and assumed utility, were seated around a table in the suite's living area. This sat between the door and a pair of armchairs on the far side of the room. Anthony sat in one, he gestured to the other to indicate I should sit, and Benito got up and closed the door behind me.

Once my bottom made contact with the chair, I asked, "Where's Jim? Where's Paolo?"

"James has gone to Davos at my request to see what he can learn about the man you killed," Anthony said. "As to Paolo's whereabouts, I can't say."

Though the men at the table seemed not to be paying the two of us any attention, focused instead on a quiet card game in progress, a subtle rigidity to their postures gave them away. I swallowed as a dull flush crept up my cheeks.

Had I been eager to get this meeting over with? I'd had one job—keeping Tony safe—and I blew it. I couldn't have cocked it up more unless I'd pulled the trigger myself. The old man sitting across from me, though bowed with grief and weariness, looked hopping mad.

He let me squirm for a moment longer, then asked, "Would you like some coffee?"

"No, thank you."

"You believe I want to talk about what happened last night," he guessed.

"Don't you?"

"No. Perhaps, but not right now. You are familiar with Camposanto's work. You've worked with him for several years, yes?"

"Oh, um… about a year and a half. Why?" Before he could answer that, I forced myself to say, "I'm not giving you information about the FBI."

He granted me a sarcastic smile. "I'm not interested in the FBI. I want to know the real reason my cousin Emilio traveled to Buenos Aires, Argentina in nineteen sixty-two, and I believe you know."

Seeing the naked shock on my face, Anthony sat back in his chair and gave me some time to think. I couldn't believe it. It didn't track. Yes, I'd known Anthony was part of The Family, but he belonged to the section of the family tree that had never left Italy. If he didn't know Emilio went to Argentina to visit his sister Etta, then the list of other things he couldn't possibly know expanded to lengths I simply couldn't process. I needed Jim. This was Jim's thing.

When I'd had enough time to think, Anthony nodded at the table of card players. Benito walked over without a word and stood behind my chair. I started to stand up, and he pushed me back down by the shoulders. His hands were even bigger than Luke's, and they stayed on my shoulders until Anthony gave him another nod. He let go of me but continued to hover behind my chair.

"You know, don't you?" Anthony prodded.

"I…" I swallowed, stalling for time. For all my faults, I wasn't too crazy about the idea of passing classified information to an Italian crime boss, even to save my own neck. "Could I have a drink?"

"Coffee?" Anthony asked.

I studied the array of tasty beverages on a table behind him and said, "Scotch." While Benito poured me a drink, the absence of his menacing shadow made me feel safe enough to admit, "I sure wish Jim were here."

"I understand. You're not certain whether you're permitted to disseminate this information. If my understanding of classified information is accurate, Camposanto would be the one to make that decision, yes?"

"Yes, but—"

I almost launched into a tedious explanation of original classification authorities and security clearances et cetera, but

I stopped myself when I realized Anthony didn't care. He was telling me I couldn't ask Jim's permission, but I could ask his forgiveness if I made it out of this room alive. Benito pressed a tumbler of way too much scotch into my hands and resumed his position behind my chair.

"Nineteen sixty-two," I mused, aimless. "Did Emilio ever tell you why he came to Italy?"

"Only that it was no longer safe for him in the United States, and that his family searched for him. He did not want to be found. After the internet made it possible to do so, I looked into his family and discovered what I could. The fire. His siblings' deaths. I assumed this was the impetus for his move to Italy, of course."

I knocked back a fortifying gulp of breakfast scotch and asked, "So he didn't tell you his sisters Etta and Regina made it out of the fire, too?"

It was his turn to be surprised. After some quick thinking, he asked only, "Regina?"

"Yeah, that Regina. I thought you must know."

"Regina is a very common name. I believed his two sisters to have died in nineteen forty-five." He frowned to himself. "Why would Paolo send Marcel's man to kill his own nephew?"

"You might want to pour yourself one too, Signore. This is going to be a long story."

▼

For all the information I provided, Anthony only explained one thing to me: He'd done some digging on Jim last night and learned of the family connection. Coupled with the knowledge that Marcel believed Paolo to be working with the FBI, Anthony had rightly become suspicious that Paolo had never once mentioned Jim was his nephew. So he'd sent Jim away that he might have me, the weakest link, all to himself for the morning. Crafty old codger.

What could I do? I told Anthony as little as I thought I could get away with, but it was still so much. Emilio's 1962 visit to Etta in Argentina and his resulting disgust with the Nazi-funded organized crime he found blossoming there; his decision to return to Italy without visiting Regina in Colombia, because he'd learned enough from Etta to know he'd only find more of the same; the hatred for his family which he passed along to Paolo, who took it to new extremes; Paolo's real reason for ordering the hit on Regina's son, and his subsequent hit on Etta's grandchildren, Fernando and Marisol; Marisol's flight to Regina in Colombia after her brother was killed. If Anthony was concerned that Paolo was killing off members of his family, which of course included Anthony himself and his now-dead son, he didn't mention it.

I left myself and Jim out of it, to the extent I could, but it was impossible to leave Luke out of it. Luke was Marcel's man, the trigger, the strong arm of Paolo's vendetta. He was the best Marcel had, and the use of his services was intended as a gift to celebrate the partnership between the Frenchmen and the Sardinians.

The one bright spot in my morning of shame was that I managed to follow the single instruction Jim had given me. I didn't mention Francisco Lira's watch.

11

Monday, June 21, 2021

Loopy from the scotch, I returned to Jim's room a couple hours later. I couldn't decide which I dreaded more: telling Jim what I'd done, or how Paolo would react when Anthony confronted him. It was too much to hope that Anthony would grant me the protection of an anonymous source. Even if he did, Paolo would figure out who spilled the beans.

I locked Jim's door, pulled the curtains closed, turned off the lights, and went back to bed. That was how Jim found me, mostly asleep and riddled with anxiety in his bed. I hated to do it, but I had to confess.

Once I got it all out, Jim stared at me for a solid minute and then concluded, "Huh."

I didn't ask if he was mad at me. I knew what mad looked like, and that wasn't it. Relieved, I said, "I know you're thinking super hard right now, but can you tell me what you found out in Davos?"

"What? Oh, Davos. Right. Not much. I found his room and tossed it, then checked out and got an itemized receipt. He checked in two days ago under the name Albert Foley, address in London. He paid for the room through Friday, but he didn't leave anything behind. I got a phone number, but I called it from the hotel lobby and it's not in service."

"That's it?"

"That's it. I was lucky he hadn't checked out yet."

"Oh, he's checked out now," I shot back with grim satisfaction. I'd somewhat recovered from the shock of taking a life, considering the life had attempted to take me.

Jim said, "The London address was probably fake, but still… This doesn't look great for the brothers Marchand."

"What about the crime scene in Livigno?"

"Nothing. I watched the news for a while in the lobby, but it's not being reported. The home owners probably haven't even found the bodies yet, since he'd rented it through tonight."

"Ugh," I groaned. "I'm going to be wanted for murder. In *Italy.*"

He ran a calming hand back and forth across my back, arguing, "Not necessarily. Think about what the evidence will show, once it's all processed. The shooter will have gunshot residue on his hands and maybe even some blood splatter on his clothes, and Tony won't. Both were killed by the same caliber, and there are seven-six-two casings all over that basement. All from the same weapon, which isn't at the scene. It's not rocket surgery: He killed Tony, then someone killed him with his own weapon and fled the scene. You'll be a person of interest, certainly, but not a homicide suspect. At least not in a shooting that wasn't entirely justified."

"Wow, you've really thought this through."

"Mhm. Did you notice any cameras at the house? A smart doorbell?"

"I wasn't looking."

"He must've been waiting there for you. Maybe he walked in front of a camera. Those vacation rental hosts like to know who's coming and going."

"A man in black with an AK-47? Wouldn't they have called the cops?"

He drummed his fingers on my back and said, "Well, it's useless to speculate right now. Once I get my phone back, I'll call Ingrid and see if she can get me some information. I didn't think it was safe to call her from the hotel."

I frowned at the mention of Ingrid Breker, our Bundeskriminalamt (German FBI) contact from a one-off job in Germany last year. "She doesn't owe us one anymore," I reminded him.

"Worth a shot."

"Paolo's never going to give you back your phone. He's gonna be so mad."

"Good thing you just made friends with a bigger fish." He trailed one finger down my spine, making me shiver, and sighed, "I'm sorry I left you here alone. You must have been scared."

"I did okay. You could have hit Davos and kept on driving, so… thanks for that."

I was about to ask him whether he'd called anyone else from the hotel in Davos when someone knocked lightly on the door.

Jim went to answer it and I pulled the blankets all the way over my head, hiding. I heard the door open, then a woman saying, "Lunch is being in twenty minute. Please, where is woman from four ten?"

Recognizing the Polish woman's voice, I peeked my head out of the covers and said, "Witam."

She nodded curtly and left. As Jim closed the door, he laughed. "She doesn't seem too pleased with you. What did you say?"

"'Hello.' I'm about eighty-five percent sure she's a ringer for the Marchands. She should be thanking me. If she'd gone home with Tony last night, she'd be dead."

▼

Paolo, Enzo, and Aldo were the last to arrive in the dining room for lunch, bearing with them a storm cloud of general hostility. Tommy was notably absent, a point which Paolo was quick to address the moment he took his seat.

"Mister Holladay won't be joining us."

No one objected, though I had to ask, "You didn't kill him, did you?"

Paolo acted as though I hadn't spoken, instead asking Anthony, "Are you satisfied the tragedy last night was Regina's doing, or have you chosen to lay that transgression at my feet as well?"

Unimpressed, Anthony replied, "We hear whole story from Anna now. Then we choose blame."

Oh, good. No pressure, then. I sucked down half my water before launching into my tale, keeping my English simple for Anthony's sake—something I noticed Paolo was disinclined to do. At the conclusion of my story, Anthony plied me with a few questions and then did the same to Jim, Benito, and the Frenchman who'd come with them to get me last night. They were kind enough not to contradict anything I said. Marcel was not.

"How clever of you to position yourself to be in the house when Tony was murdered," he said softly. All eyes turned back to me, shifting from curiosity to suspicion. I didn't like the feeling, not one little bit.

Jim rushed to my defense with, "If she had something to do with this, why be there at all?"

"Your femme fatale certainly made sure we were unable to question the man," Giles said.

"What do you call this?" Jim answered, waving the hotel receipt from Davos. "We're doing our part, here, you know. If anyone else wants to pitch in, that would be fantastic."

I heard a little bit of myself in that churlish response, and it made me smile. Jim took his turn to report on what he'd learned in Davos. At the mention of the assassin's London address, Marcel shifted uncomfortably, no doubt sensing suspicion would naturally fall on him.

In anticipation of the questions about to come his way, Marcel asked, "Did you find a photograph of this Mister Foley? Identification of any sort?" At Jim's shake of the head, Marcel seemed pleased. "Well then, might he have taken another guest's keycard and brought it with him, intending to plant it at the scene to divert suspicion from himself? Perhaps to direct it at me?"

"Seems plausible," Jim allowed. "But no more plausible than it being his own keycard."

"He may have checked in under an assumed name and address," Marcel argued.

"I think we can all agree the trip to Davos yielded no actionable information," Jim said. "Certainly no proof Regina was behind what happened last night. How did she find out where Tony was staying? Why kill him? Why not follow him back here and kill Paolo instead?"

Paolo asked, "If not Regina, then who?"

"Good question," Jim said, smiling thinly. "Wasn't it your idea to send Anna with him last night? Were you hoping she'd be killed, too? If so, you might want to refresh your memory on how hard she is to kill."

I wanted to be flattered, but the masked assassin could easily have put a few rounds in my back before I knew anything was wrong. Why he hadn't, I'd probably never know, but survival via dumb luck wasn't anything I could take credit for. Paolo reacted badly to Jim's suggestion, going so far as to rise from his seat and point a maledicting finger at him.

"You know it was Regina as well as I do! Yet you hurl accusations without a thought, without reason. Is this all fun and games to you, James?"

Wryly, Jim muttered, "Not exactly."

"Can't you see he's trying to turn us all against one other?" Giles asked. "Are Marcel and I the only people at this table who see an FBI agent sitting in Camposanto's chair?"

I hated to agree with Giles, but for the life of me I couldn't think of a better explanation for Jim's continued provocations.

"Did you send someone to kill Anna in April?" Jim asked Giles, making both Marchands blink in surprise. They exchanged a glance, mirroring one another's open confusion.

"No," Marcel finally answered.

"Did you send someone to poison her in Kraków?"

"Poison? Mon Dieu. No, of course not."

"Well, someone did. Anyone here want to take credit?" Jim asked the table at large. When no one answered, he said, "From where I'm sitting, it sure looks like everyone around this table is united by one thing: Regina Lira wants to punish all of us for what happened to her son. We can all sit here squawking about who started it, or we can decide what we want to do about it."

"When did David die?" I asked. All eyes turned to me, puzzled. "David," I repeated, looking to Jim for help. "It was around the beginning of May, wasn't it?"

"That sounds right," Jim said. "What are you getting at?"

"Someone's killing off people's family. I just think David should count."

"Obviously this is Regina's doing," Paolo snapped.

Anthony seemed to come to life, gesticulating angrily at Paolo. "This is your doing." He reverted to his poor English, further stilted by wrecked nerves, to cry, "He kill her son. What she would do, Paolo, huh? Lie down? Die? You have no sense, and this is the cost. Is too high. I blame you for this, for all of it."

"That doesn't do us any good now," Paolo dismissed, as

though that could be the end of it.

"You have two sons," Anthony snarled. "Why does Regina kill *my* son? What can she has against me? I don't even know until today she is a relative."

Jim cut in, "We can't answer that, but she can. And Holladay knows how to reach her."

"What are you suggest?"

"We move again, get somewhere safe, figure out what she wants, and decide if it's possible. If all she wants is to snuff us all out, we can decide from a position of safety how to handle it."

Paolo agreed, "We should leave this place. Someone may have followed them back here from Livigno, or Davos. It's not safe to linger."

"We still have much to discuss," Marcel said. "But if you want to take your leave, I doubt anyone will stop you."

"That's right," Giles pitched in, ever willing to create friction. "Run back to whatever hole you've been hiding from Regina in while we clean up the mess you've made with your ridiculous vendetta."

"How long have you known?" I asked Marcel, in French; but Paolo was having none of that.

"Marchand, if you answer her, I will consider our partnership at an end."

Marcel's eyebrows shot up a delicate few millimeters. "Our partnership? Does that still exist?"

He knew he held all the cards. Hadn't Tony told me Marcel could get "anything" into the United States? If that wasn't a temptation beyond what Paolo could bear, the same couldn't be said of Anthony.

He said, "This is not something we can deciding in an hour, and Paolo says right. We must leave."

"What of our American friends?" Marcel asked, smiling around the word 'friends'. "Will this be good bye and good luck? Perhaps we should be deciding whether we even need the FBI's help."

To my surprise, it was Enzo who spoke up. "James is family, too. Does that count for anything anymore?"

I met his eyes, stunned, and had to be snapped at by Giles again to translate his words into English. Enzo's contribution was met with rumbles of approval from all but the Marchand brothers. Both cottoned on quickly that the ground had shifted beneath their feet. Marcel chose a firm but diplomatic answer.

"I would just as soon abjure this perverse association with American law enforcement. However, since you all seem to be in agreement, I ask only that we be allowed to go our own way at the conclusion of all this. With Lira's network in your hands, you will no longer need ours."

No one seemed eager to agree to this, but I was quick to ask, "And Luke?"

"What about him?"

"Are you going to leave him alone?"

"I have no reason to do otherwise. Better men than he have fallen prey to duplicitous little vipers such as you, Anna."

Before I could respond, Paolo demanded, "Why can the FBI not eradicate Regina's cartel? They are operating on U.S.

soil, evidently unchallenged. Send one of your drones to kill her."

"That may be satisfying, but it won't solve your problem," Jim said. "It's not as though she's personally going after us, and we don't even know where exactly in Colombia she is."

"What is she wanting?" Anthony asked, more to express frustration than to get an answer. Jim provided one anyway.

"I suspect what happened to Tony last night is what she wants."

"Maybe we're all better off looking after ourselves," I ventured.

Paolo snarled, "You and James aren't going anywhere until I have good reason to trust you again."

"If you want the FBI's help dealing with Lira, the trafficking stops," Jim said. "That's not negotiable. In case I'm not making myself clear enough, that is exactly what makes the TIC the lesser of two evils here. You all know the United States' position on that."

I had to admire him for putting it out there, but the fact that we were surrounded by representatives of the greater of two evils made me question the wisdom of doing so just now. Jim seemed perfectly sanguine in the wave of hate-filled glances his announcement unleashed. Since Paolo had our passports, all Jim and I could do was link hands underneath the table and hope for the best. I realized I was gripping his hand way too hard when his fingers gave a twinge of protest.

"That is not something we are prepared to decide today," Paolo finally said.

"What are we going to decide today?" Jim challenged.

A short, impassioned argument erupted as to where we'd go from there, and whether we'd go together. In the end, no one could refute the bare facts: first David Marchand was killed, then Tony, not to mention all the attempts on my life. Clearly Regina was being generous with her blame and vengeance.

We were sticking together, at least for the short term.

That only left the question of where we'd go, and a consensus was reached with impressive swiftness. Though the Marchands had a secure and quite comfortable manor in Lyon, France, it wasn't large enough for all of us. Marcel also believed it was under more or less permanent surveillance by Interpol, and an influx of foreign nationals in fancy cars would raise every left eyebrow in international law enforcement.

Paolo's permanent residence would have been safest, but that was because no one knew where it was. Paolo preferred that it stay that way. Jim made a feeble effort to convince everyone to go to Canada or Mexico, but that was doomed to failure.

Anthony settled the brief debate by proclaiming, "There is more than plenty room on my island, and is perfectly safe."

12
Monday, June 21, 2021

According to Jim, I ought to have been grateful rather than dismayed that we were going to some island off the southern coast of Sardinia. He argued I shouldn't let Paolo's bad mood get me down, that Anthony and the others liked me and that was a good thing. I suspected they liked me the way Marcel liked Penelope, but I didn't pursue the topic.

Really, the decision to sail to Sardinia was the only smart one to make at that point. I didn't like it, but I knew we'd be safe there from Regina if not from each other. We'd at least be more comfortable, and the Sardinians would be able to see to their business more easily. Jim, Tommy, and I were simply along for the ride. Either Marcel and Giles were too, or they were quasi-prisoners who also had ample amounts of suspicion to allay before they could safely be turned loose.

The decision made, we all got ready to depart in great haste. I had all my stuff together in no time, but Jim was taking so much care to pack that I got bored and wandered down to the empty lobby alone.

I was perusing a bookshelf full of paperbacks assembled for hotel guests' temporary use, trying to decide which was most worth stealing, when someone behind me cleared his throat to get my attention. I turned to see Anthony standing at a respectful distance. Behind him, one of his grunts was carrying his luggage outside and paid me no mind. I didn't feel threatened per se, but I still looked around to see if Jim was nearby. He wasn't.

"I would have preferred to kill him myself, of course," Anthony started in, forcing my eyes back to meet his. At first I thought he was talking about his own son, but he went on, "But you beat me to it. The important thing is that he's dead."

"I'm sorry I couldn't save your son. I…" I stumbled, wondering why I was still talking, and blundered on, "He came onto me, and I slapped him down. He walked away from me, and I should have stayed with him, but… I didn't really believe there was any danger. I'm sorry."

I hadn't liked Tony one little bit, and I thought he'd gotten precisely what he deserved, but his father's grief touched even my hard little heart. Though I didn't know Anthony, I could see a change in him since his son's murder: He walked slower and seemed smaller. His English, already so poor, was worse. Wherever the rest of us were on the sliding scale of defeat and determination, he was openly and completely broken.

"He was my only son."

"We'll figure out who's responsible and kill them back," I promised. When he didn't respond, I asked, "Did you think something like this might happen?"

"I didn't believe there was any danger. As you said, it was Paolo's idea for you to go with him. This business with Regina, everything he's kept from me…" He shook his head, changing course to ask, "You are also with the FBI?" When I didn't deny it, he asked, "Do you like it?"

I was only too happy to change the subject. "Not really."

"Would you rather work for me?"

He managed to surprise me with that one. I frowned at him, wondering if he was joking. "Um… No disrespect intended, but I'm really not a fan of what you do."

"Which part?"

"All of it. But, mostly the human trafficking."

"Ah, of course. It is distasteful, I understand. Maybe I can change your mind."

He reached for his pocket and I flinched, causing a light chuckle to shake his bony frame. From his pocket he extracted the key to the Rimac. He tossed it to me.

"Even if you don't, the car is yours. I suspect Camposanto won't let you take it back to the United States, but at least while you're here you can drive it. Think about how long you'd have to work for your FBI to get one of your own."

I studied the key fob, certain I ought to give it back but completely unwilling to. Assured I'd take the bait, Anthony drifted away toward the front doors. Jim found me in the exact same position in which Anthony had left me.

"What's this?" he asked, plucking the key fob from my hand.

I related Anthony's offer, concluding, "I'm not going to go

work for him. I wouldn't do it for a hundred Rimacs."

"You sure?" he taunted, dangling the key fob in my face and daring me to make a grab for it. I rolled my eyes.

"Yes, I'm sure. Are you going to go full Dad on me and refuse to let me drive it to the coast?"

"I would never deprive you of such a pleasure. Paolo might object, of course."

"He can ride with me. Maybe I can smooth some of his ruffled feathers."

He studied me for a moment, then passed the key back to me. "Work it out with him. I trust you."

"Gee, thanks."

Paolo grudgingly agreed to let me chauffer him to the coast in the Rimac, even implying he might be safer with me than with his sons. I was beginning to get the impression that my victory over the AK-wielding assassin had raised me significantly in his and the other Italians' estimation.

I hoped he wouldn't ask me for a blow-by-blow, which would shatter the illusion of my prowess by making it clear I'd survived by no more than chance. The gunman had chosen, for whatever reason, not to shoot me in the back when I came down the stairs, and he'd relinquished the advantage of having a gun by coming so close before even trying to fire it. He might as well have saved me the trouble and just shot himself.

Fortunately, Paolo didn't bring it up at all. He grilled me on what I'd told Anthony, demanded to know why Jim was being so intransigent, and spoke as though it were a given that I'd be staying in Italy after Jim went home. I was just glad to hear him talk about letting Jim go.

Caravan-style, we departed the lodge at 2:00 p.m. on the dot and began wending our way south, losing nearly 6,000 feet of elevation in less than five hours. With a quick stop outside Milan to charge up, we arrived at a private dock in Genoa around sundown to board the yacht that had ferried Anthony and his company to the mainland.

Thanks to Anthony calling ahead and letting her crew know we wanted to depart as soon as possible, the *Luciana Quattro* was ready and waiting for us. I didn't ask what had become of *Lucianas* one through three.

A private ferry boat moved the cars aboard in twos and threes, where they were secured in the garage below decks. The yacht's sleek tender then ferried us all aboard to find rooms while final preparations commenced. We finally weighed anchor just before eight o'clock. I was ravenous.

Our party now numbered twenty-one, not including *Luciana's* crew: Jim, Tommy, and me; Paolo, Enzo, and Aldo; Marcel, Giles, and their four grunts; Anthony, Ottavio, and four more Sardinians whose names I had yet to catch; and four men, including Benito, who'd accompanied them to Switzerland for the same purpose as the Marchands' four: muscle.

The yacht—or superyacht, to be precise—wasn't meant to be a cruise ship. She was designed to mimic a mansion, affording a single family unit and a handful of guests the same luxuries and safety of a gated estate on land. Full-time crew members had their own accommodations, which were full, and that left a mere six rooms for twenty-one people to share.

This was no small problem, even going by simple math, and one Anthony had been working out during the drive from the lodge. The grunts, as the lowest on the pecking order, were shuffled unceremoniously into crews' quarters while their former occupants were required to double- and triple-up. That got us down to fourteen people.

Jim, Tommy, and I were relegated together to a single room on the starboard side near the stern. We had one queen bed and one sofa, not to mention a private bathroom and an ocean view, so I had to admit it could have been worse. It also could have been better. Given the choice, I would rather have sailed the Mediterranean in a luxury stateroom with just Jim, no Tommy, no mafiosos, and certainly neither of the Marchands, but I wasn't about to complain. At least I wasn't sleeping outside on the poop deck.

We skipped any sort of group dinner, since we were all quite sick of one another by that point, and ate in our quarters. As the lifeboats and the tender were being closely watched, rendering escape nearly impossible, we were left to our own recognizance.

After dinner, I took a shower and then wandered out onto the deck, masochistically probing the boundaries of my aversion to deep, open water. The sea was significantly calmer than the Atlantic Ocean. The air was warmer, the ship was nicer, and in fact the only detail that hadn't improved from my trip up the Argentine coast last year after recovering the Raphael was the company.

I longed again for some way to check on certain people in Texas about whom I'd thought nearly ceaselessly for the last week. Along with giving us passports, our boss Richard Beauchamp had afforded Jim's and my phones the ability to make international calls. Luke was, in fact, just a phone call away; but Paolo still had our phones, and we were a long way from being entrusted with them.

Lost in thought, I tottered up the deck and planted myself at the bow, which seemed to me a natural thing to do. At first I stood with my back to the gently heaving waves far below, watching shadows move to and fro in the interior of the ship until I grew bored enough to turn around.

Seeing the waves tossing far below me, I mastered a juvenile urge to spit over the railing and scanned the water, almost eager for a return of that horrifying sensation of helplessness and tininess that had afflicted me off the coast of Argentina. It never came, and I found myself enjoying the tickle of fine seawater on my face and the wind whipping my hair around playfully.

Of course, the enjoyment would be short-lived.

Deafened by the elements, I didn't hear him behind me and only realized I wasn't alone when two hands appeared on the rail on either side of me. I stiffened, not sure how to deal with the situation without risking a tumble overboard.

"Hello, Anna," came Giles' voice, his lips right at my ear, his tone an unsettling parody of fondness. "Thinking of going for a swim?"

I forced myself to stay still as his body pressed against mine. As intimidation tactics went, it was weak sauce considering the target. "Sure, I was just about to jump in. Join me on three?"

He breathed a laugh into my ear and purred, "Marcel wants

to talk to you, privately. God only knows why. He does seem to enjoy the company of dumb animals."

"If he wants to talk to me, then why am I talking to you?"

"Privately, Anna. For God's sake, pay attention to what I'm saying. We're in the last room on the starboard side off the main hall. There's a nameplate on the door that says 'Anthony,' so even you can't miss it. Will you come?"

"Jim and I will try to make an appearance, if it's safe."

"Only you."

I laughed. "Don't wait up for me, Giles."

"Oh, I think I will. What is it they say? Curiosity kills the cat."

He bit me on the neck (that nearly got a rise out of me, I'll admit it) and walked away, probably quite pleased with himself. If anyone witnessed this exchange, none rushed to my side to ask what had happened. I stared out at the ocean a while longer, then made my way to my own room to tell Jim about the invite. He found me en route.

"Where'd you go?" he asked with false casualness, gently taking my arm in his.

I related the encounter with Giles word for word and action for action. Jim's grip on my arm constricted while I spoke. When I got to the end, he brushed my hair aside to examine my neck, perhaps expecting two neat little vampiric puncture wounds. The bite hadn't hurt, so I knew there was nothing to see.

Nevertheless, he spat, "I'll kill him. Where does he get off, assaulting you like that? Why didn't you knock his teeth out?"

I shrugged. "What's the point? We're all supposed to be getting along for now. I'll teach him a lesson later." Meeting his eyes and seeing that tantalizing rage bubbling just beneath the surface, I added sternly, "Don't make a big deal out of it. Please."

"I won't, as long as you promise not to wander off alone again."

"It wasn't my fault!"

"I wasn't suggesting it was."

I started to continue on, but he held me back. I knew what was coming and I steeled myself, smiling patiently as his hands slid around my face.

"Are you okay?"

"Of course I am. That was bush league."

"Don't lie to me."

"I'm *fine*," I sighed. It was a bald-faced lie, but I nearly believed it; so he did, too. The reality that I was shaken to my core by something I should have been able to laugh off was not something I cared to discuss with Jim at that moment, any more than I cared to let Giles see he'd gotten to me. "Are you going to let me go?"

"I don't like it, but I do want to know what Marcel has to say. This is your psyop. It's up to you."

"Really? You're going soft on me, Jim."

13

Tuesday, June 22, 2021

In the wee hours of Tuesday morning, I listened to the slow, shallow breathing of my two suitemates and wondered which of them was only pretending to be asleep. My money was on both.

When the clock struck three, I decided I'd waited long enough. I slipped out of bed, silent on bare feet, and crossed the room to the door. There my plan hit a snag: The doorknob wouldn't budge. We'd been locked in.

Turning, I gazed out at the night sky through the patio door and asked myself how badly I wanted to know why Marcel Marchand wished to speak to me privately. Badly enough to risk drowning? Yes. Giles was right, darn it. I was curious.

As I crossed the room again, Tommy began to stir on the couch. I stopped and waited for him to wake, but he merely turned over and went back to snoring lightly. The patio door opened with a sharp crack, but even that didn't break through Jim or Tommy's sleep. Oh, they were so totally faking it.

I stepped out into the cool, salty air and took a deep breath. This was very stupid.

Luck had favored me in one regard. I'd already taken note of which door was the Marchands', and it was on the same side of the hallway as mine, a mere three doors down. All I had to do was climb over three, five-foot, glass partitions between our patios. No problem.

Okay, problem. The sea wasn't exactly rough, but the *Luciana* was rocking from side to side rather unpredictably. If she listed too hard to starboard at the wrong moment, I'd slide right over the side and head on down to Davy Jones' Locker.

I gripped the railing, stared out over the black waves, and asked myself again why this was so important. Again I came up empty-brained, and so I climbed onto a patio chair and grasped the rounded lip of the inch-thick, tempered glass that divided my patio from the next one. For a few seconds I felt the ship moving in time to the waves, then I picked up on a rhythm I hoped would last and heaved myself over the glass just as she began tilting away from the water below me.

That worked well enough to be getting along with, and I found myself three patios down in no time. If I had any doubt about whether I was at the correct patio, the explosion of barks from the other side of the glass door banished them.

The barking ceased as abruptly as it had started, and a heartbeat later the door was thrown open and I was dragged inside.

"Are you trying to give us heart attacks?" Giles hissed. "Why didn't you come to the door?"

"I was locked inside my room. You aren't?"

His only answer was to swear emphatically. Marcel muttered something to Penelope, and she pranced over to greet me.

"Thank you for coming, Anna," he said. "Would you care to sit?"

"I'll stand, thanks. What did you want to talk about?"

"Oh, she's in a hurry to get to the point after making us wait until three in the morning!" Giles whined.

Ignoring him, Marcel said, "You asked me how long I knew. What did you mean?"

"I was wondering how long you'd known Paolo was killing off Barbers. His vendetta, as Giles said."

"What do you want with this information?"

"I dunno, Marcel. Maybe I'm just trying to establish rapport."

"Anna, I am far too tired to deal with your habitually maddening attitude."

"Yeah, well, you asked me to come here." We held a staring contest for a few seconds. I sighed and relented. "I asked because neither of you seemed that surprised when it came up. I wondered if you really knew what it meant. Because of David."

Marcel's expression shuttered in an instant. Icily, he asked, "What about David?"

"Do you think Regina killed him?"

"If you must know, I've considered it. I worked it out myself, what Paolo was up to, after he sent Luke after the Sernas. I believe Anthony would have seen what was going on too, if he'd known about the business in Argentina. Killing Lira was to our benefit, but the Serna children… They had nothing to do with anything. Paolo took an innocent teenager in hiding and turned her into a ravaging wolf, and with Regina she is hunting down everyone involved."

"So, you're not a huge fan of Paolo?"

"Paolo Barbato is useless to me. Anthony and his compatriots do not need him. He's dead weight. An insane person who has dragged all of us into a war with an equally insane and very powerful woman."

"And he's in Camposanto's back pocket," Giles added.

"So what do you want from me?" I asked.

Marcel studied me for a long moment before asking, "James wishes to know why three of the Barber children were taken that night, and why none returned, doesn't he?"

"Yes."

"This is why he indulges Paolo. Helps him, even. He wishes to speak personally with Emilio Barber."

"Yes."

"Then I have some unfortunate news you may pass along to Camposanto: Emilio Barber is dead. Regina is the last of them."

I stared at Marcel's expressionless face, looking for some sign of deception. He seemed bored. I asked, "How do you know he's dead?"

He feigned indignation. "Are you questioning my integrity, or my sources?"

"Um…"

"Take the information to Camposanto. I'm sure he'll consider the source quite as cautiously as you. Good night, Anna."

I gave Penelope a quick ear scratch, then headed for the

patio. Giles followed me outside, ruining the fortifying Mediterranean air with his stupid voice by commenting, "I'm sure I don't want to miss this."

No snappy comeback occurred to me, so I tried to ignore him while I went back through the routine of waiting for the right moment to pull myself over the wall. The sea had become choppier, the ship moving in a less predictable rhythm, but I couldn't stand there like a fool forever. I swung one leg over the wall and immediately began sliding sideways toward the black maw of water below.

"Ah, ah!" I gasped, stupidly trying not to make too much noise as I went overboard to my death.

I slipped off the wall but grabbed onto the railing, which was a couple feet lower, and sent a murderous glare up at the grinning Frenchman while strength drained from my hands.

"Are you gonna help me?"

A resounding 'no' was written plainly on his face, but at an indecipherable call from inside the room, Giles rolled his eyes and helped me clamor back up over the rail and onto the patio. Talk about one step forward, two steps back: I was no closer to my room, and now I owed *Giles* my life. Ew.

I shoved him away from me, snapping, "Thanks a lot, le moron."

"If you're not feeling very nimble at the moment, you can try the hallway," he suggested.

"I told you, our door is locked."

Nevertheless, I left through their door and tiptoed down the hallway to see just how locked mine was. Of course it made no sense for a stateroom door on a luxury yacht to lock from the outside, but I didn't realize that until I saw the metal security bar propped under the door handle. I asked Giles to replace it once I'd gone inside, wished him a terrible night, and slid back into bed next to Jim.

I was beyond exhausted, but Jim saw fit to stop feigning slumber the moment I closed my eyes and whispered, "So, what did he have to say?"

I began a mumbled recitation of the quick conversation and fell asleep before finishing, but I thought I hit the high points.

▼

Sometimes when I dream, my brain plays reruns instead of coming up with something new. I suppose it could be attributed to laziness, but I prefer to think it's my subconscious telling me a topic isn't merely a source of curiosity or befuddlement; it's important. It's not something I *could* figure out, it's something I *must* figure out.

So, riding once more through Albuquerque, New Mexico, in the cramped back seat of Marcel's Demon, with Luke at the wheel and Jim in the passenger seat, I watched the scene unfold exactly as it had before: A news van approached and passed us, and a window in the back opened so someone within could send a horizontal shower of lead over the Demon. I remembered what came next right before the man leaned out the back window with a machine pistol and opened fire. Even know what was coming, I was too slow to return fire. A bullet cracked the windshield, Luke twitched, and the scene began to melt away. The sound, the shock, the wave of emotion as I realized Luke had been shot, all were dulled as though I'd built up a resistance to them. This time, I knew it wasn't real.

I woke up more puzzled than upset. Why did I have to see that again? Why the Challenger, why Albuquerque? It wasn't lost on me that the cherry red Demon was a few decks below me, hulking there in statuesque menace, a quiet reminder that reality wasn't nearly as separate from nightmares as I would've preferred.

I sat up instead and saw the bed next to me, as well as the couch across the room, were empty.

Running a hand through my tangled hair, I grimaced, realizing I hadn't washed it in nearly a week. I took a long shower, even going so far as shaving my legs and buffing away at my feet and elbows with a fruity little jar of sugar scrub someone had left behind. Feeling like a new woman, I got dressed—rounding out my ensemble with the delicious stilettos Enzo bought me—and meandered out to the balcony.

"Holy cannoli," I moaned, not quite capturing the beauty of the scene before me.

Where we were, I could only guess. This was a sight people like me only saw in movies, or perhaps splashed across the desktop background of her grandmother's computer.

About a half mile of water, painted turquoise, salmon, lavender, and lemon yellow by the reflection of the sunrise, lay between the *Luciana* and a compact, dense little coastal city being crowded into the sea by a shoulder of low mountains behind it. Smaller pleasure crafts peppered the water, so closely packed that I wondered how they could move at all. Across the water floated sounds of the city coming awake, everything from crowing roosters to whining superchargers.

While I stood, mesmerized into reverent silence, the yacht's tender zipped toward the ship, two crewmen in clean, white uniforms returning from a trip to land. As they slowed, veering to my right to dock at *Luciana's* stern, I called down, "Where are we?"

One merely laughed, but the other shouted back, "Monaco!"

"Monaco," I repeated to myself, getting my bearings.

We'd sailed west from Genoa, and not very far, but I was certain Sardinia lay directly south of Genoa. Heck of a detour to stop for supplies, assuming that's what had happened. Perhaps Anthony was attempting to make the meandering voyage look like a pleasure cruise rather than a business trip.

I was allowed to enjoy the view for two more minutes before movement to my right caught my attention. I glanced over to see Giles three patios down, leaning over the railing like I was. He had the decency to ignore me, but my moment's peace was ruined all the same. Returning inside, I looked around the empty suite and wished Jim were there. With Tommy out of our hair, we could lock the door and spend some time pretending this was nothing more than a romantic Mediterranean vacation.

I'd have to go and find Jim myself. He was probably too busy with the villains to entertain me, but it wouldn't kill me to try. Maybe I'd get a meal out of it, if nothing else.

The doorknob turned easily, no longer jammed from out-side, so I yanked open the door without a second thought. The blow came immediately, so quickly I thought I'd whacked my-self in the jaw with the edge of the door. I caught on that it was a fist when the second one hit me, this time in the ribs. I staggered backward, the man attached to the fists bulling after me into the room.

14

Tuesday, June 22, 2021

As I staggered backward one, then two, then three steps, a voice in the back of my head told me this was the kind of fight I had to win to survive. Then conscious thought abandoned me altogether.

I grabbed the back of my head with both hands, elbows forward, and crashed into my attacker, my right elbow landing a fairly powerful blow to his sternum as my left grazed uselessly against his right bicep. Momentarily rocking back on his heels from surprise, if not actual pain, he recovered quickly and wrapped me in a crushing bear hug. He was huge, bigger than Luke, nearly as tall as Jim. I felt like a rag doll in his arms. I tried to scream as the pressure forced air from my lungs and threatened to crack my ribs, but only a wheezing gasp came out. I boxed his ears twice before jamming my thumbs into his eyes. He gave a shout of protest and let me go, only to shove me so violently that I tripped over my stupid stilettos and fell backward.

I knew how to fall, and how to get back up, but he didn't let me get to the second part. Three kicks came in quick succession while I tried to protect my ribs and more vital organs. He paused to take a breath (beating someone up really is exhausting) and I seized the moment, locking my left foot around his ankle and jerking it toward me while I kicked his shin with my right foot. He went down, arms flailing, and managed to break his fall without injuring himself. At least we made some significant noise as his left arm crashed against a table and upset its contents onto the floor. Maybe someone would hear and come to my aid—or get killed with me.

The lamp shattered, and a wicker basket full of decorative metal balls spilled its contents to roll around on the floor. I grabbed the closest ball and hurled it at his face. The grapefruit-sized projectile connected with his nose and bounced off, accomplishing little more than enraging my attacker. I tried again to regain my feet and he tackled me, definitely cracking a couple of my ribs when he landed on me. I couldn't contain a wail, turning his grunt of exertion into a cruel laugh that caused a lull in the action while we both caught our breath.

It was enough time to recognize him as one of the Marchands' grunts, but no more. His hands wrapped around my throat, squeezing with such sudden and crushing force that I knew my windpipe would collapse any moment. Even so, I had to overcome some revulsion before I stuck my thumbs in his eye sockets again—the sensation of a stranger's eyeballs squishing against my thumbs was indescribably gross. I could have sworn I was up to the second knuckle before he finally screamed and let go of my neck, reaching for my face to pay me back in kind. I bucked with every ounce of strength I had left, which was enough to force him to catch himself with his hands but not enough to wriggle out from under the massive man.

I'd already stuck my thumbs in his eyes twice, so it didn't feel that much more intrusive to shove my hand down the front of his pants, grab his balls, and twist with all my might. His whole body went rigid for a second before he tried to push himself off the ground and away from me. I wrapped my right leg around his, bucked again, rolled him over, and tried to scramble away, but his hand shot out and grabbed me by the back of my jeans.

The burn of denim raking across my bare skin finally moved me from blackout fear to rage. As he pulled me backward, I twisted around and threw an elbow across his face, catching him in the temple. Instead of protecting his head, he grabbed my waistband with his other hand and tried to force me onto my stomach. I elbowed him twice more, hitting the same spot each time, until his hands loosened enough for me to scoot backward out of his reach and get my feet under me. Somehow, against all odds, those darn stilettos were still attached to my feet.

"What—is—your *problem?*" I gasped.

We stood in unison, sizing each other up. He was between me and the open doorway, in which I noticed absolutely no one appearing to come to my aid. Blood was seeping from the corners of his eyes, and he looked a little dazed, but I didn't like my chances of getting past him. I was as gassed as I'd ever been, and now that he knew what he was up against, I wasn't likely to win another round on the floor or on my feet. There's just no replacement for size and strength—except a weapon, but I had jack squat.

I backed one step toward the patio, then turned and fled. He was on me in a flash, one hand brushing my shoulder as I threw myself into a crouch against the railing. His momentum carried him over the too-short barrier, but not before his hand locked around my upper arm. He tumbled, yelling, into the drink with me right behind him.

Fear overtook me again as I sank like a rock through shockingly cold water. The last place I wanted to be was underwater with a very strong person who clearly wanted me dead. All he had to do was keep my head under for a minute, maybe less, and I'd be done. He'd let go of me in the fall, so I started swimming before my head broke the surface, not knowing where my foe was until a powerful hand locked around my right ankle. I kicked out with my free left foot, not really aiming at anything, and was surprised when the sharp toe of my stiletto made contact with something solid. The hand around my ankle fell away, I reached the surface, and I kept swimming. I was headed toward the shore, but I didn't change course. I'd swim all the way to Monaco if I had to.

When I was forced to stop and catch my breath again, I turned to see if he was behind me. Not only was he not following me, but he wasn't looking too hot. Twenty yards away, floating face down in the water, my assailant was bumping inertly against the stationary hull of the *Luciana* as gentle waves nudged at him.

For ten seconds I tread water, waiting for someone else to

notice and do something, before I finally screamed, "Help!" I had to repeat this ten or twelve times before a man and a dog appeared on one of the balconies. They both simply stared at me.

"You useless rock eating frog kissing idiot!" I screamed at Giles, who turned and disappeared into his room.

Penelope, who was standing with her front paws on the railing, leapt over and started doggy paddling toward me. I had neither the strength nor the will to fight her, but thankfully she had better intentions. She swam right up to me, allowed me to grab onto her collar, and began to tow me toward *Luciana's* stern. I tried to paddle with my free hand, but as adrenaline leaked away I began to sense injuries that did not feel minor. I had no idea how the little Malinois was managing both of us, until I realized my legs were kicking almost on their own. My feet were bare, those beautiful Italian shoes lost to the sea forever.

When we reached the flat loading bay where the crew had tied up the tender, two men came out to haul Penelope and me aboard. One jumped in to drag my vanquished foe out of the water, laying him down right next to me like we were co-victims in some stupid accident. I tried to shove the man's motionless body away, but the attempt caused so much pain my vision began to turn black.

The crewmember who'd pulled him out of the water began administering CPR, and the other vanished inside. Penelope lay down between me and my attacker, and I closed my eyes and focused on the gentle tickle of her wet fur against my arm instead of literally anything else. The air was warm, but not warm enough to counteract the water and the shock. I must have dozed off for a second, because when I opened my eyes again, I was covered in a scratchy gray blanket, and Jim was kneeling next to me.

"That's got to be murder on your knees," I groaned.

"What?" he asked, staring at me like I was crazy. "Anna, what happened?"

"Take me back to the room," I whined, clutching my ribs while I tried to catch my breath. "Or get this piece of garbage away from me."

"Can you stand?"

"I think. Let's find out."

Jim helped me sit up, then stand up. He and the same crew-member who'd helped pull me from the water half-led, half-carried me back to the room. We all paused in the doorway, except Penelope, who trotted inside and started sniffing around like she had to make sure the room was safe.

"Isn't that Marcel's dog?" Jim asked.

"She rescued me," I whispered. Recalling Giles' somewhat different response, I snarled, "Where is that Godforsaken knuckle-dragging French—"

"I'm right here, and you're welcome for summoning help," came Giles' waspy voice from somewhere behind me.

No one acknowledged him. Jim got me into the room and onto the bed, then paused to look around in horror at the mess we'd made.

"Oh my God," he groaned, almost reproachfully. "What happened?"

I pointed at Giles, attempting to explain, but trying to talk only doubled the pain in my ribs and called attention to more pain in my jaw. My attacker had put some power into those blows, and I knew from unhappy experience that the pain would only intensify as the adrenaline wore off.

"Ribs?" Jim asked. I nodded. "Okay. Go find help, you idiot, don't just stand there!"

Giles split, and Jim ran to the bathroom and returned with a wet towel, which he pressed to the side of my head. Was I bleeding? I hadn't hit my—oh, right, I had hit the door, hadn't I? That first right hook had sent me crashing into the edge of the door head-first, hence my confusion. While I replayed the struggle in my head, Jim took a closer look at the state of me and saw the button torn off my jeans. He became unnervingly still for a moment.

"Did he…?"

"No," I gasped, wincing. That was enough talking for now.

"That was one of Marcel's guys."

No doy, I wanted to say, but I just rolled my eyes. I also wanted to ask if I'd managed to kill my attacker and, if so, how; but that would have to wait.

Giles returned minutes later with a whole gaggle of people in tow, only one of which was of interest to me. Whether the superyacht came complete with its own Dr. McCoy or just a crewmember with the stones to tend to wounds with help from Google, I didn't much care.

The person who approached me was a woman about my mother's age who must have been halfway through her morning routine when she'd been wrenched from her quarters. Her uniform jacket was half-buttoned, the left and right sides misaligned, and her shoulder-length, black hair was damp and tangled.

She pushed Jim aside and started asking me questions. What hurt? Could I breathe? Had I hit my head? What year was it? And the like. After confirming I was in no immediate danger, she asked Jim if anyone else was hurt. He didn't understand, and I didn't understand why he didn't understand, which took me a moment to process. *Duh, she's speaking Italian.*

I told her what happened as succinctly as I could, and she excused herself to go check on my attacker.

"She was asking you if anyone else was hurt," I explained to Jim.

"I'll soon die from lack of information," he said. I couldn't tell if he was trying to be funny.

In quick bursts of ten or so words, I related the tale of my narrow victory to Jim. He cut to the most obvious question.

"Why?"

"We didn't talk about that."

"He's not dead," the Dr. McCoy woman said, sweeping back into the room with her arms full of first aid supplies. "But he's got a concussion." I watched her eyes dart quickly around the dis-combobulated room, and she added, "They're restraining him."

I just hoped they stuffed him somewhere secure before he came to, if he ever did.

With Jim's help, she divested me of my ruined jeans (the real tragedy, as they were the most expensive pair I'd ever owned) and the rest of my wet clothes and got me under the covers, which hurt more than anything had so far. Once there, though, the soft embrace of the mattress and pillows made it a tad easier to breathe.

She had brought a first aid bag from which she drew two cold packs, breaking the inner seals and pressing one to each side of my ribs. She then checked the towel against my head, possibly to gauge how much blood I'd lost so far. As head wounds went, it didn't seem that bad. She told me her name was Nedda and apologized that she didn't have a third ice pack for my jaw. I lied and told her it didn't hurt that badly. It had been a glancing blow.

Nedda gave me two huge, white pills, made sure I swallowed them, and asked Jim to keep me from falling asleep. I translated, and Jim gave a tight nod, intoning a low, sincere "Grazie" as she left the room, leaving the door ajar.

From a short way down the hall, she called, "I'll be right back!"

Jim sank down onto the bed beside me, taking care not to jostle me. "Every time I leave you alone," he said flatly.

The painkillers were already kicking in, and I reached out to flick him on the arm. "Shut up. You don't have to babysit me."

He chuckled without humor. "Apparently not. That guy was twice your size, Anna. What are you?"

Leaning back as my head doubled in weight, I sighed, "A ninja."

I felt a light tap to the tip of my nose.

"Hey. No sleeping. Open your eyes."

"Yeah, yeah. I'm so tired though."

"If you close your eyes again, I'll start singing show tunes."

"Yikes."

He watched me for a few seconds, and then his gaze darted into abstraction and back. Standing up, he crossed the room to the broken lamp and retrieved a ceramic shard roughly the size and shape of a pie knife. Nedda had left her first aid kit on the floor, and Jim rifled around inside to find a small roll of white surgical tape. He wrapped it around the top half of the ceramic shard, testing the grip a few times and adding more tape.

I watched all this with frank fascination, asking when he seemed satisfied with the result, "Are you making a shiv?"

"Well, we don't have guns. This is better than nothing."

"I didn't know you were a shiv-maker."

"Anyone can be, that's the beauty of the shiv."

He handed me the makeshift weapon, which I concealed beneath the comforter. Nedda returned, asking if I'd prayed to the porcelain god yet. I answered in the negative, which seemed to please her.

She had fetched a bag of ice from the kitchen and pressed it to my jaw, where I was imagining a bruise beginning to blossom into existence. I was lucky he hadn't dislocated my jaw, I guess. She also had a bottle of water and a thermos of bone broth, which she insisted I drink slowly.

She arranged all this on the bedside table while Jim tidied up the mess of broken lamp and stupid, useless, decorative balls.

"Ask her about the guy," Jim prompted.

I did, and she said with detachment, "Your attacker is awake. Judging by the goose egg on his temple, you almost beat him to death. They tied him to a chair in the brig."

"There's a brig?" I asked, eyes wide.

"Of course, ma'am, it's a ship."

She collected her supplies and departed, reminding me at the door not to fall asleep for at least a few hours. I relayed the message to Jim, then repeated her news about the captive.

"Strange things are afoot," he mused.

"At the Circle K," I finished gravely. He stared at me. "I'm quoting a movie. Don't look at me like I have brain damage. You're the one who said 'afoot' without meaning to be funny."

"I think it's time to encourage the brothers Marchand to walk the plank," Jim said. The lack of a segue threw me off, delaying an answer.

"It's too obvious," I whispered. I was fading, and I shook my head like a dog to stay awake.

"What is?"

"Marcel sent him after me? Come on. He's evil, not stupid."

"You said Giles—"

"I was wrong. If they wanted me dead, they missed a golden opportunity last night. Remember?"

He shook his head. "You told me Marcel said Emilio was dead, and I asked if he told you how he knew, and you mumbled something incoherent and fell asleep."

"Oh." I explained the near-drowning from which Giles had saved me against his better judgment.

He frowned in distaste. "I wish you wouldn't be so blasé about these brushes with death."

"I'll be whatever I want to do," I shot back, grinning as he leveled another concerned stare at me. "Quote. You need to watch more TV."

"Are you trying to convince me you're concussed?"

"No."

"If it wasn't Marcel, then who? Maybe Giles couldn't live with the knowledge that he'd saved your life."

"No. Someone who wanted to make it look like one of them."

"Any guesses who?"

"Besides literally everyone else on this ship?" I asked. He dithered, not answering fast enough, so I asked, "How did you two get out of the room, anyway? I only almost died because someone locked us in here last night."

"The door wasn't locked, not when I left at six. I took Tommy with me," he added hastily.

"That was hours ago. What have you been doing?"

"Listening to a bunch of cranky old men arguing," he groaned. "Did you know a group of old Italian men is called a 'bloviate'?"

"Wow, harsh. I'm not sure you're Italian enough to get away with that," I chided. "What are they bloviating about?"

"They want to contact Regina, today. Before we get to the island."

"I sense I'm going to be left out."

"That's still up in the air. I don't want Regina to know you're here, but obviously I can't leave you alone."

"What's a control freak to do?" I taunted.

I was basking in his frank lack of amusement when someone knocked on the door. As it was still wide open, this was mere courtesy. Jim jumped to his feet at the sight of Marcel standing in the open doorway, Penelope heeling at his side. I didn't recall seeing the little dog leave, but she was very stealthy. The Frenchman raised his hands to signal non-aggression.

"I know you won't believe this, but Giles and I had nothing to do with what Victor did."

"Leave," Jim gritted. My hand closed around the ceramic shiv, just in case.

"I will. I simply came to deliver a peace offering." He glanced down at Penelope, who looked up at him adoringly. "Someone to watch your back. You obviously need it, and Penelope seems to feel protective toward you."

"More like someone to maul her when you blow a whistle," Jim argued.

"Nonsense. Penelope likes Anna. She's a pet, not a killer. But she will defend you, if needed."

"Why would you give her to me?" I asked.

"*Loan* her," Marcel corrected. "I can't have you getting killed before I'm ready to do it myself. After last night," he said, lowering his voice to a confiding murmur, "I would have thought that was self-evident."

"Wow, that's… honest."

Jim said, "I don't think so, Marcel. Get lost."

"No," I squeaked as Marcel shrugged and turned to go. "I want her. Please, Jim?"

"You can't be serious."

"Serious as cancer." When he failed to object further, I looked at the gently vibrating Malinois and said, "Komm."

Good girl to the core, she looked up at Marcel and waited

for his nod before loping into the room, leaping gracefully onto the bed, and stretching out next to me. She was still wet and smelled like it, but her presence felt right, a missing piece that wasn't missing anymore. I rubbed her belly, smiling as the pain in my ribs, face, and head faded to a dull roar.

"Thank you, Marcel," I said, but he was already gone.

Jim sat next to me again, eyeing the little Malinois with overt suspicion. "What is Marcel playing at?"

"Same as you, I assume. Masterminding. Puppeteering. Machiavelling."

"I hope you're right about Penelope."

"I am. She's a good girl."

The only downside to having Penelope in my room was that Jim felt safe enough leaving me with her to exclude me from the call with Regina. I groused and begged and threatened, all to no avail, and Jim left me thirty minutes later to go up to the common room and take part in the pre-call meeting. He urged me not to fall asleep, which I did less than five minutes after he left.

15

Tuesday, June 22 to
Wednesday, June 23, 2021

When I woke up, the light had shifted dramatically. Dusk had descended, plunging the unlit room into murky half-light. I'd slept the day away. Feeling blindly for Penelope, I sighed with relief at the feel of her soft, warm fur. She hadn't left my side. I groped on my other side for the lamp and clicked it on, bathing the room in a warm, comfortable glow. It was just me and the dog, Jim and Tommy nowhere in sight.

"I don't know how I'm supposed to take you to do your business," I mumbled. "Or even where."

On cue, she rolled upright and trotted to the bathroom. Moments later, I heard the unmistakable sound of tinkling. Holy crap, this dog was smart. Was she smarter than Dude? She flushed the toilet (no, really) and returned to the bed, letting out a gusty, impossibly angsty sigh.

"I'm bored, too. What is taking them so long?"

I waited and waited, and night fell. I couldn't sleep anymore, but I couldn't get out of bed. My ice packs had assumed room temperature, my water and bone broth were gone, the painkillers had worn off, I desperately needed to pee, and I was dying of hunger and thirst. When did Penelope eat? What did she eat? Had I died in my sleep, or much earlier at Victor's hands? Was any of this even real?

Motivation to stand up warred with certainty that my body wasn't quite up to it yet. Finally, something happened. Penelope's ears perked up, and a key turned in the lock. She woofed a low warning to whoever it was.

"It's just me," Jim said in the voice he reserved for talking to Dude. He propped open the door so he could carry in a huge, heavy-looking tray, smiling when he saw I was awake. "Hungry, ladies?"

"Is this real?" I mumbled.

Busy with the tray, Jim asked distractedly, "Is what real?"

"This. Am I dreaming?"

He shrugged. "Pinch yourself."

I did. Nothing changed. "Jim, she used the bathroom."

"Where?" he asked sharply, gaze sweeping the floor for puddles and piles.

"No, she used *the* bathroom. Like a little person. I thought I was seeing things."

"Holy crap."

"Will you help me up? I need to go, too."

Jim found a t-shirt and shorts for me to wriggle into, then helped me climb out of bed. Even with him being exceptionally gentle, the pain was severe, focused in my lower, right ribs where the second fist had landed. They must have been weakened by that blow and succumbed more readily than my other ribs to the subsequent traumas. Thanks to the punch to the jaw and the door to the head, I got a splitting headache as soon as I was on my feet. Had the need to pee not been so urgent, I'd have collapsed right back into bed.

Assuring Jim I didn't need his help in the bathroom, I took care of business with all the haste of an arthritic tortoise. I stripped off my shirt and examined myself in the mirror, assessing bruises and tiny cuts and a bit of dried blood in my hair. I rinsed this out, washed my face, put my shirt back on, and left the bathroom to find Jim sitting on the bed. He was watching in open-mouthed astonishment as Penelope devoured a raw Cornish game hen whole. The sound of bones crunching was indescribable.

"I thought chicken bones were verboten," I said, overawed.

"Cooked are. Raw is fine. The mess said this is what Marcel ordered for her."

"Dude would fall head over heels for her," I sighed. We watched in mutual amazement until she was finished, and then I asked, "Are you gonna tell me about the call?"

First he helped me back into bed and set a tray of food across my legs. I ate slowly for once, chewing each bite into oblivion rather than risking indigestion on top of everything else. Jim skipped the long version and gave me the CliffsNotes.

"They eventually agreed to give Tommy his phone so he could call her on speaker. She didn't answer. There were two missed calls Tommy claimed were from her, so we think she figured out he didn't have his phone."

"So that's it? No way that took all evening."

"It didn't. They've been speculating ad nauseam about what to do. I came down to check on you earlier, but you were asleep. I woke you up—not all the way, I guess—"

"I don't remember this…"

"I had to go back before I missed too much. They've been arguing for hours. I just now convinced them to call it a night."

"What's to argue about? Are they going to call her again? Are we still going to the island?"

"Everything, they haven't decided, and yes."

I destroyed a few more bites of food and asked, "Any luck with the guy whose butt I kicked?"

"You cocky little monster," he said warmly. "No one's talked to him yet. We thought we'd let him stew until we get to the island."

"He better be under guard. Whoever put him up to it—assuming anyone did—isn't going to let him talk."

"I know. Enzo's watching him now, with one of the crew. Two man teams on rotation all night. This isn't my first day, kiddo."

"Mmhm." Belatedly, I noticed the ship was in motion. I hadn't felt it start, so we'd been on the move at least since dusk. I glanced out the window, garnering zero information. "How much longer am I stuck on this tub?"

"We'll be there by noon tomorrow."

▼

His words proved slightly premature. I snapped awake before dawn the next morning, my ribs screaming for attention, my breaths coming in short, painful gasps. I held out until the sun rose, then shook Jim awake and told him I possibly needed medical attention immediately. Unfortunately, an even more immediate concern made itself known shortly after Jim found Anthony.

I was less than surprised to hear the news that my attacker, Victor, was gone. Jim went full FBI agent and examined the scene closely before questioning everyone on the ship, using me as a translator, but nothing more than the bare facts could be gathered:

Enzo's watch had ended at midnight, and he and the crewman on watch with him insisted the man was alive, restrained, and secure when they'd turned the watch over to Aldo and another crewman. They told the same story, and their watch had ended at four in the morning. Since preparations for breakfast began around the same time, and the brig was so near the kitchen that the crewmembers in the mess were as good as a change of guard, there was no third pair of watchmen.

Sometime between 4:00 a.m. and 7:30, when Anthony had gone down himself to check, Victor had vanished, dead or alive. No security cameras existed anywhere on the ship, so there was no footage to review. All Victor left behind was a pile of zip-ties that had been cut with a knife or a pair of scissors.

For my part, I was glad he was gone. Either he'd acted on

his own, in which case good riddance, or someone was pulling his strings, and that person was still around to cause problems with or without Victor. I hadn't expected Victor to tell us who it was anyway, and I hadn't relished the thought that he may be tortured for the information. Although, as the day wore on and my pain grew, I might have stooped to slicing off one or two of the guy's toes given the chance.

The severity of my injuries couldn't be ascertained by any means available on the *Luciana*. Dropping in on some random doctor along the way was ruled out, as he or she would be asking all sorts of inconvenient questions. I had to white-knuckle my way through most of the trip, which took a slight detour to Cagliari, where Anthony's trusted doctor's offices were located.

We anchored off shore, and Nedda the nurse helped me into the tender, followed by Anthony. A minor kerfuffle followed as Jim insisted on accompanying us, as did Paolo. Perhaps I'd come to think too highly of myself, but I felt like the three of them were fighting over me. True or not, the thought gave my ego a boost it obviously didn't need. It wasn't a fair fight, anyway, not with Jim among the contenders. Anthony refused to allow anyone else on the tender, and that was the end of that.

The doctor's office was so near the marina that by the time we all climbed into a cab, navigated the thick traffic, waited in a queue to be dropped off at the medical complex, and finally got out of the cab, we could've walked the distance twice. Then we waited. For four hours. It seemed the doctor had his hands full on a Wednesday.

Doctor Graziella was a kindly old man in his 70s who treated me with kid gloves, speaking to me in the most basic Italian as though I'd sustained a serious head injury or perhaps spoke at a kindergarten level. I didn't bother correcting him.

After a few X-rays and some probing for possible internal bleeding, he plied me with a week's supply of powerful opiates for the pain, made me take two, and sent me on my way.

"Cracked," I announced to Nedda and Anthony in the aptly named waiting room. I pointed at my right side. "Numbers six and seven. Everything else is fine. Nothing to do but wait for them to heal, which could take about six weeks. He told me to be more careful going down the stairs."

Deaf to my pleas to be allowed to explore the city a bit, Anthony whisked us back to the tender as though pursued by an army of assassins. I hadn't seen anything remotely suspicious or threatening in the city, though there did seem to be an unusually high concentration of restaurants on our route from the doctor back to the marina.

No one else in my company seemed to need or want food as often as I did, and when I pointed out that I'd skipped breakfast and was once more on the verge of death, Nedda was mildly surprised to find it was nearly dinnertime, and Anthony didn't even feign interest. He did offer some consolation, namely that supplies from the ship would be distributed when we got to the island, and he'd order more as soon as he could. All I had to do was tell him what I wanted, which I did with gusto.

All in all, I was glad to reach Anthony's island a couple hours after we weighed anchor in Cagliari. The trip south from Monaco had taken us away from the coast into open water, night had fallen, and I was tired of being stuffed in a fancy, tin can floating helplessly above opaque, sea-monstery depths. I needed to feel the ground beneath my feet and regain some semblance of privacy and solitude.

Luciana dropped anchor into abyss-black waters about a quarter mile from a spit of land cloaked in eerie darkness. When I was closer, borne along by the swift tender toward a dock on the south side of the island, I could see lights dotting the distance, describing a very small area indeed.

Climbing off the tender via gangplank and standing on a gently swaying dock, I realized at last why this island was so safe: Anthony wasn't sharing it with anyone. He stood next to me, watching me take it in, while the crew unloaded our luggage.

"Only eight point three square kilometers, but it's enough for my family and me. I have a private race track for the cars, of course. When you're feeling better, you can take the Rimac—"

"Cut it out," I said churlishly.

"I'm merely being a good host, introducing you to the island. I'd be happy to give you a tour tomorrow, when it's light."

"I—" I started to decline, but thought better of it. "I'd like that. Jim and I would like that."

"Do you know how to ride a horse?"

"Anthony, I'm from Texas. But I don't think I can with my ribs cracked."

"Ah, of course."

Like an exclusive island resort, the area was dotted with villas that varied in size from Anthony's own sprawling home to tiny little one-room villettas. I only knew this because Jim, Penelope, and I were driven past many of them in a golf cart on the way to the temporary abode Anthony had picked out for us: a two-room villa on the far north side of the island.

Evidently the combination of Anthony's developing fondness for me and being trapped on an island meant we were being trusted with upgraded privacy. I wasn't complaining, especially since Tommy wasn't being shoehorned in with us again, but I couldn't help but deplore Paolo's continued refusal to return our passports and phones.

While Jim carried our luggage into the house, I stayed put in the passenger seat next to Benito, who'd driven us there. Wondering if I was growing on him too, I wagered, "Can I ask you a favor?"

"You can ask," he replied, neither encouraging nor discouraging.

"Paolo has my passport. Jim and Tommy's, too. And a bunch of other stuff we'd really like to have back. But he's not in charge here, is he?"

"He isn't."

"Maybe Anthony could convince Paolo to give them back. It would be a sign of good faith."

"Is there good faith?"

"I'd like to think so."

"I will ask, but don't get your hopes up."

Jim came out to help me inside, and Benito left. The villa was built to look old on the outside, but inside it was sleek, modern, and open. Jim had turned on every single light, probably to check all the dark corners for unpleasant surprises. I waited on the couch with Penelope while he prowled through the entire villa twice more, checking the locks and turning the lights off. When we finally crawled into bed, I popped a painkiller and followed it up with two big glasses of water. Jim wouldn't let me mix wine with opiates, the fascist.

I won't lie: Falling asleep next to Jim, aching but reasonably comfortable with a Mediterranean breeze ruffling the curtains and a highly-trained guard dog posted in front of our bedroom door, I gave serious thought to the offer Anthony made back in Silvaplana.

16

Thursday, June 24, 2021

An island tour on horseback was, of course, completely out of the question. The painkiller I'd popped before bed wore off during the night, so for the second morning in a row I exploded into wakefulness with a gasp of pain. Jim stirred, woke up just enough to grab me some medicine and water from the bathroom, and cuddled up next to me for three more seconds before Penelope began to whine and scratch at the door.

"Oooooarrrgh are you kidding me," he moaned, causing me to shake with painful laughter.

"If you take her for a walk, she'll love you forever."

"She knows how to use a toilet!"

"She's basically a velociraptor, Jim. She needs to run around or she'll eat us alive."

"Marcel gave her to us to drive us crazy."

"Loaned."

"Fuuuuuuh."

After a bit more whining and moaning, he stumbled out of bed, into some shoes, and out the door, Penelope dogging his steps with apoplectic little half-barks. This left me alone in the isolated villa, but my opiates were far and away too effective to let me care about that. I heard Jim leave via the back door and fell back asleep almost immediately.

▼

A beautiful woman was standing over me when I woke up.

I blinked up at her, unused to this particular variety of vivid dreams. Maybe it was the opiates. She smiled shyly and backed up a step.

"I didn't mean to startle you," she said in Italian, her voice a gentle whisper. "Um. I'm Eva. Grandfather sent me?" She shrugged, evidently hoping that would explain her presence.

I sat up, pushed my tangled hair away from my face, and took a closer look at my visitor. Roughly my age, she carried about fifteen extra pounds very gracefully, accentuating this in a sleeveless, blue cotton dress cinched in at the waist. With chin-length, thick brown hair, no jewelry, and not a drop of makeup, she looked so charming and pretty I thought I'd die of embarrassment right then and there.

"Um," she repeated, uncomfortable under my astonished stare. "He wanted me to bring you this."

From a canvas bag she carried, she withdrew a laptop, two cell phones, three wallets, three passports, and a tangled bundle of charging cables. These she placed on the nightstand before backing toward the door.

"He requested that you not make him regret the kindness. Whatever that means."

I found my voice and asked, "Anthony? He's your grandfather?"

"Well—" she started, interrupting herself with a tight-lipped smile. "Yes. And, you are Anna?"

"That's me. Are you—was Anthony—Tony—your father?" I felt stupid just for asking. No way were there even ten years between the two of them. She shook her head, no obvious sadness marring her features at my mention of the departed.

"No. Um. I should go. It was nice to meet you, Anna."

"You too…"

I watched her disappear through the door, unconsciously leaning sideways to catch the last twitch of her skirt as she rounded the corner. A moment later I heard the door open. Eva let out a high-pitched, "Oh!" that blended into Penelope's bark of greeting. I assumed the rumbles of speech I heard constituted Eva explaining her presence and Jim responding, but I couldn't make out their words. The door closed, and Jim appeared in the doorway. He smirked knowingly at me.

"Oh my God," I mouthed.

"She's pretty," he wheedled.

"Pretty?" I laughed. "She's a snack. But you can't say that, she's probably related to you."

"He won't tempt you beyond what you can bear," Jim said piously. He looked past me and asked, "Is that what I think it is?"

"Mhm. A full complement of previously confiscated stuff. Eva brought it."

He was already plugging in his laptop and powering it up as he asked, "Why?"

"I asked Benito to ask Anthony to ask Paolo to give it back."

His eyes met mine over the edge of the laptop. "That's it? You just… asked?"

"Yeah," I said with a modest half-shrug. "I can't believe you didn't think to try that."

"You are unbelievable," he muttered.

With my patience slipping away, I listened as Jim called Beauchamp, then our BKA contact, Ingrid, to give them both a quick update on where we were and what we knew. As tuned in as I ought to have been to what Jim chose to share—or not share—with each of them, I found my attention waning.

"Can I call—my parents?" I asked, stopping myself before Luke's name popped out of my mouth.

I saw his eyebrows push together. "I know it's difficult, but I think you should wait."

"Yeah, yeah." My phone chirped, and I snapped it up as Jim lunged for it. "Why? Ow. That hurt my ribs."

"Who's it from?"

I thumbed through my notifications, replying, "Who isn't it from? My mom, Dom, Luke… Good thing I've got notification previews turned off. This thing's almost fully charged. Paolo must've been keeping it plugged in, which means he was probably keeping an eye on it."

"See if he answered any calls."

"… Nope. He had plenty of chances, though. My mother's been particularly persistent."

He checked his phone and added, "She's been after me, too." Seeing the look on my face, he warned, "Take a breath. If anything had happened, Rich would've told me."

"If he knew."

"If it were bad enough for you to worry about, he'd know."

"All right, all right."

I tossed my phone on the bed and picked up Tommy's passport instead. As Jim, then Paolo had no doubt already done, I flipped through the visa pages to see where he'd been. They were bare except for his most recent arrivals in Amsterdam, then Rome, then Florence. I flipped back to the photograph page, where a recent photo of Tommy was paired with the assumed name Martin Vanover. The passport was issued in May of this year.

"It's brand new," I sighed. "Regina must have gotten him a new one so we wouldn't know where he'd been."

Distracted, Jim mumbled, "Right."

"Well, this isn't as exciting as I thought it would be," I said, beginning the tedious process of levering my broken body out of bed. "I think I'll hobble on down to the main house and see what Eva's up to."

"Yeah. Okay."

"Or maybe I'll go see what Enzo is up to."

"Mhm."

"I bet Enzo *and* Aldo—"

"I get it, Anna. I promise I'll pay lots of attention to you after I'm done here, okay?"

Huffing all the way, I took a shower, got dressed—carefully ignoring the bruises and abrasions all over me—and found an apple and some cheese in the kitchen. I was too hungry to question where they came from or how long they'd been there.

While I ate, I cleared out the messages on my phone. Luke and Dom had checked in five and three days ago, respectively, both via text. Neither seemed to expect a response. My mother, on the other hand, had called two to three times a day since Monday morning, hadn't left a single voicemail, and had only sent one text yesterday afternoon stating, "Please call me." Only sincere respect for Jim kept me from calling her to see what was going on.

There was no coffee in the villa, so I was highly motivated to find my way to the main house. Penelope and I set off on foot in a generally southern direction, following the road we'd traveled by golf cart the previous night. The going was slow, but the island in daylight was so breathtaking I didn't feel bad about stopping to catch my breath every few minutes.

Under a cloudless, sapphire sky, the island's rolling hills were blanketed by a grey-ish green, scrubby bush. Sand and gravel crunched underfoot, reminding me of southwest Colorado. If not for the near total absence of trees, I might have been able to imagine myself back there. The few trees I did pass were the tallest things around, every one of them looking well cared for and probably older than the country I called home.

Though I passed a number of other dwellings, some of which had to be playing host to people from the *Luciana*, I didn't see anything going on. The reason why became apparent when I finally reached Anthony's home, a three-story mansion at the center of multi-acre grounds. I passed under a limestone archway and through a verdant tunnel of overhanging olive trees to get from the road to the front door. It was love at first sight, from the ivy-covered façade to the campanile rising from the back of the house.

The poorly-attended car show had moved to Anthony's house. For two seconds I deplored my inability to call Jim before I remembered my phone was in my pocket. He answered after several rings.

"Hey, where are you?" he asked.

"Anthony's house. Everyone's meeting here without you."

"No, they aren't. Benito came and got me in the Rimac after you left. Guess you took the long way here."

"You're at the house?"

"Yep. Come join us in the parlor."

I hung up, aggrieved, now feeling the ache in my ribs like a deliberate insult. Everyone else had gotten their cars off the *Luciana*, but I hadn't even thought to ask about the Rimac Anthony had supposedly given me. Apparently Benito had a spare key. Once I was nearer the front door, I spotted 'my' car under a covered portico, waiting like a stalking butler. I smiled at him, wondered what I was going to name him, and let myself and Penelope into the house.

It didn't take a detective to figure out where everyone was. I simply followed my ears to a closed door off the foyer behind which voices rose and fell in earnest argument. When I entered, the arrangement of bodies around the room made the source of the disagreement all too clear.

Tommy sat between Enzo and Aldo on a sofa in the middle of the parlor, Paolo standing behind them. The cell phone in Paolo's hand had to be Tommy's. Marcel and Giles, accompanied by only one of their grunts, stood next to a large, freestanding globe near the door. Jim stood on the other side of it. Across the room sat the rest of our unhappy group, including Anthony.

The strategic tug-of-war couldn't have been clearer, but Jim explained anyway, "It seems we're not all on the same page about giving Regina another call."

17

Thursday, June 24, 2021

I had to choose a side, but Jim seemed to be aligned with the Marchands at the moment. I considered walking over to Anthony just to see how Jim would react, but I swallowed my revulsion for the Marchands and joined Jim next to the globe.

"Why aren't we on the same page?" I asked.

Anthony answered for him, "The less we have to do with her, the better. What can she tell us that we don't already know? This is self-indulgent lunacy."

"English," Giles hissed.

I wondered why none of the other Sardinians ever spoke up, but perhaps Giles' command was also an answer. If Anthony was the best English-speaker among them, maybe they trusted him to speak on their behalf.

Anthony was gearing up for an angry reply when Tommy's phone rang in Paolo's hand. He held it up and asked, "You would have me ignore this? She's trying to send a message. Don't you want to know what the message is?"

"Ah, just answer it," Marcel snapped.

Paolo came around the sofa, put the phone on a table in the center of the room, and answered the call. He pressed the speaker button before backing away, nodding imperiously at Tommy.

"Señora?" Tommy prompted.

"Thomas. Where have you been? Are you all right?"

Her voice, flavored with a slight Colombian accent from decades as an expat, was somewhat disappointing. It was thin, high-pitched, and almost petulant. I reminded myself that Regina Lira was an old woman, and I couldn't fault her for sounding like one. Her next words were stronger, as though she'd heard the same thing I heard.

"Are you alone?"

"No, Señora," Tommy said.

Several seconds passed while she considered this. Finally, "With whom exactly do I have the pleasure of speaking?"

"Paolo Barbato," Paolo said. The way he said his own name spoke volumes about how impressed he was with himself. For what reason, I couldn't guess. No one else spoke up to be counted.

"Ah," Regina said, a smile in her voice. "So nice to finally hear your voice. Marisol is here with me. Say hello, mija."

'Mija', she called her. My daughter. The implication was clear, to me and likely to most everyone else there: What you've done to Marisol, you've done to me.

A more familiar voice intoned obediently, "Hello."

Marisol sounded desperately sad. That was a surprise, as I'd expected her to be enjoying the game of cat-and-mouse with the person responsible for turning her life upside down. I realized I was only distracting myself by focusing so intently on the minutia, and I tried to tune in to the conversation.

"Why have you called, Nephew?" Regina was asking. "Has something happened?"

Her grotesque imitation of concern caused Anthony's face to redden. He barked, "You kill my son! Why?"

"Who is that? Paolo, I thought you liked to hide alone under a rock. Who's there with you?"

"I'll let them speak for themselves," Paolo growled.

So, like students at roll call, we went around and said our names. It was tedious and stupid, but at least I learned the full names of the other Sardinians at long last: Octavio (not Ottavio) Palermo was the old man with the liver spots and the rich voice. Geo Oristano and Raphael Russo, of an age with Octavio and Anthony, had been in London at Marcel's place back in December.

That left Marco and Bambino Cagliari, who looked like father and son. The Cagliaris were the two additions to the five who'd been in London, and one of them might have been the 'documents guy' I'd heard about at Marcel's meeting. Anthony's last name turned out to be (drum roll, please) Farina. Yummy. Since I was making the attempt to learn them, their names managed to stick this time.

Marcel spoke for himself and Giles, and Enzo and Aldo said nothing. When my turn came up, Jim actually covered my mouth with one hand and shook his head. I glared at him, as did many in the group, as he recited his own name. He was the last to speak, and no one saw fit to audibly challenge him for leaving me out. No one, that is, except Regina.

"James. What a surprise. Is Anna Bowman not with you?" she asked sharply.

"Of course not," Jim answered. "Why would she be?"

"And your assassin, Jackson?"

"We've lost track of him," Jim said. "I assumed you'd caught up to him and killed him."

"Sadly, no. Paolo? I am surprised to hear so many people stand with you after what happened to young Tony Farina. Such a shame. How is my brother, Emilio?"

I couldn't stop myself glancing at Marcel as Paolo answered, "He's none of your concern."

Marcel raised his eyebrows at me as though to say, "See?" I looked away before anyone noticed the exchange. I hoped.

Regina laughed. "How sad. How spread out we all became." Her voice shrank away from the phone, possibly in an aside with someone we couldn't hear. A moment later she returned to say, "Marisol says this is a waste of time. These young people have no patience for the art of conversation. I suppose you all want to ask me something?"

Regina's invitation was met with crickets on our side of the call. We all knew whose job it was to answer that question, and everyone turned to stare expectantly at Paolo while the silence stretched on and on. After what seemed like an eternity, during which Regina waited in absolute muteness like a professional salesman, Paolo cleared his throat and asked, "What do you want from us?"

"From you, Nephew? Nothing at all. Maybe your sons? Did you hope by keeping them silent I wouldn't know of their existence? I've known for a while. But I don't think killing your sons would really make me happy. Did killing my son make you happy?"

Hardened by her not-very-veiled threat, Paolo snarled back, "Yes, it did."

An explosion of Spanish tore out of the little cell phone, not from Regina, but from Marisol. I was the only one who understood her screaming, "You son of a whore! My brother never did anything to you, you piece of scum, I hope you die a thousand times and go to hell and rot there! You animal!"

Regina let her have it all out, then said in a voice almost too low to hear, "Go rest, child. Go on, go." A pause, and Regina switched back to English to say, "I'm sorry, she's very distraught. Her brother was murdered recently, you know."

"What do you want?" Paolo repeated.

"Let me think about it. I want to see all of you. It's the twenty-first century, for God's sake! Can't we figure out how to set up a video call?"

I sensed she'd picked up on the presence of another silent participant, though whether she knew it was me wasn't clear. Jim was now in the hot seat, for some reason, and he said slowly, "I think we can manage that. It might take some time."

"Excellent. I'll await your instructions. Oh, and do be gentle with Thomas. He didn't start this."

The call ended, and Tommy stared at the phone. I could practically see the wheels turning in his head. He groaned and sat back.

Marcel moved toward the door, followed by Giles, and said to no one in particular, "Let us know when the next call is scheduled."

They departed, leaving an obvious question in their wake. When no one else asked it, I piped up. "Can't we ditch those guys? They're not bringing anything to the table."

"Marchand is our way into the United States if things don't work out with Lira," Anthony explained. "That's why we partnered with him in the first place."

"But he's so evil," I complained.

"Why don't you want Lira to know she's with us?" Geo asked in Italian, pointing a finger at me as though 'she' didn't narrow it down enough. "What are you playing at?"

I relayed his question to Jim, who shrugged, smiling to himself. "Tell him I'm playing Four-D chess."

After I'd done just that, trying not to communicate Jim's smug overtones, Anthony fired back, "No games, Camposanto."

"No. No games. Now if you'll excuse us, I've got to go figure out how to set up a secure video call."

Once we were outside, Penelope still faithfully shadowing me, I asked Jim, "Why do you look even more pleased with yourself than normal?"

"That went well, don't you think?" he non-answered.

"It went terribly!" I cried.

"Are you kidding?" Jim laughed. "That was a gold mine. An absolute information dump. Were you even listening?"

"To the same phone call?" I asked. "All I heard was showboating and horse spit."

"Pessimist."

We made it outside to the Rimac and bickered briefly over the spare key Benito had given Jim. He claimed victory by promising to explain exactly what was so interesting about the phone call, then distracted me the moment we walked into the villa by asking, "Hungry?"

Penelope responded by sitting, perking up her ears, and barking once.

"What she said," I added.

"Great, another dog that speaks English. Why don't you sit down? I'll find something."

He didn't have to tell me twice. I stretched out on the sofa and began experimentally drawing deeper and deeper breaths, testing the limits to which my cracked ribs could be stretched. Maybe I was fooling myself, but they already felt a little bit better.

Thanks to the toast, cheese, grapes, and coffee Jim found and delivered, I was fortified enough to let my thoughts drift toward other basic needs. I tossed chunks of cheese to Penelope, watching Jim work. He'd moved his laptop to a desk by the back door and was again hunched over it, muttering to himself as he did who knew what. Something to do with a video call. Something else, probably. All sorts of interlocking, overly complicated, well-meaning mischief.

Penelope barked again, startling both of us. Jim caught me staring at him and asked, "Something on your mind, Bowman?"

"My body."

He closed his laptop. "Your body?"

I tossed Penelope another piece of cheese before she started going for my fingers. "Yeah. Earlier in the shower, I took inventory. I'm wasting away, Jim."

"You are not."

This was not mere compliment-fishing on my part. Since most of my clothes were loose-fitting or stretchy, it had taken the stark view of my ribs protruding from my skin under the elevated bathroom light to see how much of a toll the last few months had taken. I'd lost some muscle tone as well, which was doubly aggravating.

"I am. This always happens when I'm stressed."

Despite his sympathetic smile, he opened his laptop and said, "I'm supposed to be setting up a secure video call with a homicidal Colombian drug lord. You're distracting me."

"Am I?"

I climbed off the couch and perched on the edge of the desk. Though Jim remained focused on his laptop screen, he slid a hand onto my leg. Warmth spread from his palm through my whole body, and I found myself thinking thoughts I hadn't entertained in a while—longer than I cared to calculate. I turned away from Jim to stare out the nearest window, hoping it was safe to carefully explore these thoughts and what they meant.

I remembered the blue negligée he'd bought me in Berlin and given me in Argentina, and for the first time I wondered what had happened to it. I'd stuffed it in a suitcase and forgotten about it. Jim's gift was lost forever, I assumed, along with everything else I'd taken down there. Pity.

Other thoughts drifted in to mix with the blue negligée.

Jim's hand lingering on the bare skin of my inner thigh. The way he looked at me when I wore that backless dress in Kraków. Watching him shave. I wasn't sure why that last one popped in, but I didn't question it.

I slid off the desk to stand behind him, wrapped my arms around his neck, and confessed, "I am thinking some wild thoughts all of a sudden."

Now I had his attention. He wrapped a hand around my arm and asked, "Oh yeah? Such as?"

"I probably shouldn't tell you," I whispered. I gave him a quick kiss to the temple and added, "So I won't. In fact, forget I said anything. I'm going to run away now."

As I retreated, he warned me, "Better make it a walk— You're injured, remember?"

18

Thursday, June 24 to Friday, June 25, 2021

Jim wasn't the only temptation I was figuratively running from as I left the villa. I also needed to distract myself from a simpler, much more wholesome urge to call my mother, something Jim still insisted was neither safe nor pressing. To make it easier on myself, I left my phone in his keeping and wandered outside again with Penelope.

I didn't have to hobble far to get to the island's north shore, where a pleasant surprise awaited me. Eva was puttering around in the shallows, stooping every few seconds to pick up something and either toss it back into the water or slip it into the same canvas bag in which she'd delivered our cell phones.

As soon as she caught sight of the woman, Penelope broke into a run, sprinting toward her with astonishing speed. I didn't see any signs of aggression, but I was still impressed when Eva straightened up, spotted the incoming furry torpedo, and maintained her perfectly relaxed, contrapposto stance in the ankle-deep water. She crouched in front of Penelope to pet her while I made a somewhat slower approach.

As soon as I was close enough to hear, Eva asked, "Are you hurt?"

"Just some cracked ribs. What are you doing?"

In answer, she stooped again and withdrew a dark green bottle from the shallows. Brushing away the sand that clung to it, she explained, "Looking for these. We get a lot of flotsam on the north side, and I like to collect the glass before it gets broken. I'm making a window out of the bottoms of the bottles." Her mouth twisted in consternation, and she added, "There's not a lot to do here."

"Don't you ever go to Sardinia? The mainland?"

"No. Never."

"You've never been off this island?" I didn't mean to sound so sad about it, but the thought of living this close to the treasures of Italy and not being able to see them nearly broke my heart.

"How did your ribs get cracked?" she shot back, her expression daring me to call her on the abrupt change in subject.

"I got in a fight. I won." I pressed my lips together, cringing internally. I was actually peacocking at this poor woman. It had been quite a while since another woman made me feel so gawky and wrong-footed. She graced me with a smile.

"Maybe you shouldn't be walking around," she said. "If you want to ride with me," she gestured at a golf cart parked on the beach several yards away, "we can take the long way back and I can show you around. There's actually a lot to do, I'm just bored of most of it."

What the heck, I had nothing better to do. I followed Eva to the cart, and Penelope helped herself to the back seat. Thanks to the sun and the recent cardio, I was at once content and uncomfortable, alert and groggy as Eva navigated a serpentine path west from the beach.

She was quiet for so long I was startled to hear her say frankly, "He's not my grandfather." She gave me an awkward smile when I failed to follow up and added, "Anthony is my father, not my grandfather. You asked earlier today didn't you? I don't know why he insists on the pretense. It's not as though his wife is unaware."

"Who's your mother, then?"

"I don't know."

Once I'd worked my own foot free of my mouth, I asked, "You really want to know how I cracked my ribs?"

"Actually, Anthony already told me about that. He was so embarrassed that it happened to you on his ship, where you were supposed to be safe."

"Not his fault."

She lapsed back into silence, still smiling placidly.

We took a different route to the villa than I had earlier that day, and Eva directed my attention to a few points of interest along the way: the racetrack, the dry dock, the stables, the chapel, the house where Tony had lived. None of it seemed to interest her much, and I wondered how anyone could confine his daughter—illegitimate or otherwise—to 8.3 square kilometers for her entire life. Regina Lira probably didn't even know Eva existed, but that couldn't have been Anthony's reason for confining her.

"Has your father told you why we're all here?" I asked on impulse, my own villa in sight on the horizon. The tour was wrapping up.

"Not really. Something to do with a business deal. He doesn't tell me much."

"What do you do all day?"

"I paint. I was going to go to college for it, but they wouldn't let me. I wanted to study in Venice."

Ah, Venice. "Too bad. Maybe you'll get to someday. I went back to college when I was nearly thirty."

Though her eyes remained on the road, they widened noticeably. "How old are you now?"

"Fifty."

"You aren't!"

"No, but I feel it right now. I'm thirty… thirty… four? I don't know. Something like that. How old are you?"

"Twenty-six."

"See? Plenty of time."

"Sure. Well, here we are." She stopped the golf cart in front of the villa and turned, reaching her hand out to Penelope. The dog sniffed it obediently and then allowed Eva to scratch her between the ears. "Bye, doggy. Bye, Anna."

I watched her drive away, disliking the knot of guilt in my tummy. Jim would not be pleased if he knew how much more attractive Anthony's offer was made by Eva's existence. Honestly, Jim would be a fool to trust me any farther than he could throw me.

Inside, Jim was still absorbed in his laptop at a desk in the living room. He looked up when I entered and said without prompting, "It's all set up. Eight o'clock tonight. We're having dinner together to discuss things… Since, you know, we haven't quite figured out what comes after ad nauseam."

"Great. I think I overdid it with the pretending not to be injured routine. I'm going to lie down."

"Want me to bring you anything?" His question pursued me into the bedroom.

I demurred, took two painkillers, closed the curtains, stripped, and let the bed engulf me.

▼

"I can't *believe* you didn't wake me up!"

"Really? You can't?"

Jim sat on the edge of the bed, looking remarkably unapologetic for someone well within arms' reach. I balled my fists, thought better of it, and settled for chugging the glass of water he'd brought me. It was past one in the morning, and I'd narrowly escaped dehydrating to death in my sleep. I glared at him over the rim.

"I didn't want Regina to see you, anyway," he said. "I thought you'd figured that out."

"Fuh. How did it go?"

"It went okay. Regina made us jump through a few hoops to prove no one was hiding off camera, though she didn't mention you or Luke again. Marisol was with her. She looked… frail. Angry. About what you'd expect. She didn't say anything. Regina did all the talking."

"What did she *say?*"

"The worst. It's open season on all of us. That's all she wants. She even copped to killing Anthony's son. It took forever to get her to even listen to any kind of peace terms, but she got there. Leaving each other alone doesn't work for her. She said she'd call off the dogs if we delivered three people: Paolo, Luke… and, uh… you."

"*Me?* What? Not you? Tommy? Marcel? No one else?"

"Evidently not."

"That's not fair!"

"I know. She also revealed something that may interest you. I asked her if she'd already started sending people after you and Luke, and she copped to that, too. Readily, like she was proud of it. Cleveland, DC, Kraków, that was all her. And Philip in Dallas, just like we suspected, though she didn't care to explain why on that one."

I thought for a moment and asked, "Not Albuquerque?"

"Nope."

So, if Regina could be believed, the transient with the knife and the affinity for the word 'skank' was just part of the local flavor. I half-laughed, saying, "Remind me to steer clear of Albuquerque."

"Noted."

"So that's it?"

"Pretty much. We asked for some time to think about it, she gave us three days, and we hung up. They argued about it for hours. I convinced them to call it a night, came back, and now I'm here."

"What's to argue about? Are they going to hand us over, or not?"

"The general consensus is no. Besides that, we don't know what to do. In three days, she goes after our families. Including yours."

I ran through Regina's list of demands—me, Paolo, Luke— and saw that one of these things didn't belong. Luke, as far as I knew, had no family. Paolo's family was all safe on this island with us. By contrast, my parents, sister, nieces, and beloved dog were all holed up together with target number three. If I were Regina, I knew where I'd strike for maximum effect. The loss of any one of them, let alone all of them, would unhinge me. I stared at Jim, briefly robbed of words.

"Jim—they're all right there together in Texas. Everyone who matters. We have to warn them—"

"Luke is—"

"Luke's just one man!"

"They'll be okay." He locked eyes with me, thought about it, and amended, "Beauchamp will make sure they're okay. They'll be safe, I promise."

"We might not have time—"

"I know."

I shuddered as his hands slid around my face, forcing me to

stay still and look up at him.

"Nothing matters more to me than you do. I'd kill everyone on this island to keep you safe, and keep you happy. I knew it might come to this, and the groundwork's already in place. All you have to do now is trust me, and breathe. Just breathe."

I breathed, and I said, "I trust you."

"It'll be okay," he repeated.

"That *witch* though," I hissed. "I don't like this one bit. Why wouldn't they hand over Paolo and me? We're nothing but baggage, and it's not like you can stop them. And I don't think anyone here really likes Paolo."

"We'll think of something else. Anthony and the rest know help is just a phone call away for us. All I have to do is call Ingrid, and she'll send someone to come get us. That I haven't done so is an act of good faith."

"So what?"

"So?" He *tsked*, smirking at me as though disappointed at my obtuseness. I thought again about smacking him, but I was too eager for him to go on. He said, "Think about what Anthony and the others want: an agreement with Marcel, and Regina out of the way so they can make the most of it. As long as they think I can and will help out with the second half of that, they're not going to risk angering me by delivering my girlfriend to someone who's going to kill her."

"Hm," I grunted.

He patted me on the unbruised side of my face. "I'm on top of it, kiddo."

"Ugh."

"I've already let Rich know about Regina's threats, and he's going to bring your family and Luke into protective custody for as long as your father will endure it. The others are doing the same, but warning their families to be careful is basically all they can do." He sighed deeply. "Regina clearly has operatives in the United States, England, and Europe. Probably elsewhere. Even if we could take her out, her operatives will still do whatever she's told them to do."

"And we don't know who she'll go after first," I added.

"Right. I think she knows we're all here—I mean where 'here' is—but I don't think anything will happen here. It's too well guarded."

"I wish we could just send Paolo packing and hope Regina hares off after him and leaves us alone."

Jim shot me a quick, searching look and then shrugged. "She still wants you and Luke."

"Yeah."

"Try to get some more sleep. We can't do anything else about it tonight."

19
Saturday, June 26, 2021

By dinnertime on Saturday, nothing had been decided. All the Sardinians had warned their families as best as they could. Some went into hiding, some dismissed the threats, and some chose to batten down the hatches wherever they were to await an attack that would hopefully never come.

Since Regina had issued her threat, we'd only put our heads together once to see if anyone had come up with a solution. That had been Friday afternoon, and it had been an utter waste of time. Most ideas were variations on a theme: pretend to hand us over, as though any old Italian man, redheaded woman, and bodybuilder could serve as stand-ins for Paolo, me, and Luke. Jim killed the idea by assuring everyone that Marisol knew what I looked like, and Regina probably did as well.

It was Marcel who finally suggested that Regina's indefinite, good behavior could easily be ensured by kidnapping Marisol. He said any one of the CIA assets we all knew were hanging out in Colombia could track her down, nab her, and deliver her to us. As plans went, it was cynical, devious, hateful, and just plain awful. I loved it, Jim hated it, and everyone else elected to withhold judgment in case something better came up. A bad move, in my opinion, as this plan would take some time to execute; and time was something we didn't have on our side.

After the Friday meeting, I pointed this out to Jim, who assured me Beauchamp was already working with the CIA to track down Regina and Marisol, helped along by some data he'd captured from the video call. Touché. As we headed to the main house for dinner Saturday night, Jim told me some progress had been made and asked me not to mention it to anyone, especially Marcel. We arrived last for the five-course meal Anthony had arranged to clear out his larder in anticipation of the delivery of fresh supplies to the island.

It wasn't as though the lot of us had nothing better to do than bask in these obscene luxuries funded by generations of criminal enterprise, but you wouldn't have known it from observing the behavior of those assembled around the table in Anthony's massive dining room.

Regina's threat had been handed down Thursday evening, and here it was Saturday—roughly twenty-four hours to go until the poop hit the fan. People had been warned, measures had been taken, and ideas had been thrown around. Was that it? Granted, everyone was still discussing the problem, but there was a fecklessness about the conversation by now. We were safe, so what more was there to do?

Playing the gracious host, Anthony had arranged for this

communal dinner on the pretense that decisions were going to be made. It was only after gallons of wine had been poured, dessert was served, and the talk around the table had reached volumes that made me dream of ear plugs, that I realized a decision *had* been made. We were calling Regina's bluff, knowing full well that it wasn't a bluff at all and someone was likely to die as a result.

Once I awoke to this, I began scanning the faces around the table, looking for an expression that might mean I wasn't the only one feeling duped. I met Marcel's eyes. Of course it would be him. I stood up, told Jim I was going to the bathroom, and left the dining room. If anyone noticed Marcel follow me, they gave no indication.

I walked out to the sunroom, where the scent of lemon trees warmed by the sun still lingered hours after nightfall. All the lights were off, and I decided to leave it that way, heightening the impression of a clandestine meeting. Marcel found me and shut the door behind him, blocking out the din from the dining room.

Hoping to cultivate an illusion of trust, I said in French, "This is ridiculous. We're seriously going to do nothing?"

He answered me in English. "Anna, I'm sorry to have to say this, but your French… it's really not that good."

"What? No one's ever said that to me before…"

"Perhaps they were trying to be nice. I do not suffer from that affliction. But, if you wish to practice, I have no objection. Your vocabulary and grammar are good, but the pronunciation…"

"*My* pronunciation? Are you serious? You sound like a Monty Python character when you speak English."

"Perhaps we should agree to disagree."

"Whatever. Now that we're all safe on this stupid island, I guess we're just supposed to stay here forever. I know you know that's ridiculous."

"It's certainly not what I want."

"I think we should move forward with your plan," I said baldly, too tired and cranky to pussyfoot around.

"Camposanto won't allow it."

"He doesn't have to."

"What do you suggest?"

I took a deep breath, expelling my next words before I could rethink them. "Jim's boss is already working on tracking her down. He may know something by now. If I can get the information to you, you can get someone to do the dirty work. You must have other operatives besides Luke."

"I do. Less skilled, but reliable enough. I already have one picked out, and he arrived in Colombia this morning. All he needs is a location." He paused, almost smiling as he evaluated me. "You could get in a lot of trouble for sharing information with me, you know. Don't think you'll be safe in an American prison once all this is over…"

"I thought we were copacetic," I complained.

"Copacetic? Because of you, my brother is dead, my best employee is lost to me, I have the FBI and MI5 breathing down my neck, and soon I must cut ties with my new business partners in Italy. Once this business with the Lira woman is over, you and I… we will just be getting started."

Though the combination of his tone, words, and nearness sent a chill down my spine, I answered coolly enough, "Consider me warned."

"When can you get this information?"

"I don't know. Know where the stables are?"

"Yes."

"Meet me there tomorrow at eleven. If I don't have it yet, I just won't show up. That's the best I can do."

"Fine. You better get back. Your souteneur will be wondering where you went," he said, using a French word for pimp.

"Screw you," I growled, complying nonetheless.

I had been gone quite a while in Jim Time, so I power-walked through the deserted house toward the dining room, praying I hadn't been missed. Somehow I knew if I tried to lie to Jim about where I'd gone, he'd see right through me. I rounded the last corner so quickly I came within an inch of taking out Eva walking the other way. We both jerked in surprise and stepped backward.

"Sorry, sorry," I panted, pressing a hand to my side where my ribs had begun to throb.

"Are you all right?"

"Just overexerted." I sidestepped and continued on, trying to walk slower. She turned and walked with me.

"I had hoped to show you some of my paintings," she said. "My studio is up on the second floor, next to my room."

I realized she was asking me to go now, and I shook my head. "Maybe tomorrow. Sorry, I'm beat. I need to sit down."

Laughing, she argued, "Well, I have chairs."

We both stopped mid-step as Jim emerged from the dining room and spotted us. He looked from me to Eva and back, rapidly coming to a conclusion that, while wrong, would at least be a reasonable excuse for why I looked so guilty.

Eva mumbled, "Well, er, tomorrow, then. Good night, Anna."

She whisked away and I continued on, grinning at Jim. "It's not what it looks like," I whispered. "I just bumped into her on my way back from the bathroom."

"Are you coming back to dinner?"

"No, I think I'll go back to the villa. I'm exhausted. You and the boys carry on."

I fetched Penelope from the courtyard where she'd taken her dinner, trusting to her to guide me back along the dark, roughly two-kilometer path to the villa.

Pickpocketing isn't exactly on my résumé, but I know the basic mechanics: contact, misdirection, luck. Jim's gaze had been focused on Eva's retreating figure, and there was nothing suspicious about me brushing against him and using the movement to feel him up just a tiny bit, as though trying to reclaim his attention. Luck came in when he focused on my wandering left hand rather than my right hand, which darted smoothly into his left front pocket and back out again with his cell phone as my prize. For the entire walk back, I fully expected him to come running after me, but my luck held out.

Back at the villa, I got to work on the pin code. Angling the cheap smart phone's screen this way and that to see the fingerprint smudges, I eventually concluded that one, two, nine, and zero were my numbers. Assuming he'd gone for the full eight-digit pin, I played around with possible sources of inspiration until I was about 99% sure December 29, 2020 was the winner. 12, 29, 2020.

I tried the obvious first, wiped out, and considered for a moment before trying 29, 12, 2020. No dice. One try left. I had to assume I had the date right, because if not I was screwed anyway. Year, month, day? He could be insufferably pedantic, though, so I tried 0-2-0-2-9-2-2-1. The fully backward American date worked, and I almost imagined his phone giving a little scoff of indignance as it unlocked for me.

Secure in the belief that his phone could be neither stolen nor broken into, Jim had nevertheless gone to significant lengths to sanitize it. There were no calls, texts, or contacts, and even the oh-so helpful feature that automatically created a list of favorite phone numbers had been disabled. Fortunately, I'd been required to memorize Beauchamp's phone number upon receipt of our burner phones, and I was just dumb enough to text him the question, "Location?"

He texted back so quickly I nearly laughed aloud, stopping only when I realized his reply wasn't helpful. "Almost. Expect an email tomorrow morning."

Jim seemed like the type not to bother answering that, so I deleted the texts and plugged his phone in to the charger on his side of the bed. I had no hope of breaking into his laptop, even though it was just a garden variety civilian number and didn't require his PIV to sign in. I found it powered down and closed on the desk where I'd last seen him using it, and the sight was discouraging. No way he'd leave it right there, unguarded and in plain sight, unless it was even more secure than his phone.

I was tired anyway, and I had hours and hours to figure it out, so I curled up on the couch with a glass of wine and watched Italian C-SPAN until sleep took me.

20
Sunday, June 27, 2021

My eyes fluttered open and sought the face of my watch: 5:41 in the morning.

Today's the day.

I sat up carefully, gazing around the quiet living room. The TV was off, and I was half-covered by a blanket from the bedroom. Penelope feigned sleep on the couch next to me, one eye halfway open and fixed on me. What had I slept through? With a slow sigh, I leaned my head back and pictured the scene, letting anxiety help me with the details.

Jim would have noticed his phone missing from his pocket last night, probably within minutes of me taking it. He'd returned from dinner to find me asleep on the couch, his phone plugged in on the nightstand. My Jim was smarter than the average bear; he'd know at once that I'd taken it. Rather than waking me up to confront me, he'd grabbed a blanket off the bed and tucked me in. Then he'd turned off the TV and gone to bed.

191

Were this my standard brand of selfish but ultimately harmless mischief, maybe it wouldn't matter what Jim thought of my actions; but this was real. I was halfway through committing a felony. For once it wasn't selfish, though. Regina and Marisol chose to put my family in their crosshairs, and now they were going to pay, plain and simple.

Well, plain and complicated. To finish committing my felony, I had to get my hands on the information Marcel needed. Either Jim would catch me red-handed or he wouldn't, but I had to try.

I got up to use the bathroom and let Penelope out, using the light to check Jim's bedside table and confirm his phone was still where I'd left it. I showered, got dressed, let Penelope back in, and made myself a cup of coffee to wash down more painkillers.

Dawn was breaking, Jim was still asleep, and his laptop was still on the desk, taunting me.

I'd told Marcel to meet me at 11:00—a random, rectally-derived deadline if ever there was one—and I knew Beauchamp would be emailing Regina's location to Jim this morning, if he had it. If Beauchamp had meant morning in Washington, DC, I was screwed. That would be well after my rendezvous with Marcel. But if he'd meant Sardinia time, we were still in business. I only had to see this promised email.

Hacking the phone had been fun, but I wasn't excited about the laptop. Time was slipping away while I sipped at my coffee and tried to gin myself up. Finally, I closed the bedroom door to make it harder for Jim to sneak up on me, and I sat down at the desk.

I opened Jim's laptop as gingerly as though I were removing the outer casing of a bomb. I powered it on, running into the first road block when a light blue screen appeared prompting me for a pin in the name of something called Bitlocker. I tried the combination from Jim's phone, 0-2-0-2-9-2-2-1, and was astonished when it worked.

"Oh, he is so onto me," I moaned as the same eight digits logged me into his user profile.

The computer was stripped to the bone, only a handful of programs installed. Of course Jim had Solitaire, so I opened a game and made a few perfunctory moves. It was the closest thing to an alibi I could come up with.

Jim must have already connected to the internet through his phone, so at least I didn't have to deal with that. I couldn't find a desktop email app, so I looked for a web browser and found only one option: a TOR browser. Knowing what I'd see, I checked his browser history anyway and confirmed it was empty. The TOR browser was a vault of secrecy. There were no frequently visited sites, no stored passwords, no auto-fill hints in the URL bar. I drummed my fingers on the keyboard, my gaze darting down to the clock. It was 6:07.

I could burn five more hours trying and failing with this hacker business, or I could ask the only other person who knew what I needed to know. Tiptoeing back into the bedroom, I unlocked Jim's phone and composed another text to Beauchamp.

"Usual email?"

That was very Jim-like. Terse, efficient. Beauchamp wouldn't find it at all odd that Jim was being impatient and pushy.

I stood there by the bed, nerves twitching, for what felt like an hour before Beauchamp finally texted back one word: "Posteo."

I had no idea what that meant, but I deleted the texts anyway and returned to the living room. A quick internet search was all it took to get me to posteo.de, where an email login bar was splashed across the top of the page. That was a great leap forward, but with no hope of guessing the rest of the email address, let alone the password, I was once more stuck.

I clicked on the 'Forgot Password' link and tried the obvious just for grins: jim@posteo.de, plus the number for Jim's burner phone. The username 'jim' didn't work, but the form didn't give me any grief about '@posteo.de'. I tried 'james' 'camposanto' 'jcamposanto' and 'james.camposanto', clicking my tongue in annoyance when the site informed me I was in time-out for one hour. Too many attempts.

I shut down the laptop and went to fetch another cup of coffee, noting the time: 6:10. Hopefully I'd be able to try again before Jim woke up, but if not, I'd take it as a sign and forget this whole messy business.

To kill time, I took Penelope outside and wandered up to the northernmost tip of the island to watch the sun rise. She gamboled around in the water for about half an hour, overjoyed to be engaged in an activity that wasn't sleeping, eating, or waiting around for humans to talk about human things.

Across the water, I could barely make out lights flickering along the thread-like strip between sea and sky as Cagliari came alive. At seven o'clock, I picked my way back to the villa, slipped inside to grab a towel, and gave Penelope a thorough dry-off before letting her back inside. All was still dark and quiet. Jim was practically sleeping the day away.

I knew what username I wanted to try next and did so the moment the clock struck 7:10: CheckpointCharlie@posteo.de. Two seconds after I clicked Submit, Jim's phone buzzed in the bedroom. I snuck back in, scoped out the reset code, and deleted the text, feeling at once smug and puzzled while the man with the answers to this new riddle slept peacefully through.

What could possibly be so significant about that night in Berlin, December 29, 2020? I reviewed the memory again. Jim and I had walked to Checkpoint Charlie, nearly kissed, been hooted at by a drunk guy, and then moved on after Jim admonished me against starting a street brawl that might make us late for dinner with Ingrid. Jim hadn't said or done anything that made me think the date would stick in his brain at all, let alone to this extent.

Well, that wasn't technically true. A few months ago, Jim had committed everything he knew to paper by writing names, dates, and events on sticky notes and arranging them as though on a map. December 29, 2020 at Checkpoint Charlie was one of those dates. I hadn't known when I first saw the map, and hadn't asked, why he felt the occasion was worth noting.

Trying not to get distracted, I reset Jim's email password and finally logged in to his super-secret, secure Inbox. There was one message. Sent eleven minutes ago from bettyboop81@ posteo.de, it bore the snarky subject line "vacation home." Excited, I nearly opened the email before a rare, pragmatic thought stopped me. I opened the settings instead, disabled automatic read receipts, and went back to the Inbox to open the email. I scanned through it and felt a slow smile spreading across my face.

"Hola, Regina," I breathed.

I grabbed a pencil and a piece of paper from inside the desk and executed a hasty sketch of the satellite image Beauchamp had sent. I added the GPS coordinates to the bottom and called it good. There was more information in the email, but nothing Marcel needed to know. I marked the email as Unread, re-enabled read receipts, logged out, made sure Jim's browser history was still empty, and turned off the laptop. Slick as snake snot.

As quickly as triumph flared inside me, it faded away again. Had I thought *that* would be the hard part? I was wrong. Now that I had classified information burning a hole in my pocket, and my discretion was the only thing standing between Marisol Serna and Marcel's second-best brute, I was in agony.

I had hours to change my mind, and I did, eighteen times before Jim woke up at eight. When I heard him stirring, I got off the couch and went into the kitchen to make breakfast. Try as I might to play it cool, my body betrayed me the moment I heard his footsteps in the kitchen behind me. I was stiff as a board when his hands slid onto my shoulders.

His lips brushed my temple, and he asked, "Need more drugs?"

"No," I replied automatically, correcting myself with, "Well, yes, but I have to wait. I just took some a couple hours ago."

"How bad does it hurt?"

Any second now, Jim would start interrogating me, and I'd blow the whole thing by confessing like a Catholic with a hangover. I drew in a deep breath and let it out slowly.

"Bad."

"I'm sorry." He kissed me again. "I can probably handle scrambling eggs and toasting toast, if you want to rest."

"No, thanks. I've been resting since I woke up. I need a distraction." I pushed the eggs around for a few seconds, scrambling for something to say, then asked too eagerly, "How did the rest of dinner go? When did you get back?"

"Around midnight. You didn't miss much more than… well… How can I describe it?" His hands slid down to my waist. Could he see the scrap of paper in my pocket? He asked, "You know when you fill a balloon full of air, then let it go instead of tying it off?"

I conveyed my understanding by blowing a long, loud raspberry.

"Exactly."

"Are there a few details you don't want to share with me?" I prodded. "Perhaps relating to Paolo and his earlier request?"

Jim blew his own raspberry right into my ear, and I elbowed him in the ribs.

"He didn't bring it up again," Jim said. "If he does, it won't be with me. He'll come to you, like Anthony did."

"And what should I say?"

He pressed one hand to my chest and said with mock seriousness, "Follow your heart."

"My heart has a German Shepherd-shaped hole in it."

That earned me another kiss to the temple, which I concluded was one kiss too many. Jim was many things, but overly affectionate wasn't one of them. I didn't call him on his act, and he didn't mention the cell phone, so we got through the morning the only way we could: watching TV. Our semi-cozy, listless viewing of *Fawlty Towers* reruns on the BBC ended when I announced my intention at 10:30 to walk Penelope out to the stables for some mutually-needed exercise and a meet-and-greet with the horses.

Marcel was waiting for me at the entrance to the stables, pacing awkwardly on his bum leg and glancing at his watch like he had a nervous tic.

When he spotted me, he stopped pacing and crossed his arms, as though to convey the sentiment, "What took you so long?" I couldn't hold back a smile as Penelope broke away from me and sprinted toward him at Mach 37. I reached him seconds later and wordlessly handed over my all-important scrap of paper.

"What's this?" he asked, studying it with a jaundiced eye.

"You're welcome. I saw the satellite image, but I couldn't spend much time with it. The GPS coordinates are really all your guy should need, but I sketched out the lay of the land as best I could for reference. Looks pretty remote, unsurprisingly."

"She's here?"

"According to the FBI's best and brightest."

"How did they learn this?"

"Magic, I don't know. Take it or leave it. I did my part."

"I won't forget this, Anna."

"So, what? I've earned myself a quick death?"

"You've earned my silence. No one will ever know how I came by this information, not even Giles."

"Jim will figure it out."

"Perhaps he loves you enough to forgive you, in time."

"Perhaps. Just make sure your guy in Colombia moves quick. When it's time for everyone to learn what you did, I might even stick up for you. They already know I liked your plan."

"Thank you."

"You're welcome. And take Penelope back, for God's sake. She adores you, for some reason."

Marcel and the world's smartest dog took their leave, and I wandered inside the stables, thinking about what I'd done. About half the stalls were occupied with horses, all enjoying a meal of fragrant hay. Each one I passed poked its head over the stall door to see who was disturbing their lunchtime, and a few let me pet them on the nose. They kept me calm, allowing me to think things through.

Technically speaking, the email from Beauchamp (bettyboop81) to Jim was not classified. It bore no classification markings, and the German Posteo email service, while scrupulously secure, was not appropriate for the transmission of classified information.

Nevertheless, any reasonable employee or former employee of the FBI, or anyone who'd ever held a security clearance, would know handing over information that *should* be classified, to a foreign national and a known criminal at that, was a big bad. Let's not even talk about the shady things I'd done to gain access.

Now that I'd crossed that line, what else might I do? I stopped in front of a striking Palomino mare, slid my hand onto her warm nose, and considered my situation.

I still had the key to the Rimac. It wouldn't be difficult to get Eva to let me into the garage where it was stored. I'd have to get myself and the hypercar to the mainland somehow, but hey, I was surrounded by human traffickers. They were pretty good at that. Maybe they'd let me take Eva with me, and I could feel good about rescuing a genuine damsel in distress from her island solitude.

As long as the Rimac's electric motor held out, and I avoided law enforcement, I could be halfway to Munich by this time tomorrow. I could find a way to get ahold of Ingrid, though I wasn't sure how. I could work for the BKA, and they would keep me safe, and I would keep Eva safe. I wasn't exactly an important person, but surely Germany could find some use for me. I knew a lot about the inner workings of the FBI, and—

Whoa.

I took a literal and mental step back, blinking in surprise at the direction my thoughts had taken. Had I really come to hate the FBI that much? Any such thoughts had been nowhere near the surface, if they existed at all. I stuffed my treasonous thoughts into a mental lock box and threw away the key.

The walk back to the villa was long, thanks to my aching ribs and bruised conscience. Tommy was on my mind for some reason, and I realized I hadn't seen him at dinner last night. I found Jim lounging on the couch and asked if he knew anything about Tommy's whereabouts, interrupting an intense, app-based language lesson in progress.

He tossed his phone aside, sighing in Italian, "I don't know."

"Wow," I gasped, firing back, "Soon you'll be fluent, a real Italian!"

While he puzzled over this, I dismissed myself to the kitchen to find some lunch. The supplies Anthony had ordered were due to arrive tomorrow, and the stores from the *Luciana* were running out. Standing between the open doors of the fridge and pondering my limited options, I heard the language lesson resume in the living room.

What I needed was a job, not a meal. Since I didn't have a job, I settled on drinking a glass of wine, taking two more painkillers, and stretching out on the couch next to Jim. Thanks to the misuse of pharmaceuticals, I fell asleep hard and awoke feeling no pain half an hour later. Jim was gone, but I heard him rummaging around in the kitchen and got up to join him. He was arranging papers over the surface of the kitchen table.

"Your map," I said, startling him.

I wasn't surprised he'd brought it to Italy. He seemed quite attached to it.

"Yeah. I figured it couldn't hurt to look over it again. Where's Penelope?"

"With Marcel," I said, letting my sadness show through and hoping it obfuscated my guilt. "She saw him when we were at the stables, and she ran to him. I figured she's where she wants to be."

"Too bad. I was getting attached to her."

"Me, too. What about Tommy?" I asked, to which Jim

shrugged. "I just want to make sure he's contained, you know? Especially now that we don't have Penelope guarding us."

"It's an island, he can't go anywhere."

His nonchalant attitude didn't fool me, but I let it go. I picked up a legal pad, flipped to a blank page, and started doing something I should've done months ago.

"What are you writing?" Jim asked, most of his attention on his own task.

"I'm trying to remember the notes I made in London and gave to Marcel. There may be something useful in there."

I worked away in silence until my hand hurt too much to continue. I'd already seen something of interest, something I'd forgotten about until it appeared on the paper.

"Jim?"

"Mm?"

"Do you know why Paolo boycotted the meeting in London? Anthony said Paolo didn't trust Marcel. Is that it?"

"I assume Paolo didn't think the meeting was important enough to venture out of hiding, but I'm sure it's also true that he didn't trust Marcel. Once Marcel decided to overlook my involvement and partner up, things cooled down."

"Why did Marcel accept that? Luke said it was the money, but Marcel doesn't seem that dumb."

"You can thank Dominique for that."

I blinked at him, not comprehending. "Dom? What do you mean? Dom... is the leak?"

21

Sunday, June 27, 2021

"Yes and no." Jim smiled knowingly at me. "You didn't still think it was Rich, did you?"

"No, but I'd believe it was him before I'd believe *Dom*... I'd believe *you* were the leak before I believed it was her!"

"That's fair." I watched him position a few more papers on the table, apparently in no hurry to elaborate. "You're right about Dom, though. She's only doing it because I asked her to."

"But you said you had a leak way before Dom came into the picture."

"True."

"You can't keep beating around the bush. Tell me about this stupid leak already!"

"Fine. I was hoping you'd figure it out on your own..."

"Like the Raphael?" I scoffed. "That was never going to happen. You need clues to solve a mystery."

"I guess so. Where to start?" He fussed with his papers

again while I audibly tapped my foot. "I told you we hired Dom because she was your neighbor, right?"

"Yes."

"We had to make room for her, so we had to let someone else go. It was an easy decision. My old assistant, Will Gragg, was a disaster. Security violations, reprimands, and the man couldn't get along with anyone. He was an arrogant jerk."

I raised my eyebrows but elected not to point out the obvious.

"He held on as long as he did because his work was fine, even above average. But he got a DUI in March twenty nineteen, and we knew his clearance would be suspended, maybe even revoked, so we let him go in August and immediately hired Dom. Gragg must have been cultivated by Paolo separately from me, maybe when Paolo realized I wasn't going to give up Fernando. We didn't know for several months that the leak had stopped, though. You got the short end of that stick."

"Because you thought you couldn't tell me about Frères Enterprises?" I guessed. I'd had to discover the existence of Marcel's London-based front business, and its connection to Luke, all on my own last year no thanks to Jim.

He said, "Right in one. By then you were in London and Gragg was long gone, but we didn't know the flow of information to Paolo had already been cut off. Rich was the one finally who put it together and decided to dig into Gragg's credential use history and other communications."

"If you knew there was a leak, why didn't you do all that sooner?"

"Investigate everyone in the unit?" Jim asked.

"Sure." I reached out and pushed a piece of paper askew with one finger. "There can't have been that many suspects."

He moved the paper back into place before replying, "When we first discovered there was a leak, we cast a wide net and didn't catch anything. Theoretically, *if* someone had to employ legally questionable methods to prove Gragg was passing information to Paolo, that someone would've needed a solid reason to focus on a specific subject."

"Mhm."

"Dom was the only person in the office who couldn't have been the original leak, even if Gragg had help. Before I went to Argentina for the last time, I asked Dom to impersonate Gragg and contact Paolo through an offsite server."

"The one at Beauchamp's house," I said, but Jim shook his head.

"It's at Dom's dad's house."

I argued, "Luke said that kid who works for Marcel linked the server to Beauchamp's address in Maryland."

"Either he got it wrong, or someone lied. Think about how many times that information changed hands before it finally got to us."

"Okay, fine," I relented. "But why have Dom impersonate this Gragg guy? Did Paolo trust him?"

"Yes, and we needed to know if Gragg was still communicating with Paolo after we let him go."

"What did she tell Paolo?" I asked, thinking of Luke. "Luke said Paolo told him not to come to Italy without the Raphael. If you had Dom tell Paolo about the painting—"

"I didn't. She couldn't have told Paolo about the Raphael, because at the time, she didn't know. All she told him was that Gragg got fired but was still in touch with someone in the office, meaning herself. She re-opened the communication lines as Gragg, then started contacting Paolo as herself. Paolo is still courting her, being cautious. She's given him some useless bits of information about me. All made up, of course. Dom is the reason Marcel hasn't come right out and demanded that Anthony sever ties with Paolo."

"Because Paolo thinks he has a source at the FBI, which Anthony doesn't. What sort of made up information?"

"Oh, you know. Paolo likes to feel like he's got the upper hand. She told him I'm about to get fired over an affair with a subordinate. That I'm a hopeless alcoholic teetering on the edge of unemployment and bankruptcy… Things like that."

"That's going to backfire on you," I warned. "A man like that doesn't sound all that useful."

"Aren't you perceptive," he said gravely. I didn't get the impression this was news to Jim. "Anyway, now that Dom's read in on everything, she's been able to pass Paolo more specific information. She told him Rich gave me an ultimatum: Either I fire you, or he fires me. She came up with that one herself."

"To what end?"

"Now? Now… it depends."

"On?"

"On whether Emilio really is dead." Jim stuck down three more sticky notes, then seemed to win some kind of internal struggle. He shifted abruptly to, "Luke told us that kid—Marcel's hacker whiz—wasn't able to read Paolo's emails because they were encrypted, right?"

I thought back to the conversation in Chile, trying to remember. Jim's index finger was resting on the note that read '9/4/2020: PL tries to kill AB'. Assuming Philip's attempt on my life had something to do with Jim's new train of thought, I tried to jump aboard by saying, "Yeah, I think so."

"But wouldn't that same kid—or the other one, Luke said there were two—have been the one who helped Marcel encrypt them in the first place?"

"Probably…"

He thought for another long moment, then asked, "When did he get access to Paolo's email traffic?"

"I don't remember. I don't think Luke said specifically. After Luke left Colorado, and before we went to Chile."

"Not after Chile?"

"No, he identified Beauchamp after Chile, but he was in Paolo's computer way before that."

"Before Philip tried to kill you?"

"I… I don't know. I don't remember. Why?"

"Paolo and Marcel communicate almost exclusively through email. If that kid was listening in, he knew about the hit on Fernando and Marisol sooner than most. Even before Luke did."

"And then Regina knew Luke was there because of the watch," I added, starting to catch on. We'd never figured out why Regina sent Philip after me, or whether the timing was related to Paolo ordering the deaths of her niece and nephew. There was one person who might know, though, and Jim's next words echoed my thoughts.

"We need to talk to Marcel. I need to tell Rich."

Jim sat down in front of his laptop, which he'd moved to the kitchen table. I watched helplessly, knowing what was about to happen. He tried to log into his email, entered his old password three times in a row, and got locked out for one hour just like I had.

"Of course," he grumbled, far less concerned than I'd anticipated. "I guess Rich will have to wait. I can't put this in a text. Let's go see Marcel."

Thanks to Eva's tour, I knew which dwelling Marcel and Giles were using, and I guided Jim there on foot. The ten-minute walk gave me time to prepare myself for Marcel's likely reaction to finding Jim on his doorstep mere hours after receiving sensitive information from me.

Jim knocked on the door and stepped back, compelling me to stay behind him, which was just as well. Giles answered the door, his gaze sliding past Jim to land on me with a distinctly spiteful cast.

"What?"

"We need to talk to Marcel. It's important."

From the way Giles' eyes narrowed, I knew Marcel had already looped him in despite his assurances to the contrary. Hoping to communicate that this wasn't the reason for our visit, I silently shook my head behind Jim's back. Giles seemed to get the message, standing back from the door to allow us to enter.

Their villa was twice the size of ours, two stories rather than one. At the foot of the stairs, Giles called, "Marcel, you've got company!"

He disappeared into the house, leaving us feeling awkward by the stairs until a door opened above. Penelope dashed down to greet us, followed by Marcel at a much more sedate pace. He stopped on the bottom stair and locked eyes with me.

"To what do I owe the pleasure?"

Jim's answer couldn't have been more ambiguous. "I need your help with an information leak."

Still tucked behind Jim, I frantically made the 'cut it' sign across my throat as Marcel started to respond. I would've bet money he'd been about to say, "I don't know what Anna has told you…" when he caught on and changed course.

"I don't know what an… information leak means. What information?"

"Can we sit down?" Jim asked.

"I suppose so."

Marcel led the way to a small parlor and invited us to sit, stiffly offering us something to drink. We both declined, and Jim launched into a condensed version of our earlier conversation. Though he tried to skate around Luke and David's involvement, our information could only have come from them.

Giles appeared in the doorway while Jim was talking, responding to the tale with, "Impossible. It's a lie. David would not have done this."

"He was working for MI5," Jim said. "Obviously his loyalty wasn't to you anymore. Maybe you should've kept your dirty little hands out of the human trafficking cookie jar."

While Giles and Jim stared each other down, I checked on Marcel. He hadn't said a word since offering us a drink, and now his face was ashen. He met my eyes.

"He helped Luke in London, didn't he?"

I nodded.

"He was a good man. A fool."

Giles muttered something unintelligible.

"Why have you brought this information to me?" Marcel asked Jim. "Do you think I care for the minutiae of this ridiculous feud?"

Jim insisted, "You should care if someone in your organization is passing information to Regina. We've been wondering how Regina knew about the hit on Fernando and Marisol, and you were the middle man. Unless you think it was David—which I seriously doubt—it's a problem for all of us, right now."

And, I realized with a sharp breath, the Marisol operation would be in jeopardy if Marcel's communications weren't private. Giles saw the problem too and was good enough to voice this concern to Marcel in French, causing Marcel to rise from his seat and say only, "This is preposterous."

"At least look into it," Jim argued. "If you and Paolo have been on a party line all this time, we need to know sooner than later."

"If she knew, why did she not warn them? The Sernas?" Marcel argued.

"I don't know. Maybe she didn't know how imminent the threat was until Luke got there himself. She may very well have tried, but by then it was too late."

"I see…"

"We should assume she's privy to everything else you and Paolo have discussed over email. It's possible other lines of communication have been tapped as well."

Marcel nodded. "I will look into it. Thank you for letting me know."

That was that. The walk back took a little longer, thanks to my painkillers wearing off. I melted down into the couch right away, halfway wishing Jim would get lost so I'd have no one to moan and groan at. He brought me some water and an ice pack and resumed his seat before his computer.

"Twenty more minutes," he groused, presumably referring to his email time-out.

Thinking of another deadline, I asked, "When exactly did Regina give her ultimatum?"

"Eight fifty-one. We've got a few more hours, assuming she was being literal on the three days."

I stewed in it for twenty more minutes, when Jim recaptured my attention by finally getting back into his email the same way I had, by resetting the password. He saw the email from Beauchamp and announced, "That trick with the video call paid off. Beauchamp's friends in cyber tracked down Regina's location in Colombia."

"You're kidding." I wandered over to the desk, the better to pantomime surprise at this brand new information.

"She's near the Peruvian border, in a compound that's just about invisible from a bird's eye view. She's dug in like a tick. Rich wants to storm the place."

"To what end?"

"Leverage. If we have her, maybe we can call off the hits. At least we can trip her up for a while. But it's going to take a couple days to put something together. That's too late."

"So my family…?"

"I don't know. She's been striking out one at a time, Tony being the latest example. But after drawing this line in the sand, who knows. She may take out multiple targets at once."

"So my family…?" I repeated, uncomfortably aware of my own heartbeat.

"Beauchamp already sent someone to take them into protective custody."

"Are they in custody yet?"

"I'll find out."

While Jim composed an email to Beauchamp, I returned to the sofa and slipped into a light doze. I was mentally, emotionally, and physically exhausted. Sometime later, a light summer rainfall started up outside, drawing me out of my comfortable lack of thoughts.

I sat up, asking, "What time is it? How much longer do we have?"

"It's almost seven," Jim said. "If anything does happen, we might not know for a while."

"My family?"

"I haven't heard back yet."

To distract myself, I decided to put together a dinner using the last of our supplies. This was no small feat, as we were by then reduced to such niche commodities as capers, sour milk, and baking soda, along with assorted canned goods.

I won't say the resultant dish was delicious, but it was palatable; and, thanks to the wine we still had on hand, good spirits prevailed against all odds. For a couple more hours I was able to think about something besides Regina's threats and Marcel's plans. At nine o'clock, we received word from Anthony via a text to Jim's phone: We were all expected at his house for breakfast tomorrow. He had important news to share. End of message.

Still waiting to hear from Beauchamp, Jim and I went to bed. We'd imbibed so much wine that even Jim was a little tipsy, evidenced by an unusually mawkish mood that only surfaced when red wine had flowed in abundance. He appeared to be asleep already when I climbed into bed, but as soon as I was comfortable he rolled over and wrapped his arms around me from behind. He planted a few kisses on my neck and whispered, "Try not to worry. Everything will be okay."

"I seriously doubt that."

"Don't you trust me?"

"Yes." I paused, waiting for more wheedling, which never came. "I'm curious about something."

"I bet you are."

"One of the dates on your map is December twenty-ninth, at Checkpoint Charlie. What's the significance of that?"

He was silent for so long I wondered if he'd fallen asleep. I realized he was awake when his arms tightened a little, his lips brushing against my neck again. "Do you remember that night?" he asked.

"Of course. We met with Ingrid right after and got my Fritz

assignment. Visiting the checkpoint seemed like more of a touristy thing."

I felt him nod. "I've been there before, when I was sixteen. My mom had just died of breast cancer, and my dad thought dragging me around Europe would cheer us up."

"Did it?"

"Not even a little. But it was a diversion, and we got to spend some time together. He took me to Berlin for our last stop, and we went to see Checkpoint Charlie the night before we flew home. This was nineteen ninety-four, mind you. The Cold War was barely over. I didn't really care, but my dad did, and he told me the whole history and why the site was important and why I *should* care.

"At the time, all I cared about was the swim team and getting laid. I decided I wanted to do more with my life. By the time I graduated high school, I'd decided to join the FBI."

"Isn't it funny how these stories become legends in one's old age?"

"I'm serious, Anna. I made a big decision that night. If I hadn't joined the FBI, I never would've met you. I took you there because it was important to me, because you're important to me. I made another big decision that night. About you."

Oh, boy. "Jim."

"I'm not asking. I'm just saying, that's when I decided."

"That was months ago."

"What's a few months when I've been waiting for you for over forty years?"

"Jim... I had no idea you were so sentimental."

"You get that way in your old age."

With difficulty, I turned over within his embrace so that I was facing him. I didn't have the ability, drunk or sober, to articulate my feelings the way he had. Instead I kissed him, trying to convey by touch alone that just because I was nowhere near ready for this didn't mean I loved him any less.

Sentimentality was rapidly devolving into good old-fashioned desire, where I was much more comfortable, when Jim's phone buzzed. He ignored it until I groaned, "It's probably important."

It was. The text from Beauchamp said only, "News," which incited Jim to check his email again. I watched his eyes track back and forth across the screen, his expression darkening in direct correlation to my pulse speeding up.

He met my eyes over the screen and said, "Your parents and Dude are fine. Come read this."

Nerves atwitch, I traded places with him and read, "Be advised on 26 June at approx. 5:00 p.m., Bruce and Evelyn Bowman and Anna's dog were transported to a secure location without incident. All are well. Prior to transport, it was discovered that Emily Bowman had escaped from the Red River County Jail on 9 June. Upon making contact with Bruce Bowman to arrange transport and ascertain Emily's whereabouts, I was informed that on the evening of 20 June, Luke Jackson and Emily Bowman took Emma Bowman (8) and Ellie Bowman (6), as well as Evelyn Bowman's vehicle and several hundred dollars in cash, and disappeared from the residence. Whereabouts of all are unknown. An Amber Alert has been issued for the two minor children. Evelyn's car was recovered in Tyler, Texas, the following afternoon. ETA for move in Colombia tentatively set for 1 July."

22

Monday, June 28, 2021

After finishing Beauchamp's email, I'd put myself in lockdown mode for the first time in years.

Lockdown mode was a defense mechanism I'd perfected 16 years ago, when I woke up in a hospital bed after emergency surgery and was informed by a misty-eyed nurse that the doctor had to remove my uterus. At 17 years old, I'd been six weeks pregnant when I'd gone into surgery, my first and last child never to grow larger than a grain of rice. I had cried for four minutes exactly and was dry-eyed and as cold and hard as granite when my mom and Emily had come in to see me. I had sorted through my emotions later, after they'd had a chance to scab over a bit.

So, on Monday morning, I walked with Jim to Anthony's house for this all-important breakfast we'd been invited to. None of our so-called companions needed to know what Luke and Emily had done, so I didn't plan to mention it or provoke suspicion by showing a single emotion. Perhaps one or two people noticed the storm clouds hanging over Jim's head. *I was fine. I did not, in fact, care at all.*

Regina's deadline had passed yesterday evening, and as far as anyone could tell, nothing had happened. Perhaps her crosshairs had been on my family, and her plan, once foiled, would take some time to change. We were far from off the hook.

Once everyone, even Tommy, was assembled and breakfast was served, Anthony called us all to order. Then, to the puzzlement of all but yours truly, he turned the floor over to Marcel, who rose to his feet. I stared at my plate, hardly breathing while he spoke.

"The news is good. Last night, my operative in Colombia located Regina Lira's compound and was able to get inside, abduct Marisol Serna, and escape before his presence was discovered. He is on his way here now, with Miss Serna. They should be here by this time tomorrow. I recommend contacting Regina immediately to make a new deal: If any threats are carried out against us or our families, the girl dies."

I felt Jim's gaze boring into me long before Marcel was finished. I could almost hear his mind whirring as he put the pieces together.

Paolo exploded with questions the moment Marcel sat down.

"How did your operative find the compound? Was Regina there? Tell me where this place is!"

"I will do no such thing," Marcel said serenely. "And if you attempt to question my operative, I will consider it an act of aggression and terminate our partnership. We're all in this mess because of you, Barbato, and you're the only one who still cares about killing Regina."

Before Paolo could argue, Jim said, "The important thing is, now we have leverage to use against Regina. All we have to do is play our cards right, and this will all be over."

Though Paolo crossed his arms and proceeded to look like he'd swallowed a whole lemon tree, he fell silent. The remainder of the gathering was used to game out exactly how to use Marcel's news to our greatest advantage.

I might have gotten away with my little bit of subterfuge if it hadn't been for Giles, that miserable wretch. While talk milled around me and I attempted to tune it out, Giles stared at me until I was forced to meet his gaze. He winked at me. Jim saw.

After a frozen moment, Jim stood up and left the dining room without a word. Since he'd been elected the videoconferencing expert, his departure was somewhat disruptive. When it became clear I wasn't going after him, Enzo stepped up with a mumbled, "I'll get him."

When he'd gone, I hissed at Giles, "You're a wretched insect, you know that?"

"Whatever do you mean?"

"You and I are gonna rumble, Giles. Count on it."

"Rumble? How quaint."

"Shut up, both of you," Marcel snapped.

Jim returned a few minutes later, Enzo right behind him. Ignoring a handful of questions directed at him, Jim stretched his arm over the back of my chair and put his lips to my ear to say, "Tell me you didn't have a hand in this."

I shook my head tightly, staring straight ahead. He took my chin and forced me to look at him.

"Why did you ask me about Checkpoint Charlie?"

"Because I saw it on your map," I breathed.

"And because that date is the pin to unlock my phone and my computer?"

I didn't answer, but the look on my face was enough. For an agonizing moment I braced for the explosion, already marshalling my defenses. Then he smiled at me. Was I having a stroke, or did he actually look proud?

Still so quietly that only I could hear, he said, "You never cease to amaze me, kiddo."

"You're not mad?"

"I'm incensed. But I'm impressed. I knew you stole my phone, but then what? You hacked into my computer and email, and snuck off to deliver the information to Marcel?"

"She threatened my family, Jim."

"I know." He turned away, still smiling, and whispered, "I expected nothing less."

I was so flummoxed I could only stare at Jim as he rejoined the conversation, leaving his arm across the back of my chair and adopting an attitude of benign contentment. I felt a phantom tug on my sleeve and turned to face Tommy, who was sitting on Jim's other side. He was staring at me, an expression of horrified disbelief transforming as I watched into ice cold loathing. It was a look I hadn't seen since Houston. I didn't know why, but I knew without a doubt that Tommy was once again my number one problem.

I turned away, wondering how to deal with this development. Nothing occurred to me, but I was able to hold a quick aside with Jim while Tommy was dialing Regina's number and putting the call on speaker.

"Tommy knows I had a part in this. He's mad. Beyond mad. He looks like he wants to kill me."

"We'll deal with it," Jim whispered back.

The call to Regina went to voicemail, and Tommy said only, "They want to meet again." Paolo ended the call, pocketed the phone, and started to leave with his entourage.

As chairs began scraping back all around the table, Jim stood as well and said, "Hold on, Paolo. We need to talk."

He nodded, stone faced, and told Enzo and Aldo to take Tommy back to their villa. I would've preferred to keep him in my sights, but Jim didn't protest, so I kept quiet. The room cleared until only Anthony, Paolo, Jim, Marcel, and I were left. No one questioned Marcel's presence.

"There's some kind of problem with Tommy," Jim told the assembled 'captains.' "He has a history of violent behavior, specifically toward Anna. We're not sure what, but something just set him off."

"This is why he stare at you?" Anthony asked me.

"You noticed?"

"It is hard not to."

"I know you're keeping a close eye on him," Jim said to Paolo. "But the kid is dangerous. I think he should be kept locked up."

"Kill him," Marcel said, as flippantly as though choosing

between chicken and fish. "He has been as useful as we have reason to expect. Why keep him around, potentially causing trouble?"

Jim said, "We don't know what else he knows."

"So find out," Marcel shot back.

"What, torture him?" I squeaked. "No way!"

"Do you have a better idea?" Marcel asked.

"No."

Anthony spoke up again in his halting English. "There is place on island where we can keep. The same place I have to use for the Serna girl. Is good?"

"I don't want him hurt," I said.

Marcel asked, "Why do you care?"

"Why do you care that I care? And why are you even here right now?"

Over the tail end of my words, Jim said, "Yes, Anthony. I think that's the best solution for now. Thank you." Anthony nodded.

Petulantly, Paolo said, "The boy is my responsibility. He is already under guard. He'll stay with me."

Switching to his native tongue, Anthony shot back, "This is my island, cousin. The security of everyone here is my responsibility. This isn't a matter for negotiation. What if he does escape, and something happens to Anna?"

He waved an arm toward me, clueing Jim into the meaning of his words. I fought back a smile as I watched Jim's hopeless attempts to decipher the old man's rapid Italian.

"She's already been attacked once. Don't act like a fool,"

Anthony finished.

Casting a dour look at me, Paolo grumbled, "Fine. I will allow your men take him to this secure location of yours, if you care to tell me where it is."

"Anna?" Marcel asked impatiently.

I repeated the conversation in English for Marcel and Jim, adding, "Two old men bickering like toddlers over a toy sounded a lot better in Italian, didn't it?"

"Anna," Jim moaned.

"Okay, fine, only Paolo was acting like a toddler," I said with an apologetic smile at Anthony.

"Anna, your opinion is not needed here," Paolo hissed.

In Italian, hands and all, I fired back, "Neither is yours. This whole thing is your fault, and instead of apologizing and trying to help, you're swinging your salami around and daring everyone to measure it! What is wrong with you?"

Paolo was silent for a long moment before turning to Anthony and saying, "Call me with the location."

He left, followed a few seconds later by Marcel. When it was just Jim, Anthony, and me, Jim asked, "What did you say to him?"

"That this is all his fault and he's an idiot."

"Ah. This may come as a shock to you, but he's not accustomed to being spoken to like that."

"Ask me if I give a crap."

Anthony came to my defense with, "She only tell him what he need to hear. James, I may have word with you in private?" In Italian, he told me, "Anna, you may wait here while the young man is secured. I believe Eva has been wanting to show you her paintings."

I heard zero question marks there. At a curt nod from Jim, I trudged away alone to find Eva as ordered. I spotted her and an old woman I didn't recognize eating breakfast in a small court-yard off the living room, but I kept walking, not feeling partic-ularly sociable. Eva must have seen me slink past, because she caught up to me moments later and impudently took my arm.

"There you are. Why do you look so sad?"

Did I? I shrugged. "Long night. Where are these paintings I've heard so much about?"

She beamed at me, revealing dimples in her cheeks. "Up here, I'll show you."

She led me to the stairs and let go of my arm, climbing too quickly for me to keep up. Flat ground was fine, but raising my legs to navigate the stairs was like a knife in my side every other step. Stopping half a flight above me, Eva put her hands on her hips to watch my progress.

I'm only human, so when I paused to rest, I took the chance to size her up again. In tight jeans and a white blouse unbuttoned past her sternum, again barefoot, she struck a pretty picture as she smiled down at me and waited. Once I reached her, she looped her arm through mine again and guided me at a slower pace to her studio on the east side of the house.

I wasn't all that eager to view the art gallery, honestly. I'd been picturing some pretty banal pieces. Landscapes, still lifes of fruit and flowers, maybe a tasteful nude or two. Worst case, some O'Keeffe knock-offs screaming vagina at me from every direction at once. I stopped at the doorway while Eva whisked inside, trying to reorient myself as I took in a view of at least two dozen finished and unfinished paintings. These were not the products of a workaday painter pining for art school.

My eyes were drawn first to a massive canvas in the far corner, no less than five by eight feet, its inky black background covered to the edges of the field with shapes and symbols so tiny and intricate she must have drawn them in with a pen. Nearer the door, I saw a half-finished piece in a completely different vein, splashes of spray-paint like color dashed onto the canvas to confuse the crisp lines of a young woman's profile.

Another piece depicted a flock of geese flying through a thunderstorm, one caught in a lightning strike. I was tempted to ask if this one was a joke, but I held my tongue. True artists never, ever joked around, right? My favorite, after a first pass of the room, was a whirling mass of cretaceous carnivores ripping apart a man I was almost certain was a member of the Italian parliament. I'd fallen asleep watching him blabber on about some political garbage just the other night. His viscera were depicted with frightening accuracy and detail.

Eva watched me in tense silence until I finished looking around the room and gaped at her.

"You like them?" she asked.

"They're incredible."

"Really? I can't figure out what my style is. Sometimes I like to be really precise, but then I just lose it and have to make a mess. Maybe variety is my style."

"You are absurdly talented," I said, my gaze drawn back to

the dinosaur painting. I could almost hear the screams. "What do your parents think?"

"Well, who knows what my mother thinks," she said with a laugh, making me grimace. "No, it's okay. I know what you meant. They don't like most of it. Sometimes I paint something stupid to make them happy. A family portrait, a ship in a storm. Nonsense."

Nodding vacantly, I walked over to the huge painting in the corner to take a closer look. All the symbols were silver, gold, or bronze. I couldn't find any two alike, but I started to see the ghost of a pattern forming the longer I looked.

I felt Eva behind me and was surprised and delighted when she caught a lock of my hair between her fingers and tugged lightly at it.

"Your hair is so beautiful. I couldn't mix this color if I tried for weeks."

"The folks at Revlon could probably help you out." At her frown of confusion, I added, "I went blonde and had to dye it back. Long story."

She breathed a laugh, twisting my hair around her finger before letting it go. "Do you paint? You have a degree in art, don't you?"

"How do you know that?"

"I saw you on the news. You found the Raphael."

"Oh, right. It was art history, actually. I prefer to leave art making to the real talent, like you."

"What would you write about me, in the history of art?"

"Hm," I pretended to give this some thought, turning reluctantly away from the painting to study her. "Italian, born circa nineteen ninety-five, stylistically hard to pin down, achieved worldwide fame after graduating from the most prestigious art school in Italy and breaking free of the influence of her evil father, who kept her locked up on a tiny island all by herself."

Her grin faded. "He's not evil. He just wants to keep me safe."

"Two things can be true at the same time."

"He's not evil," she repeated firmly. Her smile reappeared, a little uncertain now. "You think I don't know what he does. Right? You think I'm naïve or stupid or something."

"I don't think you're stupid at all…" I hesitated, looking around the room and feeling my gaze settle again on the dinosaur painting. "But if you're not as innocent as you seem, I'm in deep trouble."

"Why?"

We both turned toward the open door as someone called my name from downstairs. The voice was faint, but I was pretty sure it was Jim.

Grateful for the escape, I told Eva, "Oh, let's save that for another time. Thanks for showing me your paintings."

"You're welcome," she lilted, turning back to the symbol painting and picking up a metallic gold pen. I backed away, watching her work for a moment, then turned and fled as Jim called me again.

23

Monday, June 28, 2021

Thanks to the news about Marisol, Tommy's over-the-top reaction, and my brief stint as helpless putty in Eva's hands, I'd managed to go the whole morning without wasting a single thought on Luke and Emily. The look on Jim's face, when I spotted him at the foot of the stairs, ended my winning streak.

"What happened? Is Emily—"

"It's not about your sister. They can't find Tommy. Paolo left a couple of Anthony's men at their villa to guard him, and when he went back to get him, both guards were dead and Tommy was gone."

I reached the bottom of the stairs and demanded, "Enzo and Aldo? Are they okay? They were guarding him—"

"They're fine, but Aldo got knocked out cold. He must have seen what happened, but he says he doesn't remember anything."

Fury rising, I snarled, "There's no way that little ferret killed two men and knocked out a third all by himself. No *freaking* way."

"Whatever happened, he's gone. Anthony wants us both to stay here until he's found."

I narrowed my eyes at him and asked, "What were you two talking about before this happened?"

"He asked me to keep it to myself."

"Oh, no," I sighed in a sarcastic mockery of concern. "But you *hate* keeping secrets!"

Jim studied me with concern, his grey eyes far too probing for my tastes. He asked, "Are you okay? You've been a little detached since last night. I figured you'd be a basket case."

I rolled one shoulder in a shrug so nonchalant I couldn't be bothered with both shoulders; also my right side was one big mass of pain. "This is how it is with Emily. She's a chaos demon. You never see it coming, but when it happens, it makes perfect sense. At least they're safe."

"That's… pragmatic." He paused. "I told Rich to stand down. Now that Marcel's guy has infiltrated Regina's compound, security will tighten up. We can't have people getting killed, not when we already have Marisol in hand."

"Makes sense." I looked around the foyer, which was empty but for the two of us. "I don't really want to hang around here while they look for Tommy. We should be helping."

Addressing my cracked ribs, Jim mused, "I'm not sure how helpful we can really be."

He was right, but I wasn't about to say that. Instead I asked, "Where's Anthony now?"

Nodding behind me, down the hallway that led deeper into the house than I'd ventured so far, Jim said, "He went that way.

He told me to stay in the front rooms."

"So stay in the front rooms. I'll be right back." He looked like he was about to argue, so I added, "You said you trust me. Don't take it back."

"Don't do anything I wouldn't do."

Leaving Jim there to sprout a few more grey hairs, I followed the hallway back into the house and began hearing voices somewhere ahead of me. The noise led me to a pair of locked, double doors, behind which I could hear a flurry of activity. I knocked on the doors and stepped back, hands folded politely in front of me.

It took a while, but soon the door cracked open. I was pleased to see a familiar face on the other side of it, but Benito was less pleased to see me.

"What do you want?"

"A gun and a golf cart."

"Absolutely not."

He started to close the door and I darted forward, pleading, "Let me help. Please. I'm the one losing sleep until he's found. That psycho has it in for me."

"Be that as it may, there's no way Anthony will let me give you a gun."

"But it can't hurt to ask, right?"

Though he shook his head, he sighed, "Just a second," before shutting the door in my face.

I turned my back to the door while I waited, finding the lonely hallway somewhat menacing without Jim there to watch my six. Tommy could be anywhere, and I didn't know whether he wanted to hide, escape, or cut my throat from ear to ear. I hoped Jim had a better idea of his motivations than I did in that moment.

The door creaked back open. I turned to see Benito and Anthony, the former holding a Beretta M9 in a black leather holster. I couldn't believe my eyes.

Anthony said, "You will use this for self-defense only and will give it back the very moment Benito or I or any of my men ask for it. Understood?"

"Yes."

The old man nodded, and Benito handed over the holstered pistol and a set of keys, which I assumed were for a golf cart.

"The supplies are being unloaded now at the wet dock on the south side of the island. You and Camposanto can keep an eye on the dock to make sure Thomas isn't able to escape the island in the confusion. Thank you for your assistance," he added with a grudging half smile.

I wasn't wearing a belt, so I stuffed the holstered M9 into my waistband and returned to the foyer. The moment Jim spotted me and the bulky addition to my wardrobe, he let out a low whistle.

"You never cease to amaze me."

Grinning, I repeated Anthony's stern directions. "Let's stop by the villa first, though. I need a belt."

"I already have a belt," Jim pointed out.

"Anthony gave it to me, not you."

"Fine, then I'm driving."

I handed over the keys, and Jim led me to a row of parked

golf carts on the side of the house. Matching the number on the keychain to the decal on the side of one cart, he started it up and began to navigate the narrow path to our villa.

After a few minutes of silence, during which I assumed from Jim's expression that he was deep in very serious thought, I asked, "Did you tell Beauchamp what I did?"

"I did not. That'll be our little secret, okay? He can be touchy about the unauthorized disclosure of classified information to foreign nationals."

"There weren't any classification markings," I grumbled, unable to resist the urge to be pedantic.

"Don't make me change my mind."

We arrived outside the villa and fell silent, individually assessing the danger. It had come to feel like home, albeit temporary, but now it felt more like a trap. I unholstered the M9 and checked the magazine to make sure it was full before chambering a round. I left the safety off, at least until we were sure the villa was safe. After a brief squabble about me waiting in the golf cart, which I of course won, we crept inside on high alert.

Jim found me a belt, I popped a couple of pills, and we made our getaway. I waited until we were out of sight of the villa to trip the M9's safety and get it situated in its holster on my borrowed belt. I moved it from my appendix to the more familiar four o'clock position behind my right hip, untucking my shirt to conceal the weapon.

The full-sized Beretta felt unfamiliar and bulky, making me pine for the Glock 29 I'd left behind in the States. Once we knew for sure we were getting on a plane and leaving the country, Jim had given my Glock and his Kimber 1911 to an agent from the Dallas office for safekeeping. I assumed Luke still had the little .380 Jim had taken from Tommy, but even if he didn't, my dad had plenty of firepower at the house. I wondered if Luke had stolen any guns while Emily was grabbing the cash, but I shut those thoughts down immediately.

If Tommy was around, he didn't show himself. Knowing I'd have to sleep in our villa tonight, I fervently hoped Tommy would turn up between now and then.

We arrived at the wet dock a few minutes later. While the painkillers took their sweet time kicking in, I was happy to use Jim for support as we climbed out of the golf cart and descended the gentle slope toward the dock. I was expecting to see a smaller craft like the *Luciana's* tender disgorging the proceeds from an epic grocery store run. Instead, a massive cargo vessel was anchored about a quarter mile off shore. Smaller, flat-bottomed boats were ferrying crates and workers to and from the ship.

Not only were they delivering supplies to the island, they were offloading them from the island as well. The crates that came from the ship were being loaded onto a couple of work trucks, which were already nearly full. As we watched, a third work truck arrived, and the driver began assisting the others in removing several smaller crates. These were added to a pile of goods ready to be loaded onto the flat-bottomed boat, once it was emptied. There were no fewer than 50 men milling around, shouting and laughing as they worked.

"Is this what you expected?" I asked Jim.

"Not really. I wonder what's in the crates heading out?"

I scanned the busy workers and saw no one of import. A few faces I recognized from among Anthony's staff, and many more had presumably arrived via cargo ship and would be departing the same way.

I said, "Let's go take a closer look."

We picked our way down to the nearest truck, the one that had just arrived, and casually eased into the ongoing activity. No one paid us the slightest attention. The drugs kicked in all at once, and I realized I probably should've eaten something before I took them. It was too late now.

Each of the smaller crates was about the size of a banker's box but made of raw wood, a logo and Italian words burned into the side, an additional paper label glued next to the logo. I scanned the labels eagerly, disappointed to find the crates contained wine and olives. Boring. I passed my findings on to Jim, who didn't seem all that surprised.

"There's a working vineyard here. Must be an olive grove, too. I suppose they would need a legitimate business operation."

"You suppose? I thought you knew what was going on here."

"I haven't had time to become an expert," he said, acerbic. Clearly I'd plucked a nerve. "I'm more interested in what's in those larger crates."

The crates to which he referred were indeed much larger, six feet to a side, about eight feet tall, and requiring a forklift to move. I started toward the nearest one but was forced to stop by Jim's hand around my arm. He tensed, clocking a man walking toward us with less than friendly intent.

"What are you doing?" the man asked in Italian—no, wait. I blinked at him, slow to catch on. Spanish.

"We're looking for someone," I said, forcing a smile. A couple of yards from us, he focused on me and froze in his tracks. He backed away.

"This is a dangerous area to be wandering around. Keep your distance, please, and stay out of the way."

"We will," I promised. "Sorry."

"What was that about?" Jim asked as the man retreated. "Do you know that guy?"

"No, why?"

"He recognized you. Didn't you see that? He recognized you and backed away. What was he saying?"

"He was only telling us to stay out of the way." I closed my eyes, trying to reassemble his face from the brief, opiate-fuddled glimpse. I definitely didn't know him. And why would I? "Maybe he didn't recognize me. Maybe he just decided we were people he shouldn't be yelling at."

Curiosity burning, we nevertheless backed away as ordered and watched the loading-unloading process until it was complete. I counted five truck loads going out, seven coming in, and obviously more of both before Jim and I got there. I never spotted Tommy, but I had to admit it would've been all too easy for him to get lost in the shuffle.

One of those seven-plus trucks had contained the burrata mozzarella and black truffle oil I'd brazenly demanded of Anthony, and I found myself unable to think about anything else as

Jim bundled me into the golf cart and took off behind the last truck leaving the dock. He was much more interested in what we'd just seen.

"Curious that Anthony would let us see that. We know they're moving people, probably not between the island and Sardinia, but definitely from Sardinia to the mainland. They've got the wine and olive business running in the foreground, looking legitimate, but there's no way this little island can produce enough of either to net Anthony and the others this kind of profit. I'd say whatever else they've got going on has to be on Sardinia, but what was in those larger crates? That's something that either came from this island, or to it at an earlier date. From Libya? Egypt maybe? Crap, it could be anything. Think about where they started. Anna, are you listening to me?"

"Mmhm."

"Is any of this even mildly interesting to you?"

"Honestly?"

He vented a quick sigh. "Never mind. We've got more pressing concerns. I wonder if they've found Tommy yet."

"I hope he escaped on that boat," I mused. "I never want to see that little wiener again."

My eyelids felt heavy, and I was still having visions of mozzarella on toast. Jim finally accepted that I was a lost cause, falling into private contemplation. Faster than the golf cart by far, the trucks outpaced us and were lost to sight by the time we got back to Anthony's house. We could hear the hustle and bustle of unloading around the back of the house, so Jim maneuvered the golf cart that way.

I was fairly certain we were sticking our noses where they wouldn't be welcome, but Jim's body language betrayed no such reservations. He parked the cart, helped me out, and let me lean on him while he found a spot from which to watch the unloading process.

Several large crates had already been unloaded and were neatly arranged along one side of the concrete driveway. Most were untouched, but one was open, revealing a dozen young citrus trees packed in curling bundles of wood shavings that were spilling out onto the concrete.

I watched listlessly as a young man pulled one of the trees out and started wrestling it around the side of the house. My gaze snapped away from him, back to the interior of the crate. Jim's attention was focused elsewhere, so he didn't see it. I wasn't sure *I* was really seeing it. I really, *really* hoped I wasn't seeing it.

Barely visible between two canvas-covered bundles of tree roots, something long and white had shifted slightly when the tree was removed. The longer I looked, standing at a distance of about fifteen yards, the more it looked like a forearm. Five fingers ending in black nail polish stood out against the wood shavings. The other end of the arm was lost in shadow amongst the young trees. I stared at it for so long that Jim left off his own source of interest and peered at me.

"What?"

"Either I'm tripping balls, or there's a body in that crate."

▼

Octavio's daughter, Gia Palermo, had left work at her office in Sassari on Saturday afternoon and called her father on the way home to let him know she was okay. After learning of Regina's threats, Gia had made a habit of checking in with her father.

She'd missed a lunch date on Sunday with her boyfriend, but this didn't come to light until after her body was found. Her check-in Sunday night had taken the form of a brief text message, which in retrospect was an obvious red flag. Best we could figure, after Octavio's frantic search for information Monday afternoon, was she'd been taken from her home, where she lived alone, on Saturday night and killed sometime Sunday.

Her body bore no signs of abuse, only a single bullet wound over her heart. Jim had insisted on seeing her, and he'd dubbed it a contact or near-contact shot. I confess myself relieved by the manner of her death, having imagined far more grisly methods being wielded by a Colombian drug lord.

The only message Regina had chosen to send with her death was a piece of paper pinned to her shirt. It bore the words 'Tuesday at 10' three times in English, Italian, and French.

Dismissing warnings that he was putting himself in further danger, Octavio whisked her body away to Cagliari for burial. He was mum as to his exact course of action. Obviously, taking his daughter to a hospital or mortuary would raise quite a lot of interest because of the plainly criminal way in which she'd died, and that interest would sooner or later find its way to the island. I suspected my Sardinian friends knew of more discreet means by which to dispose of their dead. I didn't really want to know.

The discovery of Gia's body had chased away the lingering

effects of my opiate-and-empty-stomach cocktail, leaving me jittery and in a great deal of pain. I kept these complaints to myself, trying to stay out of the way while Anthony's house buzzed with activity. Everyone had congregated there again, checking up on family members via phone and putting their heads together about what to do.

By dinnertime, the only person who couldn't be tracked down for a wellness check, besides Emily, Luke, and the girls of course, was Russo's wife in Porto Pino. He left to check on her in person, and we all dispersed to pull ourselves together for dinner.

Tommy was still nowhere to be found, and Benito had confiscated the M9. We could now contact Regina without involving Tommy if needed, but no one doubted he was using his freedom to attempt contact with her. If he'd known about Gia's kidnap and murder, it made all kinds of sense for him to make himself scarce, but what else he may have been up to was anyone's guess.

Over an especially fancy surf 'n' turf dinner in which no one showed much interest, opinions varied wildly about what to do. Knowing Marcel's man was on his way with Marisol gave the discussion a particularly frenetic edge.

Many wanted Marisol maimed or even killed in retribution for Gia, but cooler heads prevailed. We only had one Marisol, compared to dozens and dozens of potential targets for Regina's wrath. We would proceed with the Tuesday morning video call with Regina, show off our hostage, and go forward from there.

All we had to do was stay alive until said hostage arrived.

As dessert was being served, a message arrived for Anthony and he announced to the table at large, "They found him."

24

Monday, June 28 to
Tuesday, June 29, 2021

Where Tommy spent the majority of his absence, he wouldn't say, but it was Penelope who ultimately saved the day when Tommy attempted to break into Marcel and Giles' villa and discovered how protective the little Malinois could be. She had literally treed him, like a raccoon, and her incessant barking had drawn the attention of the men out roving the island for Tommy.

Penelope was excited but unharmed and immensely proud of herself, and Tommy was none the worse for his brief, solo adventure. Refusing to utter a word, he was dragged to the holding area intended for Marisol. Jim and I demanded to be taken there, and Anthony agreed.

I got my first glimpse of the vineyard, bathed in darkness, its dimensions unknowable, as Anthony, Jim, and I arrived in a golf cart driven by Benito. Anthony had flat refused to allow anyone else access to Tommy, knowing full well that nearly everyone on the island would have happily snuffed him out if given half a chance. Since Jim and I were openly against any snuffing, regardless of our feelings toward Tommy, we were considered safe.

Anthony led the way to a long, low building which hugged the northern edge of the vineyard. It looked relatively new, especially in contrast to the established grape vines beyond, visible by the light pouring from windows spaced evenly along the building's length. I knew Jim would be making note of these details and decided to leave that to him.

Inside, a metal staircase descended to a subterranean-level fermenting and storage area, all sleek and modern and scrupulously clean. I smelled not only fermenting wine but olives and possibly tomatoes. Anthony's humble little island was busy indeed.

One end of the building was walled off into what I assumed was a suite of offices. A door at the other end opened onto another staircase, this one ending in a solid, wooden door complete with an iron grate over a square opening about six inches to a side. Light was issuing from behind the door, but no sound.

Anthony sent Benito down the stairs first to see what the prisoner was up to before he opened the door. He peeped through the grate, saw nothing of concern, and unlocked the door. Jim and Anthony descended the stairs, and I hesitated for only a moment before following.

After the briefest of glances at Tommy to make sure he was safe, in both senses of the word, I looked around to see what this convenient prison really was: a cellar for hundreds and hundreds of bottles of wine. They lined the walls in various states of inaccessibility, the finest of them displayed in a glass case on the far wall. I couldn't even ballpark the value of the collection, only that it was worth keeping under lock and key.

Tommy was handcuffed to a metal pole set in the middle of one wall. He was sitting on the concrete floor, leaning against a stack of now-familiar hand crates, a half-empty bottle of water by his foot. Either he hadn't realized he was within reach of some very expensive bottles of vino, or he simply didn't feel like destroying them. We were lucky he wasn't suicidal, with all that glass around. He cast a surly glare over his visitors and settled on Anthony.

"Do you know what I'd be wondering if I were you?" he asked lightly, as though picking up the thread of a recent conversation. When Anthony didn't answer, Tommy went on, "If Paolo is so obsessed with pruning his family tree, why hasn't he gone after you? You are related through his grandfather, aren't you?"

"Perhaps his goals haven't been made clear to you."

"But they have to you?"

"Why were you trying to get into Marcel's villa?" Jim asked.

"I was hungry."

"Why'd you run off in the first place?" I pressed. "Did you know about Gia?"

"Gia who?"

"Have you been talking with Regina," Jim said, not even bothering to make it a question.

Tommy shrugged. "I couldn't get to a phone. Why did you help Marcel?" he asked me, losing a touch of the casual façade he was faking so hard.

"We didn't have time to pussyfoot around," I hedged. "Why do you care?"

He held my gaze for several seconds and said in a voice I knew too well, "If anything happens to her, you die."

We left it at that, knowing any further attempts at questioning would be fruitless. I had been intending to inquire after what sort of treatment Tommy could expect as far as food, water, bathroom breaks, and the like; but the death threat somewhat diluted my interest. Benito searched Tommy's pockets and came up with a pocket knife he'd somehow acquired, and that was that. We all went our separate ways, Jim and I retiring to our villa to get some rest.

The supplies we'd ordered had been delivered in our absence, stacked on the kitchen counter or shuffled into the fridge as necessary. Jim wasn't thrilled that someone had been in the villa, but I only had eyes for the mozzarella. I made a beeline for the fridge, found the treasured cheese, tore off a chuck, and popped it into my mouth. I moaned with pleasure.

Jim poked his head into the kitchen, asking, "Why do I suddenly feel left out?"

"I'm just eating cheese. Don't mind us."

"How many of those pills do you have left?"

"Twelve, why?"

He held up the pill bottle and shook it. "You sure?"

Feeling vaguely defensive, I snatched the bottle out of his

hand and dumped the contents on the counter. I counted sixteen pills, then counted again twice more to be sure. They all looked exactly the same, tiny white pills with '5mg' stamped into one side.

"No, there were twelve. I'm absolutely certain. I've been rationing it."

"Someone's been in here, and not just in the kitchen. Do me a huge favor and don't take any more of those."

"Aw, no," I moaned, already feeling a plaintive twinge of pain in my side. "You think there are four bonus pills in here?"

"If we're lucky, that's the only thing they tampered with."

"Who?"

"Tommy? I don't know. Obviously whoever delivered the supplies can come and go as they please."

My thoughts tiptoed back to the mozzarella in the fridge, and I asked, "You think the food's safe to eat?"

"I guess we'll find out," he said, eying me significantly.

"What about your notes?" I asked, glancing at the kitchen table.

"They're all in English and reasonably encoded, if that's the right word. Still, it's a find."

"I *hate* it here."

"Me, too. Just try to get some rest. We're not waiting until ten. We're calling Regina as soon as Marcel's guy gets here. I want you there for it."

I took a hot shower, drank a glass of wine, and burrowed into the bed, willing myself to sleep, but it was no good. My whole body ached, and my thoughts were like a dryer full of mismatched socks spinning around at 1,000 rpm.

I gave up after about an hour and went into the living room, where Jim was watching TV on low volume, his attention on his laptop on the coffee table in front of him. I recognized the secure email he'd been using to communicate with Beauchamp, but either no new messages had arrived since Jim's update this morning, or he'd already read and deleted them.

"Why aren't you resting?" I asked.

"Not tired."

He looked up at me and gave me a cautious half-smile. "Why aren't *you* resting?"

I shut the laptop, ever conscious of the webcam, and sat down next to him.

"I don't want to hear any guff from you, buddy," I whispered. "Everything already hurts as much as possible, and I can't take anything for it. This is the next best thing."

He opened his mouth, probably to give me guff, and I kissed him before he could speak. He hadn't shaved his face today, and the sandpaper texture of his chin was unexpectedly gratifying. There was no use denying it now; I wanted him like I hadn't wanted anyone in years. Only the pain in my torso kept me from acting on it. Once the effort of sitting up became too much, I lay down with my legs across his lap and finally drifted to sleep.

▼

This time when the gunman leaned out of the Channel 221 news van with his boxy, evil-looking machine pistol, he sent not one round but dozens peppering across the windshield of the Demon. None of them seemed to hit Luke, Jim, or me; but he kept firing and firing until the concussive report of the weapon forced me to abandon sleep and accept that the sounds did not exist only in my head.

I sat up, dizzy and disoriented, re-identifying the bangs not as automatic weapons fire but a much slower, less insistent pounding of someone knocking on the door. Jim came around with me, having apparently fallen asleep sitting up with his head leaned back across the sofa. He rubbed his neck ruefully, waiting for me to move my legs off his lap before he headed for the door.

"Don't—" I started, but he waved one hand at me.

"I know, I know," he whispered. Bereft of his sidearm, his hands formed an automatic, loose imitation of holding a gun at low ready as he edged toward the door. Rather than opening it, he moved to a nearby window and peeked out. "It's one of Anthony's guys."

I felt an instinct to flee, though I wasn't sure from what. I stayed on the couch and listened. Jim opened the door, ending the knocks and allowing the man outside to say, "I'm sorry to disturb you. Anthony wants everyone at the house. They're here."

"What did he say?" Jim called to me.

I translated, then smiled to myself as Jim whipped out his beginner Italian to reply, "Grazie. Uh—ci saremo pronto," to the messenger. Jim closed the door and came back into the living room, looking smug.

"Close." I couldn't help but correct him. "Presto, not pronto."

"He got the idea."

"You're a quick study."

We threw on some shoes, Jim grabbed his laptop, and we left the villa to find the messenger still there, waiting for us next to one of Anthony's ubiquitous golf carts. He got us to the house in a couple of minutes, and Jim and I were among the first to arrive in the formal parlor where we'd already agreed to host the video call. Marcel and Giles were there, accompanied by the two newest arrivals.

Marcel's operative was a surprise, given that Luke was the only other one I'd met. Where Luke was hulking and tall, this man was gracile, no more than five feet, six inches of stringy muscle. He was white, about 30, with dirty blonde hair worn a bit too long, pale blue eyes returning my gaze from under a heavy brow ridge.

With arms slightly too long for his frame, big hands, and a pair of overlarge ears that had probably earned him some cruel nicknames in school, I thought he looked remarkably like an ape. He nodded at me, unsmiling, merely a gesture to acknowledge my inordinate interest.

Next to him, tethered to him by a hand clenched tightly around her upper arm, was the woman I assumed to be Marisol. She had a black pillow case over her head and was as still as a statue, dressed in pajamas that had not weathered the trip well at all.

Below the hem of her cotton shorts, her legs were scuffed with dirt, her knees scraped, an abrasion barely beginning to heal over her left ankle. Her bare arms were in no better shape, and her t-shirt was torn at the collar. She must have put up a serious fight, just like I'd taught her so long ago.

Marcel pulled the pillow case off her head, presumably to allow Jim and me to identify her. In addition to the pillow case, someone had wrapped a scarf around her eyes. I recognized her in the instant before my heart sank even further: I saw a cut on her forehead, blood in her nostrils, her upper lip fat and busted from some impact. She looked like she'd been in a car accident.

"What happened to her?" Jim demanded, echoing my thoughts.

Marcel and the unnamed man exchanged a look, the latter unsure whether to respond.

"She fought," Marcel answered.

I approached her cautiously, seeing when I was within a couple feet of her and her kidnapper that she was trembling. I met the man's eyes, asking, "What did you do to her?"

Marisol reacted to my voice, turning her head toward me, the pace of her breathing picking up. The man smiled at me, a twisting of the mouth that only made his features more brutal.

"Nothing she didn't like," he finally said. He let go of her arm and reached up to stroke her hair.

"Anna!" Jim warned, knowing what I was about to do even before I did.

My right palm crashed into his nose at an upward angle and he reeled backward, reaching toward Marisol for support;

but she'd skipped blindly away at Jim's warning. I sent my shin straight up into the A formed by his legs, and his nose met my knee with crushing force as he reflexively leaned forward, grappling protectively at his crouch. He went down face first, groaning, blood gushing from his ruined nose.

No one had raised a finger to stop me, and I might have carried on until he was dead if that last flying knee hadn't caused me to double over in agony. Clutching my right side and trying not to take the deep breaths my body craved, I turned and left the parlor.

As I stalked down the hall, I heard Giles say, "Wow."

25

Tuesday, June 29, 2021

Jim found me in a nearby bathroom, sitting on the floor, sobbing. I try to save the waterworks for only the bleakest of moments, which had been coming up more and more often lately. Each sob felt like a dagger to my ribs, and I was struggling to get control of myself when I felt his hand on the top of my head.

"Everything that's happened to her is my fault," I gasped. "I told Marcel how to find her. I helped you and Luke kill her brother. She's just a kid, Jim. What kind of animal could do that to her?"

He sat down next to me, wrapping one hand around my ankle in a gesture he'd certainly learned from Luke. His hand was smaller, a normal size, but the pressure was bracing.

"This is war, Anna. Wars have casualties. We didn't start this."

"Paolo started it," I whispered obediently, desperate to let him convince me someone else was responsible for Marisol's suffering.

"I'm glad you understand that. I'm about to ask you to do something you won't like. I need you to trust me."

Jim hurriedly briefed me on the key points of his strategy. He was right: I didn't like it, not one bit; but I agreed to it all the same, if only to end this once and for all.

Jim returned with me to the parlor, only to find Marisol, Giles, and Marcel's operative missing.

Marcel volunteered, "Anthony's wife took her to get cleaned up. I'm sorry, Anna, but you failed to kill my employee as I'm sure you intended. Giles is taking him back to the villa."

"Thanks for the update," I snapped.

Jim took his chance, while Marisol was out of the room, to get a consensus from the others gathered in the parlor. He presented almost the same strategy to them that he'd described to me, and all agreed to try it. A short time later, Marisol was led back into the room by Anthony's wife, who quickly took her leave again without speaking to or even looking at anyone.

When the video feed from Colombia flickered to life on Jim's laptop, followed a heartbeat later by an identical, larger image on the TV to which he'd connected an HDMI cable, I studied Regina Lira's face while her gaze swept the room around me.

Unlike her brother, Emilio, the Regina who'd appeared on her father's missing children poster had been an awkward, rather mean-looking child with a hawklike face and soulless eyes. It's entirely possible I had attributed too much of the adult to the innocent child's likeness in my memory. Knowing she'd grow up to be the villain, I'd disliked the seven-year-old girl on principle.

The old woman centered in the flatscreen before me was

identifiably that same person, but age had been kinder to her than I'd anticipated. She looked much more like the Regina in Etta's photograph, a beautiful young girl who'd decided to age gracefully rather than kicking and screaming as so many do. She'd grown into her nose and eyebrows, and like Paolo her hair had turned a silvery gray. Pushing 84 now, she could easily have passed for 70, her eyes flashing with youthful vigor that currently took the form of unspeakable rage.

Distorted by the camera's angle, it was difficult to tell on which of us her gaze alighted, but Marisol was my guess. She was sitting between Marcel and Paolo, her wrists tied to the arms of her chair and a gag tied in her mouth.

The old woman had found her a change of clothes, washed her face and arms, and brushed her hair. The effect of this perfunctory care was pathetic, Marisol's superficial wounds all the more shocking against the backdrop of her detangled hair and clean, borrowed clothes. Rather than staring up at Regina on the screen, Marisol's gaze was downcast, her shoulders slumped.

Regina finally found her voice to ask, "Who did that to her? Mija, mírame. Estás bien?"

Marisol looked up, nodded her head, and lowered it again. Something in the rigidity of her movements made me wonder if she was putting on an act. The girl was frightened and hurt, but totally cowed? Somehow I didn't think so.

"You have killed Marcel's brother, Anthony's son, and now Palermo's daughter," Paolo said, forcing Regina's eyes to move. The shift made it easier to guess who she was looking at as her gaze then roved over the assemblage. I thought she paused a little at me, but she didn't say anything about the addition. "By my count, Aunt, you are ahead by one. Should I kill Marisol now, to even the score? Maybe then we can call a halt to this."

"If you harm one hair on her head, I'll hunt you all down like dogs," she snarled, letting her composure slip just a bit before taking a deep breath. She leaned back, away from the camera. "But you already know that, don't you? So what do you want?"

"Luke Jackson is the one who killed your son, and your nephew," Marcel said. "He has been found and brought here, and he's currently under guard on the island. We are willing to give you him. Only him."

I held my breath as Marcel spoke, begging Regina not to look at me. He'd delivered the lie with practiced ease, but I knew my reddening face would give us away.

"Paolo is responsible," Regina hissed.

"Only Jackson," Marcel repeated. "We will deliver him, and we will hold Marisol to ensure your continued good behavior. That is the new deal, take it or leave it."

"You expect me to agree to this, to Marisol remaining a prisoner there? For how long? Look how she's been treated! How can I trust you with her?"

"You tell us," Paolo invited.

Regina's gaze fell on me again. "Shouldn't I have a hostage of my own?"

Before anyone else could answer, Jim barked, "Anna's not part of any deal. Period."

"You're right," Regina agreed, waving her hand over the

camera as though to wipe me away. "She doesn't matter. Mari wanted her included, but I couldn't care less either way. I can accept Mister Jackson… as a hostage. After a time, perhaps an exchange? I will not agree to any deal that doesn't include Paolo. You started this, Nephew. How long will you hide from the consequences of what you've done? Or better to ask, how long will everyone else consent to hide you?"

Again, Marcel stepped in to reiterate, "Only Jackson. You have three days to decide."

She glared at him, sweeping the room once more to ask, "Where is Thomas?"

"We don't know," Jim answered. "We haven't seen him for days. A supply ship came to the island this morning, as you know. We think he might have left on it."

She said only, "You'll hear from me," before the screen went black and the call ended. I exhaled loudly into the thick silence following her departure.

"How did you know she would believe we have Luke?" Marcel asked Jim, looking a bit too perceptive for my taste.

"Why wouldn't she? She doesn't know where he is. We managed to nab Marisol right out from under her nose."

"You're lying," the Frenchman hissed. "You've been playing your own game this whole time, right? Why wouldn't you?"

"Why would I? What would that accomplish, Marcel? Go ahead, I think we're all eager to hear your wisdom on the matter."

He said nothing, merely glaring at a spot just over Jim's head.

"I didn't think so. Just so we're clear, if your man or anyone else lays another finger on Marisol, I'll feed you your own eye-balls. Understand?"

Icily, Marcel answered, "Tell me how you knew Regina would believe me, and perhaps I'll understand."

With a loaded glance at me, Jim sighed and said, "I would think you of all people would be aware of Jackson's magpie-like behavior. It's what led Regina to you in the first place."

"What does that mean?"

From his pocket, Jim withdrew a heavy silver watch, which he placed on the arm of my chair. I assumed that meant we were done not telling anyone about Lira's watch. Excitement and terror flooded through me as Jim began to explain.

"Luke took this from Lira when he killed him, as a souvenir. It's got an anti-theft device. We figured it out when Tommy kept turning up like a bad penny. He's been tracking it with his phone for over a year. We managed to muffle the signal with some Southern engineering, but before Anna and I went to bed last night, I turned it back on."

Marcel's eyes widened in anger, and Paolo snapped, "Why would you do this without telling us? You're saying Regina can now see that this watch is here on the island?"

"Yes. It's not like she didn't already know we were here. Even if Tommy didn't find a way to tell her, it doesn't take an idiot to figure it out. Why send Palermo's daughter here?"

"Now she believes all three of the people she wants are right here on this island!" Paolo argued. "She'll send someone for us."

"Not with a sword hanging over Marisol's neck."

"I don't believe it," Giles said, motioning toward the watch. "This is some trick. So you have a watch. The watch is not Luke."

"See for yourself," Jim countered, pulling Tommy's phone from his pocket and tossing it to Giles. "The app shows you where the watch is now, and where it's been. All you need is Tommy's thumbprint. I'd suggest leaving it attached to his hand, in case we need it again later."

Studying the phone, Giles said, "I was thinking just the opposite."

"Severed fingers rot, idiot. Just threaten to cut it off unless he gives you the pin code to turn off the fingerprint lock."

"Fine," Marcel snapped, taking the phone from his brother. "Giles, you stay here and make sure that watch doesn't move. Anthony, I would like to visit our prisoner, if I may."

Anthony agreed, and he and Marcel departed for the vineyard. They left a strained silence in their wake, broken only by a creaking of wood as Marisol shifted uncomfortably in her chair. I couldn't believe no one had objected to her hearing Jim's big reveal, but then again he'd hardly given anyone a chance to mention it.

"Can't you take that gag out of her mouth?" I asked. "And why does she have to be tied up? Are you big, bad men all afraid of her or something?"

"Christian said she was almost more than he could handle," Giles argued. "You taught her a few tricks, didn't you?"

I was astonished that someone had decided to name that apelike creature 'Christian'. I shot back, "Of course I taught her some tricks. She's been hunted like an animal her entire life. That doesn't mean she needs to stay trussed up like this. You should all be ashamed of yourselves."

"That's enough, Anna," Jim muttered.

"Strong words, from the person who played such an instrumental role in finding her," Giles said with relish. I met Marisol's disbelieving gaze for as long as I could.

"I wouldn't have, if I'd known you be such savages about it."

Probably just to stop the bickering, Paolo reached over and pulled down the gag around Marisol's mouth. She thanked him frostily and said to me, "Don't do me any more favors, puta."

I deserved that, but it still stung. "Jim and I are the only ones here who give two craps about you," I answered. "Don't forget that."

She chose not to reply. Anthony and Marcel were gone for so long I was starting to wonder if something had happened to them. I wasn't the only one, either. After forty minutes of their absence, Marco ordered his son, Bambino, to go and check on them. Minutes ticked by, and I desperately needed sleep when all three finally returned. Marcel wasn't done yet.

"We've seen it stay still. Now I want to see it move."

"What difference does it make?" Jim argued. "Regina can see that the watch is here, and she thinks it means Luke is here."

"Move it," Marcel insisted.

Jim looked at me again, "Do the honors?"

I picked up the watch and walked around the perimeter of the house, relishing the solitude and the chill of the early morning air. According to Lira's watch, it was almost 6:00 a.m. in Central Time, to which I assumed Luke had set it when he'd arrived in Oklahoma. I'd lost track of the exact time difference, but I knew it was sometime after midnight here.

Doubts plagued me, things I might have voiced to Jim if I'd had the chance. What if Tommy had already told Regina that we'd figured out the GPS transmitter in the watch? He'd still had a cell phone when we'd discussed it back in Oklahoma. What if Regina realized the significance of the signal camping out in Oklahoma, disappearing, and then suddenly reappearing in the Mediterranean right when we needed her to think we'd brought Luke here? Had she only pretended to accept our lie about Luke, already wise to Jim's chicanery?

A full circuit of the massive house wasn't enough time to settle on a satisfactory answer to any of these questions. I had to trust that Jim knew what he was doing.

Back inside, I found that my circumambulation keeping pace with the watch's blipping signal on Tommy's phone had already convinced the Marchands and everyone else that Jim's news was genuine. I gave the watch back to Jim, who put it on above his own watch, and Marcel returned Tommy's unlocked phone.

"Where is Christian now?" Jim asked, not addressing anyone in particular. I hadn't given the man a second thought, but Marisol had to spend the night somewhere, so I could see why Jim would want to know.

"He's at our villa, resting before he returns home," Marcel answered. He fixed me with a very strange look and asked, "How different would this story be, I wonder, if I'd sent him to kill Lira instead of sending Luke?"

I briefly pictured turning around in the doorway to Luke's little shack in Colorado and seeing Christian, rather than Luke, watching me from the shadows. I shuddered delicately and answered, "I guess we'll never know."

Jim was still focused on more tangible concerns. "Anthony, what about Marisol? Do you have another space for her, since Tommy's at the vineyard?"

"We are needing one? Are you fearing the boy harms her, or other way around?"

"Not necessarily."

"What, throw them in there together?" I asked. "That seems like a bad idea."

"I'm sorry Anna," Anthony said to me in Italian, feigning chagrin. "I haven't yet broken ground on the jail I intend to build."

"Too bad."

The matter thus settled, I demanded to be allowed to accompany Marisol to the vineyard. I wanted to see how she and Tommy would react to one another, perhaps circumventing something unfortunate if the reaction was too bad on either side.

After the obligatory peek through the grate to make sure Tommy wasn't waiting inside the door with a broken wine bottle, we were allowed into the room. I went in first, and then Jim brought Marisol inside. Tommy was still seated in the same attitude, his hand cuffed around the metal pole.

Neither Marisol nor Tommy batted an eye when they saw each other. Marisol, her hands bound in front of her with handcuffs, dragged herself to the corner farthest from Tommy, slid down into a crouch, and pressed her face to her knees. Tommy gave no indication, by word or expression, that he objected to her having freedom of movement that might allow her to attack him if she were so inclined.

Maybe if I'd been less sleep deprived, I'd have seen what was really going on, but who knows. We left them there, returned to our villa, and went to bed.

26
Tuesday, June 29, 2021

Jim and I slept like the dead until 11:30 that morning, when the incessant buzzing of his phone forced us into consciousness. I threw an arm over my eyes to block out the sun while I listened to his side of the call.

"Hello? … Did he now… Okay, why? … Yeah, text it to me. Thanks. Bye."

"Who was that?" I mumbled, not caring at all.

"Anthony. He wants us to see the security camera feed from last night. From the vineyard."

"Oh?" I sat up, looking over Jim's shoulder. It took a few seconds, but eventually a text came through containing a video clip. Jim opened it.

I sputtered, "Oh my God, did he use his phone to take a video of his computer screen?"

"Shush."

There was no sound, but I shushed anyway. From a camera that appeared to be positioned directly over the door, we watched as I entered the wine cellar, followed by Jim and Marisol. Tommy was visible at the lower right corner of the video, and Marisol took up a position near the center on the left. The camera was aimed at the case of super pricy vintages, so we were lucky Tommy made it into the frame at all. Jim and I left, and for a few minutes neither Tommy nor Marisol moved.

I was beginning to get bored when Marisol lifted her head off of her knees and said something to Tommy. If he answered, it wasn't visible on screen. Marisol stood up and walked to the door, passing out of the frame for a moment.

When she returned, she wasn't in her own corner but in Tommy's. She threw her handcuffed hands around his neck and began to shudder with sobs while he held onto her with his free hand. They kissed, then slipped out of the bottom of the frame, nothing visible but Tommy's hand still bound to the metal pole. The video ended there.

"Holy act of congress, Batman," I whispered.

"Interesting," Jim said. He called Anthony back. "Think we should separate them? … No, I didn't… I have no idea. Maybe he spent some time in Colombia? … It would… Uh huh."

"What did he say?"

"That this changes things. After you got the truth—so to speak—out of him in Dallas, I thought it was possible, even likely that he was still lying about Miami… but if he's got something going on with Marisol, I'd say that's the case solved. He's been to Colombia."

"Maybe Regina found out they were together and tried to

stop them, and that's why he came to us, to use us to get Marisol out of there."

"There's no way he could have known that would happen, though."

"Yeah… So if he's doing all of it for Regina, what's the end game? Why didn't he just kill Luke and me in Texas, then go after Paolo?"

"I don't know. Let's ask him."

I caught a gleam in Jim's eyes, a familiar warning that I was falling for an act. For several seconds I studied him, torn between calling him out and playing along to let him have his moment. I chose the latter, inured by then to the fact that, like them or not, Jim's plans seemed to work out for the best… eventually.

Anthony agreed to meet us at the vineyard so we could talk to Tommy, and Jim only deepened my considerable suspicions by asking him to bring Marcel along. While we walked to the vineyard, my curiosity bubbled over.

"What are you up to?"

"I'm not sure." He sounded sincere.

"Regina has to know that we know about the watch. And what about all that time it was just resolutely blinking away in Oklahoma? No way she hasn't noticed that it teleported here *right* before we 'captured' Luke…"

He grinned at me, softening his harsh response: "Do me a huge favor, and don't say any of that out loud ever again."

"You're loving this, aren't you?"

"Who doesn't love it when a good plan comes together?" He scoffed, adding, "Not sure why I'm asking you. A *plan*, kiddo, is something people make *before* they act. Sometimes whole minutes before they act."

"Let me try: In five seconds, I'm going to kick you in the shin."

Though he scoffed again, he pointedly put a few feet between us for the rest of the walk. My plan fell through.

We waited outside the locked winery building for about five minutes before Anthony, Marcel, and Benito appeared to let us in. I hovered at the bottom of the stairs to the smaller storage room, next to Benito, while the others filed inside. Tommy was supine, apparently dozing, while Marisol had pressed herself against the back corner and was eyeing us with trepidation.

"A word, Tommy," Jim said, loudly enough that he couldn't continue feigning slumber.

He sat up, making quite a show of getting comfortable before he replied, "What now?"

"We need to know what you've been telling Regina since we got to Italy."

"What am I, your secretary? You've heard every call I've made to her, since that first one in Switzerland."

Jim's next move was an unpleasant surprise. He turned to look thoughtfully at Marisol, then asked, "Marcel, would it be all right if Anthony's man here took Marisol back to your villa for now, while we talk to Tommy? I don't want her here for this."

I watched Tommy while Jim spoke, noting tiny reactions I could easily have missed before: slight coloring of the cheeks, eyes dilating, rigidity freezing his posture. He was truly concerned for Marisol, protective and jealous. Could it be possible that he loved her? The thought of Tommy genuinely caring about anyone made me sick to my stomach.

"Isn't Christian there?" I supplied helpfully.

"I believe so," Jim said.

Catching on, Marcel nodded and voiced no objection to the fact that he'd been dragged down here just to listen to two minutes of posturing. When the three of them were gone and only Jim, Anthony, Tommy, and I were left, Tommy asked, "So are you gonna torture me, now? A little waterboarding before breakfast?"

"What have you told Regina?" Jim repeated.

"Nothing. I haven't talked to her since I called her and left a voicemail. I couldn't find a phone."

Jim pulled out his phone, bringing up the video Anthony had sent him that morning. He held it in front of Tommy's face, letting it play through to the end. Tommy said nothing.

"Back in my day, you needed to spend some time with a girl to get her to that point. Phone calls just wouldn't cut it. How many times have you been to Colombia, Tommy?"

"Zero."

"Try again."

"I'm not saying there's something to tell, but why would I even talk to you? No way I'm getting off this island either way."

"It's up to you where Marisol spends the night tonight. Talk to us, and she's safe here with you. Keep jerking us around, and she gets some more quality time with Christian."

Tommy's eyes flashed to me, and I hastily rearranged my expression. It was too late. He laughed bitterly. "Anna beat the crap out of him, right? Mari told me. She's not going to let you do that."

"It's not up to her," Jim argued.

I fumed, knowing this was true. "Tommy, just tell us. Please. If she stays at Marcel's, she'll get hurt again, and I'll end up killing someone for it, and everyone's going to get mad at each other and start fighting and forget all about you, and you'll just starve to death down here."

"Maybe you could leave this part to me," Jim said sternly, turning to wink at me.

I interpreted his wink as discreet approval and mumbled, "Whatever."

"Who cares if I went to Colombia?" Tommy spat. "You already found out where Regina's compound is, and you don't need my help getting inside even if I'd give it. I went there a couple times. Big deal."

"She must have trusted you, to bring you there when she'd put so much effort into staying hidden. After Marisol's parents died, and Etta cut off all contact, Regina went to ground too, didn't she?"

"Obviously."

"Does she move around a lot?"

"I don't know. I guess... She must not have been there long. Tres Islas—the cartel, not the town—it's pretty new, right? She must have had to start over."

"But you don't know for sure?"

"I never asked her."

"She must think pretty highly of you, to let you mess around with Marisol."

"Who cares?" Tommy demanded, frustration bursting to the surface. "What are you getting at? Regina trusts me? She doesn't trust anyone. That whole compound is rigged to explode if she gets it in her head it's time to go."

"Is that so?" Jim asked.

Though he was facing away from me, I heard the ring of victory in Jim's voice and almost lost the thread of the conversation, trying to figure out what Tommy had said that was so important.

Jim was asking, "It's like a game of Battleship, isn't it? Ever since Marisol's parents. Emilio and Paolo on one side, Regina and Etta on the other."

"I guess so. I know she was trying to find Paolo. I wanted to tell her about the house in Florence, but I told you, I couldn't find a phone. She's probably tracking my cell just like she's tracking the watch, so it doesn't really matter what I told her or didn't tell her, does it?"

"Maybe you should ask her that," Jim said. He turned to go so abruptly that Anthony and I were both surprised, trying not to look too undignified as we hurried after him. Just outside the winery, we bumped into Benito and Marcel. Marisol was secured between them, looking impatient. Jim didn't seem at all surprised to find them there.

"We're done with him for now," Jim said.

"Please lock the door, Benito," Anthony directed at his goon, who nodded and released Marisol, moving toward the winery and reaching for his keys.

Marcel seemed to notice that he was now holding a tiger by the tail, and he started to ask for help; but, just like I'd taught her, Marisol had patiently waited her turn and was already moving.

She stomped downward on Marcel's bad knee, and he crumpled. As Benito whirled to grab her again, she kicked him in the groin and made a mad grab for the keys in his hand as he bucked backward. I had no inclination to dive into the fray, but Jim held me back all the same. Anthony too had stepped back in a very wise retreat.

Swift as a deer, Marisol twisted the key ring out of Benito's hand, darted around us into the winery, and shut the door behind her. We all heard the click as she locked us out.

27

Tuesday, June 29, 2021

Over Marcel's swearing and Benito's groaning, I found myself cackling with delight. Marisol had done it all with her hands cuffed together, and I suspected the keys to her own and Tommy's cuffs were on the key ring she'd just snatched.

"You have created a monster, Anna," Marcel moaned.

"Her brother made me teach her," I said by way of my defense. "Is there another way out? We can't let her turn Tommy loose. He's been all over this island. He might already have a place to hide."

"This is the only door," Anthony answered. "They will have to come out this way." He glanced uncertainly at Benito, adding, "Still, you should go around back, check the windows. They could break out."

Benito hurried to comply, already recovered from Marisol's groin kick. It was disappointing, but that trick rarely ended a fight the way it does in the movies. Now, a good solid knee to the face… My ribs gave a twitch of protest as I reveled in the memory. Benito made a full circuit of the building and returned looking bemused.

"I looked in every window, no sign of them. Want me to go inside and check?"

He did, returning minutes later with Marisol in tow. She was smiling placidly, still cuffed.

"Where's Tommy?" Jim asked.

"No te comprendo," she replied calmly. In Spanish, I repeated Jim's question, knowing she understood both times but hoping she'd be more likely to answer only to me. She fixed her unnerving gaze on me and said only, "If you kill Christian for me, all will be forgiven."

"Consider it done," I said without hesitation.

"What about Christian?" Marcel snapped.

Without looking away from Marisol, I 'translated', "She thinks Tommy will try to find him. She told him what Christian did."

Anthony asked, "How did he get out of the building?"

"Through a window," Marisol said happily, comprendoing perfectly now.

While Anthony set about organizing another search party for Tommy, Jim asked, "What are we supposed to do with her now? We can't leave her out here all by herself."

"Wasn't that the original plan?" I shot back. I fancied myself about halfway caught up with what Jim was up to, and I suspected Marisol's part in it wasn't over. "As long as Tommy didn't run off with any of those keys, she'll be secure in there."

"I would prefer to keep her close, now that Tommy is running around," Marcel said. "Christian is leaving this afternoon. Once he's gone, I would like her moved to our villa."

Whether Anthony interpreted this as a request or an order, he nodded dismissively. I exchanged a look with Jim, wondering if we were on the right track.

"We need to talk to her too," he said over my head, addressing Marcel. "Just Anna and me."

Marcel said, "I'm not comfortable with that. You're obviously up to something, Camposanto, and I suspect it won't be to my liking."

"Marisol can't tell us anything that would be to your detriment," Jim answered. "Just give us a few minutes."

I wondered if Marcel picked up on the fact that Jim hadn't denied he was up to something. The Frenchman said only, "Ten minutes. Remember that she is my hostage, and my responsibility."

Jim and I escorted Marisol back down to the storage room, where Benito locked us all inside before stomping back up the stairs. Marisol followed his progress by sound, looking pleased with herself. When his footsteps had faded away, Jim asked, "Are they treating you okay?"

"Honestly? Better than Fernando did."

"We need to know what happened after he was killed. Will you tell us?"

"Why should I? What do I get out of it?"

"I assure you, Marisol, if you stay on this island, eventually you will be killed."

"I assure you, *James*," she snarled back, mocking his stern tone, "I already know that. What are you going to do, help me escape?"

"Of course we are." He sounded genuinely indignant. "How could you think we'd do anything else?"

"Well—how? And why? It's your fault I'm here in the first place!"

"Will you tell us what happened in Argentina, or not?"

"There's hardly anything to tell. Before your murderer even got there, Fernando killed Daniel. When the others found out, they went crazy. Fernando shot Leandro. Mario went upstairs to let Anna go. The others ran away. Then he came." She swallowed, paused to compose herself, and went on, "Mario and Martín mopped up the bodies, and we buried them. We were still trying to figure out what to do when Tommy found us. Regina sent him with some others to come help. They were too late, but at least we had somewhere to go. I've been in Colombia with her until that *chimp* puta came in the middle of the night and took me."

"And Tommy was there with you? The whole time?"

"Off and on."

"Does Regina trust him?"

"I don't know. She seems to like him. She told me once that he reminded her of a boy she knew in school, back in the United States."

"No kidding…"

"Is that what this is about?" Marisol asked sharply, losing patience with us. "Why don't you just ask Tommy?"

"We did. I wanted to hear it from you."

The door opened without warning to admit Benito and Marcel, the latter saying curtly, "Time's up."

"We're done here," Jim said. He left the little storage room and I followed, all the way up the stairs and through the winery, until he paused just inside the door. In a conspiratorial whisper, he said, "I need you to talk your way into viewing the security camera footage from last night, when Marcel came here with Tommy's phone. Can you do that?"

"Probably. What am I looking for?"

"I'm not sure yet. Meet me back at the villa when you're done."

"Yes, sir," I mumbled, following him through the door to find Anthony waiting outside. He wasn't alone, having been joined already by a cadre of men on golf carts, ATVs, and even a couple on horseback. I felt a pang of jealously as I studied the animals, all sleek muscle and shiny manes. I wouldn't be getting on one myself for several weeks at least, long after I left this place.

With all the authority of a man used to getting his way, Jim told Benito, "I'll join you. Anna can go with Anthony back to the house."

Benito passed me the keys to his golf cart without argument, and that was that. Anthony and I climbed in and set off.

Since I was driving, it was easy enough to get lost in my own thoughts while the old man rode silently next to me. The morning's excitement had been a useful distraction, but now my right side was screaming for painkillers again, and it was all I could do to keep from crying out every time we hit a rock or took a sharp turn. Eventually Anthony could ignore my obvious discomfort no longer.

"Doctor Graziella gave you medication for the pain, yes? Why aren't you taking it?"

"Someone tampered with it. We think it happened when they delivered the supplies yesterday."

Though he didn't show the slightest surprise at this news, he said, "I will send for a refill. Do you need anything else?"

Smirking, I tried, "I wouldn't mind getting my hands on that M9 again."

"You don't need it. Two attacks in as many days, against bigger and stronger men, one of them armed—I'm impressed."

I was tired of insisting my victories were as much the product of blind luck as skill, so I asked, "Do you want to know how I did it?"

"Please."

I described both fights in vivid detail, skating over the discovery of his son's body of course, and found myself enjoying the blow-by-blow in spite of the pain still gnawing at me. By the time I finished, Anthony was smiling.

"What?" I asked.

"Your Italian is very good. Your hands—you must have had a good teacher."

"He told me no one would understand my accent if I didn't use my hands."

Anthony laughed. "He was right. Tell me, what do you do for the FBI that requires you to know how to fight or communicate with anyone?"

"Anyone west of Istanbul," I corrected. "I used to be an intelligence analyst. I wanted to be an agent. Now I just… I guess I just deal with whatever Jim gets me mixed up in."

"Have you thought about my offer?"

I focused on navigating a blind turn around a massive, gnarled old olive tree, taking some time to think. What would Jim say?

"I have thought about it. It's not something I would ever do, but I'm still tempted. I guess that's how good little worker bees like me get drawn into criminal enterprises."

"You won't be treated as a pawn in someone else's schemes if you work for me," he promised. He knew more than he let on about my relationship with Jim.

"That's especially tempting. Are you looking for a yes or no right now?"

"No. But I do enjoy your company. I hope you won't begrudge me a few more insights."

"No more classified information," I cautioned.

"I wouldn't dream of asking."

Liar, liar, pantaloni in fiamme. We were almost to the villa, so I decided to go for broke. "We can talk more later if you want, but first, I was hoping to take a look at your security camera feed from last night."

"Oh?"

"Jim wants me to."

I was way too fatigued for anything but the direct approach, but of course I'd allow Jim to infer that I'd sweet-talked my heart out. Either way would've sufficed, most likely. Anthony studied my impassive profile for a few moments before saying, "All right."

After dropping Anthony off at the front of the house, parking the golf cart, and finding him again in the foyer, I decided to push my luck a bit more and ask, "Did you ask Eva to try to make me want to stay here?"

"Eva? Certainly not. The girl does as she pleases."

"Do you still want me to?"

His gaze swept over me once, openly evaluating. A strange sensation of disappointment and rejection suddenly nagged at me, but he said only, "James won't allow it."

"It's not up to him. He doesn't understand what it's like for me. After that business with the Raphael... I feel so used up. The FBI has no use for me anymore. Jim is just being selfish."

"Luciana believes it would be a mistake to employ you. She believes you would only stay here to gather information, to act against us when we no longer have a common enemy."

I tried to match a face to the name Luciana and asked hesitantly, "Your... your boat?"

"My wife."

Ah, of course. I'd seen the old woman how many times, and never once had someone referred to her by name. Come to think of it, I'd never even heard her speak. I said, "That makes more sense. And I can see why she'd think that."

"Come inside, it's getting hot out here. We can discuss this later, if you wish."

I took that as a sign that the offer was still on the table.

Anthony led me through the house to the same heavy, locked double doors behind which I'd found him earlier. He opened them to reveal the sanctum sanctorum, the holiest of holies, the control center.

We were roughly in the center of the big house, no windows affording natural light or the opportunity for someone to break in the old-fashioned way. The only way in or out seemed to be the double doors, which opened onto a long, high-ceilinged room some 50 by 25 feet, three arched openings along each of the longer walls giving way to rooms that would be called side chapels, if this were a church.

On the far wall, opposite the double doors, another pair of doors stood open to allow the glow of technology to spill out into the main room. Anthony had placed the beating heart of his operation right here, and I couldn't believe he was letting me see it, just because I'd asked.

Granted, there wasn't that much to see. It was, on the surface, a large office, with desks, storage, computers, phones, and the like. It didn't scream 'evil lair' by any means, especially not with Anthony's olive and wine business in plain sight.

As we passed through the main room to the opposite end, I saw that the last niche on the right was closed off by retrofitted metal doors. Here were all the firearms, an arsenal of handguns, rifles, shotguns, ammunition, and even a rocket launcher unless my eyes deceived me.

"For emergencies only, of course," Anthony said flatly, discouraging further covetous staring. He ushered me into the far room. "Here we are."

28

Tuesday, June 29, 2021

Anthony pulled out a chair for me, and I sat in front of a wide, curved monitor dominated by a view of a pristine garage, rows of gleaming cars sitting idle. I spotted the Rimac at the far end just before Anthony used the mouse to select a different thumbnail image at the bottom of the screen.

The wine storage cellar appeared, the lack of movement within making the camera's feed look like a still image. Anthony was standing so close to me that I felt him tense up.

"Where is the Serna girl?"

"There," I said, pointing to the bottom of the frame. A brown shoulder moved into the picture and out again. "She's standing right in front of the door. Can we go back to last night?"

He demonstrated the controls and then let me drive, and I moved the image back in time to midnight. I had to fast-forward about ten minutes, to when Marcel and Anthony appeared on the screen and began talking to Tommy. Tommy's phone was visible in Marcel's right hand, and without any attempt at caution the Frenchman reached for Tommy's cuffed right hand and pressed Tommy's thumb to the bottom of the phone to unlock it.

Tommy looked bored by the whole thing, studying the fingernails of his left hand while Marcel thumbed through his phone. The Anthony on the video, his back to the camera, must have said something, because Marcel glanced at him, and Tommy nodded his head slowly. Marcel studied the screen for a long time, his lips moving with what I assumed were questions for Tommy. Tommy gave short, disinterested answers.

I sighed. "I wish there was sound."

"He was turning off the fingerprint security as James suggested. Then he was asking Tommy about the application that tracks Lira's watch."

"And Tommy wasn't giving you any trouble about it?"

"He seemed quite apathetic."

I fell silent, reminding myself that Anthony didn't need to know every twist and turn of my thought process. Judging by how long Marcel poured through Tommy's phone, I had to conclude he was tracking Luke's movements from the time he left Houston until now. It would have been eye-opening information for Luke's former employer. To my surprise, Anthony and Marcel left after only spending about fifteen minutes with Tommy.

The real-life Anthony sensed my confusion and volunteered, "Marcel wanted to go to his villa before we returned to the house. We were there twenty, maybe twenty-five minutes. He wanted to check on Christian and his pet dog, evidently."

"You waited outside?"

"I waited downstairs."

"Do you mind if I take a look at what happened earlier today?"

"I'm curious to see as well."

I fast-forwarded through what looked like a lot of nothing, broken only by the reunion scene I'd already watched. I overshot the escape, backed up to a frame where Jim and I were still there, and held my breath as the moment unfolded in real time.

As Jim held the phone in front of Tommy's face, replaying the tender love scene for him, I thought I understood why Marisol was hiding just out of frame in the present. Tommy saw the limits of the camera's view, and he must have told Marisol. Had that been Jim's intention? I couldn't see why.

The action moved on, and I was forced to abandon these thoughts. Marisol burst into the room, unlocked Tommy's handcuffs, and helped him to his feet. He pulled her out of frame immediately. I didn't see anything else until Jim and I returned with Marisol a few minutes later.

"Well…" I sighed, sitting back. "There's not much to see. May I ask what these other cameras are pointed at?"

Anthony clicked through the thumbnails one by one, describing them as he went. "The garage you saw. Here's the front of the house, and the back. The dock. The wine room, the stables, my son's house, front and back, and the last one just outside those double doors. Luciana wants me to install many more cameras, inside the house and even on the yacht, but I think so many eyes watching from every angle would make this island like some kind of prison. What do you think?"

I was so taken aback by his question that I turned around in the chair and stared up at him. "More cameras means less privacy. Some people take that very personally. Disgruntlement will ensue."

"I see."

"If Luciana doesn't trust someone on the island, more cameras won't change that."

"I agree."

I turned back to the screens, catching a flash of movement in one of the thumbnails. I clicked it, bringing up a view of the stables. Anthony and I watched Eva enter, looking back and forth as she passed the horses in their stalls. Anthony sighed.

"I told her to stay in the house. Willful girl."

"I'll go keep an eye on her. Don't worry, I'm sure Tommy has no interest in hurting her. He probably just wants to get off the island. Can you text Jim and tell him where I went?"

"I will. Thank you, Anna."

I took my leave, going on foot as fast as I dared. By the time I walked into the stables, Eva had already chosen her mount and was nearly finished saddling up. She'd selected the same Palomino mare I'd been admiring earlier, its silky blonde mane and tail flashing in the ambient sunlight with every movement.

Eva turned at the sound of my entrance, and I was suddenly very conscious of the camera that I now knew was situated under the eave of the door. There was only one way in, and I wasn't thrilled with the stables' half-lit interior. Though two rows of clerestory windows let in plenty of light to see the open corridor between the stalls, the stalls themselves were lost in murky half-light. If I were Tommy, I'd consider the stables a prime hiding spot.

"Didn't Anthony tell you to stay at the house?" I asked, trying out a bossy tone. She was not impressed.

"Maybe. So what?"

"That kid who came to the island with us, Tommy, is on the loose. He's actually pretty dangerous. Anthony wanted me to keep an eye on you until he's caught again. That is, assuming you won't just go back to the house."

"You can't ride," she argued coyly. "So I don't think you'll be able to keep your eyes on me."

"Let's do something else. Maybe you can show me the cars in your dad's garage."

"Cars don't interest me."

I'd been approaching her slowly, trying not to spook the horse. As soon as I was close enough, I took the reins out of her hand and impishly tugged at a lock of her hair.

"Don't be difficult," I wheedled, coaxing an unwilling smile out of her. "I told Anthony I'd keep you safe."

"All right. Let me put her through her paces, at least. It's cruel to get her all tacked up and then not ride her."

"Stay where I can see you," I relented.

She led the mare outside and climbed on, and I watched patiently while Eva trotted her around for a few minutes. At the last, she urged the mare into a gallop and guided her on a huge circle in front of the stables. She trotted back, dismounting next to me, and passed me the reins.

"Okay, Anna. Let me get her squared away, and I'll show you father's cars."

"And the racetrack?" I ventured.

"If you're nice."

With visions of supercars dancing in my head, I watched Eva remove the mare's saddle and other tack, increasingly impatient as she brushed her down and fed her a carrot. It was all charmingly bucolic, but that Rimac wasn't going to ogle itself.

I was composing a polite version of "hurry the heck up" when a shadow briefly darkened the door, forcing my attention away from Eva. Hoping to see Jim, there to gripe at me for not returning to the villa as ordered, I felt my pace quicken at the sight of the empty doorway.

I tugged at Eva's sleeve, whispering, "I think we have a problem."

To her credit, Eva accepted the warning in my tone immediately and didn't complain as I dragged her away from the door. She pointed me toward a tool box in the last stall, and while she kept an eye on the entrance, I rooted around inside for some kind of defensive weapon.

I found a short, square-tipped knife with a curving handle. Once I'd wrapped my fingers around it, the grip was completely hidden, the blade protruding from my fist like a talon.

"What do you need that for?" Eva whispered.

"Hopefully nothing. He might've seen us and run off, but if he's out there waiting for us then he's looking for trouble. Stay behind me."

We crept toward the door, stopping when I knew we were

close enough to the camera for Anthony, if he was watching, to see that I'd armed myself. "Tommy?" I called. "You out there?"

Crickets. I hated everything about this. Either he was long gone, or he was waiting in ambush just outside. Without knowing which side of the doorway he was hiding behind, I was pretty much asking for injury if I passed closer to one side than the other. I'd have to go right through the middle and hope he hadn't armed himself with anything longer than a baseball bat.

I was still deliberating what to do with Eva while I made my move when a figure appeared in the doorway, making us both yelp with fright; but it was just Jim.

He took in the scene at a glance: Me in code orange, the equine equivalent of a prison shank in my hand, while Eva cowered behind me. He didn't laugh, but I could tell he wanted to.

"What's wrong with you two?"

Slipping the knife into my pocket and praying the movement was hidden from the camera, I explained, "We thought we saw Tommy. Have they found him yet?"

"No. I was headed back to the villa when Anthony told me where you were. Should I leave you two alone?"

Though I'd been conversing with Eva exclusively in Italian, I had no reason to believe she didn't understand English. I glanced at her, wondering if she'd understood Jim's words or his suggestive tone, but she was looking around boredly.

Catching my gaze, she asked, "Can we go to the garage now? Is he coming with us?"

"I told Anthony I'd keep an eye on her until Tommy's caught," I told Jim. To Eva, I answered, "He'll probably insist."

"She's a big girl, Anna, she can take care of herself."

"Don't be like that. We were just going to look at Anthony's cars. You can come with us."

"This isn't a good time to play with Anthony's toys," he said, becoming stern. "Bring her back to the villa, if it's that important."

I conveyed Jim's suggestion to Eva, who grimaced, answering, "I'd rather go home."

She consented to being escorted there, at least. I waited until Jim and I were on the way back to our own villa to snap, "So you can trust me to run your errands for you, but you can't trust me with a pretty girl?"

"A pretty girl is literally the last thing I'd trust you with," he shot back, totally unrepentant. "Did you see the video?"

"Yes."

"And?"

In clipped tones, I described what I'd seen, becoming distracted from my bad mood as Jim reacted to the new information. He seemed pleased, not the least bit surprised to learn about Marcel and Anthony's side trip to Marcel's villa.

I asked, "Did you show Tommy that video so that he'd tell Marisol how to hide from the camera?"

"That was more of a side benefit."

"Well, it worked. She's camped out in front of the door, so it looks like the camera's watching an empty room."

I saved my breath for the rest of the walk, desperately wishing I could take one of the pills Doctor Graziella had given me. To circumvent the eventuality that I'd play the odds and take one of the pills, knowing there was only a twenty-five percent chance it would kill me, I went straight to the bathroom and flushed them all down the toilet.

29

Tuesday, June 29 to
Thursday, July 1, 2021

The search for Tommy continued while everyone on the island counted down the days until Regina's latest deadline. Russo returned on Tuesday afternoon, his wife in tow, which unleashed all sorts of grumbling. If Russo was allowed to bring his wife to the safety of the island, why couldn't other family members be given the same option?

Anthony was forced to grant permission, but only one person heeded the warnings. Bambino's fiancée purportedly arrived on Wednesday, though no one saw her and she wasn't permitted to leave her villa. Octavio returned shortly afterward from his unhappy errand, slightly shrunken but otherwise unaffected by the ordeal of burying his daughter in what I assumed were tragically clandestine circumstances. I wasn't sure how many other people remained in danger, only that our Italian friends were one seriously nervous bunch.

I wasn't much better. My parents and Dude could only stay in federal custody for so long, and I had no doubt my father was already trying to talk his way out of it. According to Beauchamp, the manhunt for Emily, Luke, and the girls was proving just as fruitless as I'd known it would, which I'd decided to be happy about. That first wave of anger and hurt at what they'd done had washed over me, leaving me somewhat ambivalent about the whole affair.

On the one hand, kidnapping my nieces and stealing from my parents was objectively bad; but on the other, I knew Emily would keep the girls happy and Luke would keep them all safe. As long as they avoided a Bonnie and Clyde situation with law enforcement, they were actually better off than my parents and Dude were.

What exactly was going on between Luke and Emily, I couldn't bring myself to care about it. I cared more about my mom, whose gentle heart had surely been broken by the loss of her granddaughters. Perhaps I wasn't happy, but I wasn't angry anymore.

Christian left the island on the same boat that brought Russo's wife to it, and with him went my chances of redeeming myself in Marisol's eyes. Not that I'd ever intended to kill the man in cold blood, but I'd been hoping he'd try something and give me a reason. Maybe if I was really lucky, after all this was over, Marcel would send him to kill me and I'd get another chance.

Wherever Tommy was hiding, I felt certain he was watching Marisol from a safe distance and knew when she was moved from the winery to Marcel and Giles' villa. The three remaining goons the Marchands had brought to the island, who'd been billeted in a nearby villa, moved in to the Marchands' to keep an eye on Marisol.

Jim didn't appear overly concerned about Tommy, but I was of a different mind. I frequently felt that someone was watching us while we were at home in our villa, and every walk to or from Anthony's house was ten minutes of pure anxiety that got really old really fast. By Wednesday, Anthony had loaned me a golf cart for my own personal use. He was still refusing to give me a gun.

I went to bed early Wednesday night, the better to be awake and alert for the midnight call with Regina. It had been over a week since Victor had cracked two of my ribs, and though the pain was less acute, I was still fragile. The bruise on my jaw and the abrasion on my head had faded and begun to heal, respectively, but it was the ribs that frustrated me.

For weeks yet, I'd be unable to run, fight, exercise, take really deep breaths, or even eat with too much gusto. On Wednesday, I'd attempted to work out some of my nerves on Anthony's racetrack, but even driving had been too much of a strain.

My one comfort was that Anthony, as promised, had requested a new bottle of painkillers from Doctor Graziella to replace my tainted one. Those had arrived with the doctor himself on Wednesday morning. After my checkup, I kept the bottle in my pocket at all times. The good doctor had departed the island in high dudgeon, no longer keen on treating me like a little baby once he saw how poorly I'd followed his instructions to take it easy. He'd all but ordered Anthony to strap me to a bed.

The murder of Gia Palermo had overshadowed much of what Jim and I had seen on the dock, but Octavio's return triggered a mental review of the day. I drifted to sleep Wednesday night with a face shimmering before my mind's eye: the man who'd approached Jim and me at the dock, who Jim insisted had recognized me and backed away to prevent me doing the same.

Annoyed at my continued failure to place him, I'd mulled over Jim's map before crawling into bed. I was certain something would come to me while I slept. I simply had to have seen him during one of the events marked out on Jim's meticulous notes.

Jim shook me awake later that night so we could head to Anthony's house. I was none the wiser for my attempts to figure out who the mystery man was, having dreamed about racing cars and hand-to-claw combat with velociraptors instead of the man from the dock. Stupid opiates.

▼

Despite the late hour, no one looked sleepy as we gathered once more in Anthony's house in front of the TV. Somehow I knew, no matter what transpired, this would be our last video call with Regina Lira.

As the call connected and Regina's face appeared on the screen, I was unnerved to see that the rage she'd displayed last time had been replaced by a cool, serene smile. Either she'd medicated herself to stave off the stress of worrying about Marisol, or she felt she'd gained the upper hand since we last spoke.

Marcel, the de facto spokesperson since he'd captured Marisol and offered up Luke as a sacrifice, opened the discussion for us by asking, "Have you had enough time to consider our offer?"

"More than enough. Please pass my apologies to Marisol. I don't believe you'll hurt her, and if you do, my operatives in the United States and Europe will tear your lives apart one person at a time. No, I'm afraid I will settle for nothing less than Paolo's head on a platter, and I see no need to waste further time with this back-and-forth. I only joined you tonight as a courtesy, to let you all know that the farther you are from my nephew, the safer you will be."

She let us all contemplate that for a few moments, waiting until the silence became as uncomfortable as a scream.

"Speaking of safe, Paolo—how is your father? I have no quarrel with Emilio, however he's come to feel about me, and I'd like to see him."

"He's dead," Paolo said, to general surprise. "He died of old age months ago. Pulmonary embolism. Don't worry, Regina, you won't suffer the same fate."

"We know where you are now, Regina," Jim put in, before she could react to the news. "I don't think you want to start an all-out war."

"That's true, James, you know where I am now. But tomorrow, I could be anywhere. I could be in Florence."

She didn't stay to savor the effect of her words, ending the call there and leaving us all in a state of very quiet turmoil. No one spoke for a long time, and though I tried not to stare at Jim, I found my eyes drawn inexorably to him. He had eyes only for Paolo, who appeared to be doing some very quick thinking. So was I. Hadn't Jim said everything depended on whether Emilio really was dead?

To distract myself, I glanced over at Marcel and was less than surprised to see him just as engrossed in Jim as I was. I nearly groaned out loud with the force of my longing to read both their minds. Instead I sank down into my seat and closed my eyes, the better to block out all this significant staring.

I no longer cared what happened, as long as it meant I would be getting off this island sooner than later. I wanted to rub Dude's velvety ears between my fingers and fall asleep with his massive body sprawled protectively across my feet. A real thunderstorm and some Independence Day fireworks wouldn't be too bad, either.

Paolo's voice ended the impasse as he rose to his feet. "I think we can all agree that it's time for my sons and me to be on our way. I thank you for your hospitality and protection, Cousin," he nodded at Anthony, "but Regina is right. We are now safer apart. I will contact you after we've settled into a secure location."

"She can't get to you here, Paolo," Anthony said. "Can't you see she wants you to run? For all we know, she's got a gunman waiting for you right off the coast."

"Paolo," Jim spoke up again. "We know she's going to relocate, too. Tommy as good as told us so. What if you had a way to track her?"

"Track her?" Paolo echoed. He gazed at Jim with intense dislike. "Would I need to track her if you'd simply told me where she was? But that would have been too easy, I suppose."

"I won't apologize for hoping it wouldn't come to this," Jim answered. "Now that we're here, do you want a way to find her, or not?"

Paolo swore and said, "That might be useful, but we haven't got one."

Jim audibly shook the heavy watch on his wrist. "We can."

Paolo frowned at Jim as though seeing him for the first time. "You wanted the boy to escape."

"Of course I did, and I want Marisol off this island, too. All we have to do is give her the transmitter and get out of the way. Tommy will take her and lead us straight to Regina, even if she moves."

"Regina knows about the watch," Marcel reminded him.

"I said give her the transmitter, not the whole watch."

"How?" Paolo asked, his curious tone betraying that he already approved of this plan.

"I'm not sure," Jim admitted. "I think the transmitter is powered by the same battery the watch uses, and it never needs to be charged or replaced because there's a device inside that converts kinetic energy to power and recharges the battery as you move it. It may not be possible, or feasible, to separate the transmitter from the watch. We just need to pare it down to the smallest possible size and hide it in something Marisol is likely to take with her. Inside the sole of a shoe, for instance."

"Not that you've given it much thought," Marcel quipped.

"Right."

I dozed off a few times while they were hashing out the details, but it wasn't for lack of interest. I just couldn't keep my eyes open. In the end I fell fully asleep, not to wake until Jim pulled me to my feet sometime later.

I leaned against him, mumbling, "Wa'time is it?"

"Past two. Anthony's got a guy working on Marisol's new shoes. We're going to send them home with Marcel along with another change of clothes. Hopefully Marisol won't be too suspicious when they forget to lock her door tonight."

"You think she'll know how to find Tommy?"

"I'm counting on it. Anthony and Paolo are going to make quite a show of getting a boat ready for Paolo and his sons to fly the coop. If Tommy doesn't steal it, he's an idiot."

"Guess I'll just cross my fingers, then."

We returned to our villa and got a few hours of makeup sleep, then joined together in the search for Tommy that was now no more than a well choreographed farce. Marcel reported that Marisol had accepted her new kicks with a respectable stab at gratitude and could almost certainly be counted on to make a break for it while Marcel was out walking Penelope and Giles was loudly getting drunk and playing cards with their three guards. I just hoped Marisol was the right combination of gullible and desperate to escape.

At dusk, the search wound down to only the most stalwart nighttime crew. Jim and I had dinner in our villa, just the two of us, and fell asleep in front of the TV like an old married couple.

I was jerked awake by the single most unpleasant sensation

I'd experienced to date: My head was wrenched backward by my ponytail, a cold kiss of steel pressed against my neck.

30

Thursday, July 1 to Saturday, July 3, 2021

I looked up to see Marisol standing over me, her face starkly white in the gloom of the dark living room. Jim hadn't anticipated this part.

"Did you do it? Did you kill Christian?" she asked, hissing in Spanish so quietly that Jim, who was clearly still alive because he was delicately snoring, didn't wake.

"He got away before I could."

"I should kill you now. I heard you that night, when Jackson came for us. You said something about his boss, something about a car. You knew him."

"Yes."

"You *helped* him."

"Not on purpose. He knew how to find me, the same way Tommy knew how to find him. Jim and I didn't know."

"Why didn't you let him kill me, too?"

"Are you serious?" I breathed. Trying to talk and breathe without moving my throat was starting to make me lightheaded.

Marisol whispered, "I *hated* my brother, but he was all I had. You let them destroy my life. You stole the most valuable thing in my house, my grandmother's favorite painting. All I had left were dead bodies."

"I'm sorry."

"You'll be a lot more sorry when I cut you from ear to ear," she snarled, wrenching my head back even farther so that I was unable to speak. "But Tía would be so mad at me. She has plans for you, and Jackson. Together."

In the silence following her words, I realized Jim had stopped snoring. I shut my eyes, willing him to stay still, until the pressure on my scalp and throat disappeared without any kind of warning. I heard the door slam and Jim immediately sat up, running his hands over my throat as though checking for a gushing wound.

"Are you okay?" he gasped.

"Why is she so mad at *me*, but *you* get a pass?"

"She didn't cut you?"

"No."

"God, Anna, I can't believe she did that. I'm so sorry…"

"Well, even masterminds make mistakes." As tunnel vision receded and my eyes began to work normally again, I studied his expression and added less grouchily, "Did you hear her footsteps? Definitely wearing shoes."

"Oh—good. I better let Anthony know she's in the wind. We don't want some gung ho red shirt taking her down before she and Tommy can get away."

He kissed me on the forehead and left to call Anthony. My sleep thus interrupted, probably for several days, I wandered into the kitchen and poured myself a glass of wine. Guns I could handle, bludgeons were no problem, fists and feet a delightful challenge; but knives? Knives scared me stupid.

I was shaking badly as I brought the wine glass to my lips, comprehension sinking in that one whisper of Marisol's whims might've had me bleeding out on the couch right now. She could easily have killed Jim too, which I couldn't even bear to think about.

The worst part was, we kind of deserved it.

▼

With one outstanding exception, Jim's plan had gone off without a hitch. Like a homing pigeon, Marisol had found Tommy at what must have been a pre-arranged meeting place, and the two of them had escaped the island on the boat ostensibly intended for Paolo's own escape.

We ate breakfast as a group Friday morning, the atmosphere one of general relief. Tommy was on his way back to Regina with Marisol and a tiny stowaway, and soon Paolo would be taking his leave as well. After that, Jim and I would be on our way home.

After showing Paolo the blinking red dot that now represented Tommy and Marisol's course to the mainland, Jim provided Paolo with the code and password to track the signal himself. This didn't strike me as odd at all, until we got back to our villa and my brain finally caught up.

"You don't know Regina's password," I said, making it an accusation. I thought Jim was pulling out his suitcase so he could start packing, but he extracted something from an inside pocket and pressed it into my hands. I looked down to find myself holding Lira's watch.

"Once I knew Emilio was dead, I knew what we had to do," he explained. "Tommy confirmed Regina was watching the signal. All we have to do is point her toward the right target."

Numbly, I forced, "What am I supposed to do about it?"

"I think Enzo would appreciate it if you took the time to say goodbye. They're leaving in a couple of hours."

It took a minute, but the full meaning of what I held slowly dawned on me and I said, "No." I shoved the watch back into his hands. "I'm not having any further part in this. It's wrong."

"It's war, Anna. It doesn't end until one of them is dead."

"She'll kill Enzo, too! You said he was a good guy, and he is! I can't do this."

"I don't know what to tell you. This has to happen, and you're the only one who *can* do it."

Against every instinct I held my hand out, palm up, grimacing as he dropped the heavy Rolex into my hand. I would rather he'd dropped a live spider into it.

I forced my hand closed around the watch and asked, "What am I supposed to do with this? It's not like I can put it on Enzo's wrist and they won't know what it is."

"Put it in the Alfa Romeo."

"Oh yeah? And how am I supposed to do that?"

He tapped me under the chin, saying softly, "I'm sure you'll figure something out."

"You're a jerk, Jim."

"I know."

▼

By the time I knocked on Paolo's door, at the house Tony had once called home, I had resigned myself to what I was doing. Paolo started this. Paolo had to go. Enzo… Maybe he'd get lucky, and he'd escape Regina's vengeance. All I could do was hope, and remind myself that I had my own loved ones to worry about.

Aldo answered the door, smiling automatically at me in greeting. My heart thumped painfully. It was trying to kill me to keep me from doing this.

"Is Enzo here?" I asked. "I was hoping to say goodbye."

"He's here. Come in, please."

Aldo ushered me into the house and asked me to wait in the foyer while he fetched Enzo. Tony's house was nearly as grand as his father's, though much smaller and more comfortable. I stared at the intricate pattern in the marble floor, struggling to hold on to my resolve. Though no one was in sight, I could hear the hubbub of packing and getting ready to leave, and it imbued me with a sense of urgency. Enzo appeared in the foyer, openly surprised to see me.

"I thought you'd forgotten all about me," he said.

"Jim's been like a mother hen, since, you know." I mimed punching myself in the ribs. "Since we're probably never going to see each other again, I thought maybe we could say goodbye. Properly."

He grinned, but argued, "Dad told me to stay away from you."

"And Jim told me to stay away from you. That's what makes it so much fun."

Shaking his head, he laughed, "Has anyone ever said no to you?"

Recognizing the same sentiment Jim had once expressed, I shrugged. "I'll let you know if it ever happens. I've never made out in an Alfa Romeo, either, and I don't think I'll ever get another chance."

Under the pretense of driving the Stelvio down to the dock to load it onto the ship, Enzo made a quick stop at the vineyard where he and I could enjoy a little privacy. Well, at least one of us enjoyed it.

About an hour later, I left the vineyard minus one watch, my conscience thoroughly seared and my cracked ribs throbbing. Enzo drove away in the Stelvio, and I knew I'd never see him again. As tempted as I'd been to offer him some sort of warning, I knew he'd tell Paolo, and we'd all hop right back on the same scary-go-round I'd been on since Jim had yanked me out of Christopher King's office nearly two years ago; so I'd stuffed the Rolex deep between two cushions in the Stelvio's back seat when Enzo wasn't looking.

On my way back from the vineyard, I made a pitstop at

Marcel's villa on an errand of my own. Giles once again answered the door, and I clearly hadn't grown on him. He just rolled his eyes, let me inside, and said, "He's upstairs."

I found Marcel seated behind a desk in an upstairs room, his own laptop open in front of him and Penelope curled up at his feet. She must have smelled me as soon as I walked in, because she didn't bother warning Marcel with a bark or a growl. She only wagged her tail a few times in greeting.

"What can I do for you, Anna?"

"Are we good?"

He looked up from his laptop and studied me in a way I didn't like at all. "Are we? I can't see that anything has changed."

"You're staying in business with the Sardinians, aren't you?"

"Not that it's any of your concern, but yes, I am."

"So you'll be in competition with Regina Lira, essentially."

"Until Paolo kills her."

"I think we both know that's not going to happen."

He sighed, stretched his arms and shoulders, and said comfortably, "If perchance Paolo himself goes the way of the dodo, perhaps Regina and I can come to some sort of arrangement. You and James were so helpful in letting me know that the lines were already open."

"Um… you're welcome."

"Still, I can't think of any reason I should let you live."

"I'm not boring," I offered. He shrugged in impassive agreement, and I ventured, "Tell you what: You send Christian after me, and if I win that round, we'll call it a draw."

"You cannot be serious."

"Why do people always say that to me?"

He stood, limped over to me, and held out his hand. I was only frozen by surprise for a second before I reached out and shook it firmly. "We have a deal, Anna."

"Cool. Bye, Penelope."

She wagged her tail once more, too comfortable to get up. I fled the villa with as much dignity as I could muster, hurrying back to Jim before he had too much time to imagine what sorts of trouble I could be cooking up.

Jim greeted me with strained silence, the question clouding the air between us. I just nodded, hoping it stung like crazy that I'd just let Enzo get to second base at Jim's demand.

We didn't speak to each other for the rest of the day, but I inferred from his busywork on his laptop that he was arranging for us to finally go home. He'd already disassembled his map and started packing his suitcases, so I occupied myself the same way until there was nothing left to pack. I turned on the TV, popped a painkiller, and settled in for the end.

▼

With Paolo's departure, the mood on the island became downright optimistic. I spent all day Saturday with Eva, not to mess with Jim but to cheer myself up with her sunny disposition and those adorable dimples. I just wanted to get through the day.

On July 4, 2019, I'd learned that I would not be going to Quantico to become an FBI agent. I'd been so crushed and angry, I skipped the fireworks show at the capitol, even going so far as closing my windows so I wouldn't be able to enjoy it from afar. Exactly a year later, Luke and I had kissed for the first time. Stuck in rural Colorado, I'd again missed out on the traditional fireworks display. Tomorrow, I'd be getting on a boat with Jim and sailing to Cagliari, from where we'd board a plane and begin the interminable hop-skip back to Washington, DC. Maybe, if the timing worked out right, it would still be July Fourth when we got back to the United States, and I'd get to see some fireworks for the first time in three years.

My first priority when I got my job back would be to appeal my rejection and try to get another chance to make agent. I would have to jump the line, otherwise I'd be too old to try again the normal way. If Jim and Beauchamp knew what was good for them, they'd help me.

Though I was sorely tempted to spend all night with Eva too, I returned to the villa after dinner to make my peace with Jim. After all the injustices he'd put me through, this latest outrage wasn't nearly enough to stop me loving him.

Over a bottle of the island's finest vintage, a gift from Anthony, we made up very quickly, then went to bed. I was slipping into dreamland, wrapped up in his arms with my head on his chest, when I remembered our conversation about Checkpoint Charlie.

"When are you going to ask?" I breathed, already half asleep.

He thought for a minute, caught up to me, and said, "When I know you'll say yes."

"How do you know I won't say yes now?"

"Because I know everything."

You don't know who that man at the dock was, I thought, just before sleep pulled me under.

31
Sunday, July 4, 2021

I knew this was the last time I'd have this stupid dream. Willing my brain to slow it down, I watched the man emerge from the Channel 221 news van and take aim with his nasty machine pistol. This time I caught the bullet with my abdomen, but I still had enough fight left in me to whip out my M9 and put three rounds through the Demon's windshield before I woke up.

With the impression of imperfect victory stuck fast in my emotions, I opened my eyes to a dark room. My bladder was painfully full, the most basic of urges so insistent that I didn't even lie there in denial and try to go back to sleep as I normally would. I tiptoed to the bathroom and tried to hold on to that sweet, sleepy feeling while half a bottle of wine exited me. I was not successful. Still bleary-eyed, I crept out of the bathroom and into the kitchen for a glass of water.

I will never understand how my brain works. One second I was chugging lukewarm water from the tap, and the next I was rigid with the shock of discovery. Replaying the dream in my head, I saw the gunman's face, one side blocked by the news van's window frame emblazoned with 'Channel 221,' the other by his gun at eye level. With the extraneous details cropped away, recognition came at last.

I dashed back to the bedroom, calling, "Jim, Jim I figured it out! It was the guy at the Motel 6 when Tommy and I—"

As I reached the doorway, an enraged shout cut through my words and derailed my thoughts. I stumbled into the bedroom just in time to see Jim go down, starched by a haymaker straight to the temple. He landed face-up on the bed and began groaning almost immediately, a welcome sign that he was alive and conscious after a hard reset.

I flew at the attacker, the man from the dock, the first member of the TIC I'd ever seen face-to face. I dodged his first swing but wasn't fast enough to escape the second, and it landed—you guessed it—squarely in my lower right ribs.

I screamed silently as my cracked ribs broke under his fist, and while I redefined the meaning of pain, Jim struggled to his feet. The man left me writhing on the floor and turned his attention back to Jim. They moved out of my line of sight, making an unholy racket that absolutely no one else was going to hear.

Quiet descended after only a couple of minutes, and cold fear gripped at my heart so hard I thought I'd have a heart attack. I moved from fear to rage at once, resolving that if he'd killed Jim, I'd stab the guy to death with my own broken rib.

The man returned to the bedroom and dragged me into the living room, tossing me on the couch and tying my ankles together. The pain of this treatment was so blinding I couldn't even comprehend the visual information from my eyes until he'd finished and backed away, breathing like a bellows. Jim had given him a darn good fight and was even still alive, tied to a kitchen chair and bleeding feebly from one ear. I locked eyes with him and held his gaze until the man stepped between us.

"Where is Luke Jackson?"

I looked up at him, studying his face, confirming my revelation. Definitely the same guy. He must have been sent by Regina the moment she knew we were all on the island, maybe even before Marisol was kidnapped. Something told me he was looking for Luke.

"He ran off with my sister," I spat, sobbing once as the words ripped through my broken ribs.

"Tell me, or you will watch him die," the man said, taking up a position directly behind Jim's chair. As though to underscore his threat, he placed his hands on either side of Jim's head.

"The vineyard," I forced out. "We moved—ah—moved him—after Marisol. I can take you—"

"He will take me. If Jackson isn't there, I'll come back without him, and we'll try again."

He cut the zip ties binding Jim to the chair and forced him to stand, dragging him outside before I could even catch my breath. I experienced a brief, random wave of relief that I hadn't had more to drink last night. This would be so much harder hungover.

Unconscious of the passage of time, I dragged myself into a sitting position and untied the rope around my ankles. Multiple courses of action ought to have occurred to me: Find Jim's phone and call Anthony. Hobble to the Marchands' villa, which was closest, and get help. Fire up the golf cart and make this a tiny bit easier on myself.

All I could think about was Jim and the TIC man getting to the vineyard and seeing that Luke obviously wasn't there. I armed myself with the knife I'd stolen from the stables and set off on foot, driving myself to an impossible pace.

With the moonlight waning, I was guided only by starlight as I trudged along. *Technically, moonlight and sunlight are starlight too*, I reminded myself. This and other helpful bits of nonsense managed to crowd out the pain in my side, and about halfway to the vineyard I spotted two silhouettes moving in tandem ahead of me.

I hoped Jim wasn't too addled to think of some kind of plan, because I was spent. Burying the blade of my nasty knife in the guy's neck was the new limit of my imagination.

Within a couple yards of them, I slowed my pace and focused on making no noise. If he spotted me, I had no doubt he'd kill Jim before dealing with me. I trailed them all the way to the winery's door, pausing only once to freeze next to an outcropping of rock as the man stopped and turned to scan the area. Miraculously, he failed to spot me. I could hear Jim's voice as the man tried the door handle to the winery.

"Paolo has the only key—" he started to say, only to flinch backward as the man kicked the door down. He pushed Jim ahead of him, artificial lights flaring to life through the windows. I nearly crowed at the sight. If anyone was monitoring the security camera (unlikely, but I could hope), the light was a dead give-away that someone was in the winery when they shouldn't be.

I was on the stairs, easing my way down with teeth-shattering determination not to cry out, as they moved toward the door to the wine cellar. Jim pointed out the correct door, maybe counting on that security camera the same way I was. The man pushed Jim aside as he opened the door and started down the stairs. In seconds, it would be wildly obvious that Luke was not in that room.

Putting on a turn of speed, I held my finger to my lips as Jim spotted me, and I crept up to the open door at the top of the stairs. Jim was already on the move himself, probably thinking about trapping the man on the stairs; but this guy had a good sixty pounds on Jim, and the door at the top of the stairs swung both ways, which would have been hilarious if I'd been thinking about it.

He was already on his way back up, swearing up a storm. Jim stepped in front of the doorway, drawing the man's focus and ire.

"Guess what, gringo? Your time is up."

Maybe if he'd known they would be his last words, he'd have put more thought into them. I stepped out from behind the door as he passed me, burying the curved knife to the hilt in the side of his neck. Hot blood gushed out so quickly and with such force that the knife was too slippery to hold onto, and as he twisted away I lost my grip on it.

The knife remained lodged in his neck until he, very unwisely, tore it out and had the gall to come at me with it. Between him and the stairs, I kicked him once in the chest and felt the knife slash across my ankle as I overbalanced and tumbled bum over teakettle down the stairs. The last things I remembered were hearing my own name and hoping to God the fight was over.

▼

I came to in Cagliari, which I identified immediately for the simple reason that Doctor Graziella's office smelled of peppermint. I knew I was back there before I opened my eyes, and the knowledge was deeply comforting.

All the overhead lights were off, but ambient light from the window was enough to see the necessary details: rails to either side of me, a curtain to my left, a couch to my right, and a head resting on a pair of arms next to my right thigh where the bed rail ended. Déjà vu passed through me like a malign spirit, and I shivered.

I must have made some noise too, because the head rose partway from the arms, turning toward me. Jim's expression was one of complete and utter exhaustion, his left ear still darkened by dried blood.

"Anna?"

He looked so much older than he was. I felt a wave of painful guilt, which never happened to me. Guilt, yes, but painful? It built and multiplied, my face crumpling in discomfort as the memory of each individual injury came back.

He said, "Try not to breathe too deeply. You have two broken ribs."

"No kidding."

"Thank God for morphine, right?"

"Is it still July Fourth?"

He blinked at me. "Yes. Why?"

"I was really hoping to see some fireworks."

"Anna, we're still in Italy."

"I know," I groaned. "I just meant, I thought we'd be home by now."

He took my right hand in both of his, grimacing as though he were in pain, too. He studied this hand sandwich for a full minute before saying very quietly, "Anna, Rich wants you to stay."

"Well, he can go screw himself twice. I mean—what? Since when? What are you talking about?"

"We've been talking about it for a while, and we're not going to get another chance like this. Anthony trusts you. Even Marcel seems to like you, which is a big one-eighty from where he started. You don't even have to pass yourself off as someone else. You've got the in. You need to take it."

My heart sank through my chest as I realized he was being completely serious.

"Jim… I want to go home."

"I know."

"Forget the FBI."

"Agreed."

"Don't you dare leave me here!"

"I'm not going to. Our plane leaves at six fifty tonight, and if you want to be on it, you'll be on it."

"I want to be on it," I said, almost before he'd finished speaking. He sighed heavily.

"I have to ask you to think about it. Can you?"

Mulishly, I spat, "No."

Probably just to change the subject, he said, "I lost track of Paolo on Tommy's phone. I guess Regina figured out what we were up to and changed the password. Tommy and Marisol are already in Cuba. She must have gotten them on a plane somehow."

"Good for them."

"I changed my password, too. Paolo won't be able to find them."

"He's going to be incensed."

"For the rest of his life, I'm sure."

"How did you manage that, by the way?" I asked, trying and failing to keep the ardent admiration out of my voice. He smiled at me, so pleased with himself that my heart jumped right back into my chest and settled around my naval, fluttering sickeningly.

"I saw some Rolexes for sale in Florence, decided why not? Might as well have a duplicate. I suspected Regina had been moving around all this time, staying one step ahead of Paolo, but Tommy confirmed it."

"Why hasn't Paolo gone after the Sardinians? Tommy made a great point—they're no better than Regina or Etta's husband. Why do they get a pass?"

"Paolo doesn't want to scrub the family clean. He wants power. That's all anyone wants, when you get to the heart of it."

"Bleak. Also, why go after Fernando and Marisol? They

were powerless."

"Gragg told him about the painting. Dom and Beauchamp finally found the email he was using—the petty idiot told Paolo about it for free the day he was fired. He'd known about it all along. I think Paolo wanted that painting just as much as he wanted to kill Fernando and Marisol."

"How pedestrian," I sighed airily, rolling my eyes.

My hand was still pressed between his, and my gaze fell on it as an anchor point while reality turned upside down.

I didn't so much decide to stay in Italy as come to the realization that I'd already decided to.

From the moment Regina Lira had voiced her threat against the occupants of the house in Manchester, Texas, I'd known I'd do anything in my power to protect them, up to and including espionage. That swung the pendulum in Anthony Farina's favor.

I wasn't cut out for the FBI. There were just too many rules.

Staying in Italy, I could have my cake and eat it too: I loved Italy, and I wanted to be here as a person, not as an FBI lackey; but if I went back to the States, would I even be that anymore? Refusing this assignment wouldn't win me any points, but taking it would add a big old gold star to my résumé. Maybe the gold star would be big enough to cover up what I'd done.

Jim read my mind as soon as the fat, hot tears started slipping down my cheeks. He brushed them away as fast as they came until my eyes ran dry. Back into lockdown I went.

"It would only be for two years at most," he wheedled.

I gasped as though struck. "Two *years?* Would I see you at all that whole time?"

Another sigh. "Probably not."

"God, Jim… I can't go that long without you. I can't go that long without *Dude.*"

"Two years is an outside estimate. Closer to one, most likely. I'll take care of Dude, and he'll take care of me. We'll be fine."

A pathetic sound emanated from the back of my throat, and I laid my head back, closing my eyes.

"You don't have to decide now. My flight doesn't leave for four hours."

"Four—four hours? Holy crap, how long have I been out?"

"Since we got to the hospital. Do you not remember the trip here?"

"No. I was conscious?"

"Sure seemed that way. They put you under for surgery."

I squeaked, "Surgery! For what?"

"They thought you had some internal bleeding. Had to check."

"Just rooting around in there for fun, were they?" I grumbled.

"Hey, I'm just the messenger here."

"I've never been happier to black out," I mumbled, imagining the nightmarish pain I must've been in after falling down a flight of stairs with two broken ribs. "So, no internal bleeding?"

"Amazingly, no. You're a lucky girl."

"Yeah, I feel super lucky."

Jim stayed with me, playing cards and keeping my mind occupied, until it was time for him to get on a plane. He already knew I wasn't getting on it, broken body or no, and he didn't make me say it out loud. He kissed me one last time, told me he loved me, and headed for the door.

Before he left, he turned back to me and asked, "Oh, by the way, will you marry me?"

I shot back, "The heck, Jim."

"Yes or no."

"Yes. Butthole."

"I knew you'd say that. See you later, kiddo."

Epilogue

I spent the night in the hospital and left the next morning with Benito. He helped me all the way to my villa and promised to be back at seven to take me to dinner at the big house, the subtext being whether I wanted to go or not.

In addition to all my luggage, Jim had left me several pairs of his pajamas and a photo of me and Dude that appeared to have spent some time in his wallet. I wasn't sure which was more touching, that he knew I'd stay and thought to leave it there for me, or that he had it in the first place. He'd also left my cell phone and passport et cetera, but Benito had already informed me those were in Anthony's safekeeping for now.

Anthony laid it all out for me at dinner: I would have to heal up, and then I'd begin earning my keep by acting as Anthony's escort anytime he had to leave the island. I was to be his secret weapon, a translating bodyguard who was indistinguishable from arm candy. When he was on the island, I'd focus on Eva, teaching her English and French and Krav Maga and anything else her father thought might be useful.

I was not to have any contact with Jim, who would obviously be trotting straight back to his FBI masters the moment his feet were back on U.S. soil. If I earned enough trust, Anthony would consider giving me incrementally more freedoms.

I was required to dye my hair black, the better to escape recognition associated with my Raphael, not to mention to avoid making it too easy for the crime scene techs at the house in Livigno to find a match for the owner of the red hair they'd found stuck in a pool of blood in the basement. After being beat up, torn away from Jim and Dude and my sister and everyone else, and left there to figure this out all on my own, further abusing my hair hardly registered on the injustice scale. I looked good in black, anyway.

Near the end of July, when a great deal of rest carefully interspersed with delicate bouts of physical therapy had netted me almost a full recovery, Anthony took me with him to Monaco to meet with Marcel and a German man who was slated to manage Marcel's business in Poland and the Balkans.

Lucky me, with my fluent Deutsch, I not only had to tag along but desperately wanted to. After nearly a month on that island, I was raring to go, even though it meant getting back on the *Luciana* and seeing Marcel again.

Anthony and I arrived at the Hôtel de Paris Monte-Carlo, which was exactly as magnificent as it sounds, and found our way to the sea-view restaurant on the eighth floor. We were an hour early at Anthony's insistence, but Marcel and his German friend were only about fifteen minutes behind us.

I stood to shake Marcel's hand and turned to his companion, nearly blurting out something lamentably stupid before I snapped my mouth shut and let him speak first.

"Nice to meet you, I'm Fredrich Hammel. Fritz, if you like."

"Anna," was all I could manage.

He smiled at me, and I read in his startling green eyes not only recognition but a serene lack of surprise. The last time I'd seen Fritz, I'd just finished bugging his apartment, car, and phone on behalf of the BKA. He'd known me only as Ilse, but it seemed in the intervening six or so months that he'd learned my true identity and with it, I assumed, way more than I ever thought he'd know. I certainly hadn't expected to see him again, let alone in the company of Marcel Marchand.

In German, I asked, "Can we speak privately this way?"

"I believe so. My friend doesn't speak a word of it. Does yours?"

"No. What in the world are you doing here?"

"Someone has to keep an eye on you, my Ilse."

I hope you'll forgive me for saying this, but I did *not* see that coming.

Thanks for reading! If you enjoyed *No Port in a Storm*, please take a couple minutes to leave a review or rating wherever you found it. Reviews help readers decide whether to buy my books, and every single review helps so much—even the bad ones!

Want to be the first to know when new stories come out? You can sign up for my mailing list on my website, akweller.com. You'll get my occasional newsletter, and you'll receive a link to download a free short story.

▼

About the Author

AK Weller was born and raised in Texas, moved to New Mexico, and now lives in Montana with her husband, four cats, and three dogs. She mostly enjoyed brief careers as a technical writer, private investigator, social worker, and pet sitter before finding her calling as a semi-employed writer. AK writes mysteries and thrillers while running her own graphic design business. Her favorite books to read over and over again were written by JRR Tolkien, Stieg Larsson, Sue Grafton, Michael Crichton, and JK Rowling.

▼

Also available from AK Weller

The Anna Bowman Thrillers: a 5-Book Thriller Epic

Book 1: Enemy Closer

On the run from her ex-husband, a powerful federal agent, Abigail takes shelter in a cabin in rural southwest Colorado with her trusty German Shepherd, Dude. When she learns someone else has been using the cabin to hide out too, she'll find herself stuck with a shady, surprise roommate for the summer. While they figure out how to get along, they'll learn their stories were intertwined long before they met. *Enemy Closer* is a suspense thriller that allows you to experience each new piece of information along with the characters right to the end, when you realize everything you thought you knew was a lie. A deeper story has only just begun to unfold.

Book 2: House on Fire

Thanks to her boss, shady FBI Agent Jim Camposanto, Analyst Anna Bowman finds herself the target of two different international criminal cabals. With no obvious way out of the mess she's just beginning to understand, she'll have to drag the truth out of her secretive boss and a hitman who just can't seem to shake her. Will Anna ever get to relax and feel safe with her beloved German Shepherd, Dude, or will she become addicted to Camposanto's dangerous games? Anna Bowman's misadventures continue in *House on Fire.*

Book 3: Bigger Fish

Home from her unlikely triumph in Argentina, Anna thinks her life is getting back to normal until a surprise visit from David March—and sets her on a collision course with Luke Jackson once again. With a little help from two people straight out of Anna's past, they'll unravel a mystery that takes them out of the frying pan and into the fire.

Book 4: No Port in a Storm

After unraveling a murderous family feud, FBI castoffs Anna and Jim travel to Italy to deliver a final peace offering. Amidst their fraught romance, they find no shortage of ways to make new trouble. While fostering unlikely friendships against an idyllic Mediterranean backdrop, they provoke dangerous enemies closer to home. Emily, Luke, and Dude were supposed to be safe in Texas, but suddenly they're in the crosshairs again. As tensions escalate, Jim's clever schemes are put to the test. When generations of hostility erupt into all-out war, will Jim's cunning save them, or will Anna's fighting spirit be their only way out?

▼

Coming soon from AK Weller

<u>2.15.2020</u>

In the prequel to *Enemy Closer*, Anna Bowman escapes her boring hometown and joins the FBI. After a few years as a quiet but efficient cog in the machine, she tries to achieve her childhood dream of becoming an FBI Agent, only to be rejected and bewildered. Ensnared instead in the intrigues of Agent James Camposanto, Anna will embark on an unexpected assignment in Houston, Texas with her protégé, Thomas Holladay. What really happened on February 15, 2020, in Houston, and how in the world did a divorced art historian from Manchester, Texas end up there?

<u>Friday the 14th</u>

Anna Bowman and her older sister, Emily, just wanted a fun night out to celebrate Anna's twenty-fifth birthday. While enjoying some much-needed time away from their significant others, the sisters accidentally pick up a new friend at a casino in Oklahoma. When a tongue-in-cheek plan to burn down each other's houses and collect the insurance money falls into the wrong hands, Anna and Emily will have to band together to stop an arsonist… if they decide they want to. Find out who's left standing on *Friday the 14th*.

A Last Time for Everything

A Last Time for Everything tells the tragic and unbelievable origin story of 17-year-old Anna Bowman and the events that set her on the path to joining the FBI.

Sam Walsh, PI Mysteries

Prequel - Tiger by the Tail

Private Investigator Samantha Walsh has been in denial about her true identity for 25 years. When a terrifying figure from her past explodes back into her life, Sam will have to decide how much she's willing to sacrifice to stop running from her father's killers in *Tiger by the Tail*.

#1 - Sam vs. the Black Hat

Newly independent PI Sam Walsh needs clients, and she can't afford to be picky. When her old boss sends a prospective client her way, Sam takes the case - a classic cheating spouse - against her better judgment. Caught between a dishonest client and a dangerous, shadowy foe, Sam will either solve her first case or die trying. Sue Grafton's iconic Kinsey Millhone is catapulted into twenty-first century Texas suburbia in book one of the Sam Walsh, PI Mysteries.

Short Stories

<u>Underworld: A Short Suspense Thriller</u>

Underworld follows mystery woman Seffy Nix as she moves into a 140-year-old mansion that seems to be haunted by a slovenly, inconsiderate ghost bent on distracting her from the mission that brought her to small-town Helena, Montana.

<u>The Beast and the Books: A Short Monster Story</u>

All alone one night, Rodney is clearing out a storage unit. His biggest problem is his wife's massive book collection, at least until the lights go out and he realizes he's not alone. Something is living deep in the bowels of the storage facility, and it's about to make a break for freedom. Unfortunately for Rodney, he's right in the creature's path.

<u>Anywhere But Home: A Memoir</u>

A short memoir about budding author AK Weller's increasingly nonsensical attempts to fill a void in her life caused by an abusive relationship. From Oklahoma to Texas to Colorado, she hops from one distraction to another until she realizes the answer to her problem is starting over.

332

High school junior Miguel thought getting an underage drinking charge would derail his life at New Mexico Military Institute in Roswell, but when his new friends draw him into their world of pranks and mischief, he'll discover there's a lot more going on at NMMI than he ever imagined. Will Miguel maintain his hard-won GPA and graduate with a diploma that will open doors for him to wherever he wants to go, all while learning how to mix a little fun into his busy life? Will his new friends have his back when things start to get spooky?

▼

Keep turning for a sneak peak at the next
chapter of Anna's story: *Moth Island.*

1

Saturday, April 1, 2023

Joint Base Andrews, Maryland

Have you ever had one of those moments that forces you to stop, look around yourself, take it all in, and ask: How in the world did I end up here?

When the C-17's wheels met the ground, the whole plane and everyone in it, including me, gave one great, teeth-rattling bounce. I closed my eyes.

The young airmen around me were all whooping and chattering, their collective volume nearly drowning out the drone of the engines and the squeal of rubber. A tsunami of sound crashed through the interior of the cargo plane, accompanied by a sudden, violent deceleration that nearly flung me into my neighbor's lap. Only the harness around my shoulders and hips kept me in my seat.

I opened my eyes to see the other passengers' mouths moving, still cheering and carrying on. I couldn't hear anything but the deafening roar of air around the plane. How could they hear themselves, let alone each other?

No one was paying me any mind as we bumped along the runway, losing speed more gradually now. I felt so apart from the grinning, laughing, uniformed men and women that I might as well have been a different species. There I sat, shivering in my borrowed USAF PT outfit, trying to remember how old I was, wondering when I could go home and where home even was—and that was when it hit me.

How did I end up here?

Almost two years ago, I'd woken up in a hospital bed in Cagliari, Sardinia and decided to accept the biggest challenge of my life. Now I was done, I was home, and the intervening months were already blurring together. A rapid mental review revealed long stretches of time where I couldn't recall exactly what I'd done, and important events that I couldn't match up with any specific date.

I wished I could return to that hospital room in July 2021 and tell myself to pay more attention to what day it was.

The C-17 taxied for so long that I started to worry we'd just take off again. This was all a cruel joke, and I was going to end up right back in Italy to deal with the consequences of my actions. Only the continued smiles on the faces around me convinced me I could relax and stop fearing the worst. Sound levels slowly returned to normal, and at last we came to a lurching stop. The fuselage was filled with metallic clicks as a hundred people began removing their harnesses at the same time. I figured it was safe for me to follow suit.

Everyone stood, stretched, and started freeing their luggage from the racks above their heads. Since I had no luggage, I inched toward the rear of the plane. There was probably a pecking order dictating who was allowed off the cargo plane first, but I was prepared to violate all sorts of unwritten rules to reunite my feet with the earth as soon as humanly possible.

I found a painted line that ran across the floor and up the wall to a sign that read, "WAIT HERE FOR AFT RAMP DOOR TO OPEN." I was going to miss the clear, simple instructions I'd been able to follow since arriving at Ramstein Air Base in Germany yesterday. At least, I was pretty sure that was yesterday.

I placed my toes just across this magic line and waited. People began crowding behind me, jostling with one another to be closer to the exit.

The young airman who'd been sitting next to me sidled up behind me and said, "Watch out, Diana. You're over the line. People have been executed for less."

I didn't know why he was calling me Diana, and at that point I didn't care to ask again. I took a full step forward and said, "I'm a civilian. I'll do what I want."

"Aha!" he exclaimed. "I knew it. Gotta be CIA. That's okay, I know you can't tell me."

With a scream of machinery, the aft ramp door started to open, its hinge less than an inch from my toes. Someone with a booming radio voice took it upon himself to announce, "Ladies and gentlemen, welcome to Joint Base Andrews. Local time is seven twenty a.m., and the temperature on the ground is a balmy two million degrees. Please remember to take all your worthless, smelly crap with you when exiting the plane. Thank you for flying Air Force Air. We know you had no choice in the matter, and it shows."

Appreciative laughter followed. Even I let a smile creep onto my face, but it faltered as the door clanged to the ground and I saw what was waiting for us on the tarmac.

Something told me the besuited bald man with cheap sunglasses and an expensive, poorly-concealed sidearm wasn't there for any of the airmen. I started down the ramp toward him, and he removed his sunglasses to fix me with an evaluating, carefully neutral expression.

When I was close enough, he asked, "Anna Bowman?"

I was tempted to shake my head and keep walking, but I knew he knew who I was. I stopped a yard from him and was about to answer when someone slapped me on the back—hard.

"Hey, Diana, your real name is Anna! I was pretty close, huh?"

"Uncanny," I replied. I waved, he waved back, and then he was gone.

The bald man didn't say a word until the last person to file past us was out of earshot. Finally, "Miss Bowman, I'm U.S. Marshal Gary Pleasant. I'm here to escort you to the FBI."

Though I shook his outstretched hand, I argued, "Can't I go home first? I need a shower, and…" I trailed into defeated silence. His expression was not encouraging.

"I'm afraid that's not possible. My instructions were to transport you to the FBI without delay."

"What's the big emergency?"

"I haven't been given that information. If you'll follow me, I have a car waiting."

Since I clearly didn't have a say in the matter, I didn't say anything. I followed the marshal to a black SUV parked next to a fuel truck near the nose of the still-idling C-17. The sound of the engines was cut off abruptly when Pleasant shut me into the back seat. I hadn't noticed until then how loud it was on the tarmac.

He climbed into the driver's seat, and away we went. Once we were off the tarmac and had shuffled into traffic on a normal road, he switched on the AC and glanced at me in the rear view mirror.

"Getting any air back there?"

"No. I don't need any. I'm still thawing out."

"Okay."

He didn't speak again until we stopped in front of the J. Edgar Hoover building in Washington, DC. The silent half hour had not been enjoyable. My mind had skipped from one wild idea to the next, desperate to prepare me for what was waiting for me at the FBI. I felt like I was in trouble, or I was about to be—but for what? Had my sister done something crazy again? Had my mission been deemed a failure, and my fault at that? Was I about to learn some terrible news that had to be given to me inside a cleared facility?

That last possibility was almost too terrifying to consider.

I had expected my boss, FBI Agent James Camposanto, to be waiting for me where Pleasant had been standing. Had something happened to him?

Ushered inside by Pleasant, I shuddered in the too-cool air and tried not to meet anyone's eyes. The FBI wasn't as crowded as it would be on a weekday, but there were still plenty of important-looking people to gawk at me. I looked like a prisoner in my sweat pants, t-shirt, and tousled hair, and I halfway wondered whether I was a prisoner. At least I wasn't in cuffs. I did have to wear a visitor badge which proclaimed in huge, red, bold letters that I wasn't allowed out of sight of a cleared escort.

But Jim still wasn't there. All the way up to the sixth floor to the open door of a conference room, his continued absence gnawed at me. Jim should have been tearing apart the C-17 to get to me the moment it touched the ground, but he wasn't even at the FBI. Either he couldn't get to me, or he didn't know where I was. I refused to consider any other explanation.

I entered the room at Pleasant's instruction, but he didn't follow me inside. Seven people were already seated around the boat-sized conference table. Only one looked at me.

A lean man with short, grey hair and excellent posture threw me a steely smile and motioned toward a seat at the opposite end of the table, as far from the door as possible.

"Miss Bowman, good morning. Please have a seat. Can I get you anything? Water, coffee?"

Before answering, I twisted around to look for Pleasant. He'd vanished without a word.

I said, "I just want to know why I'm here. Where's Agent

Camposanto? Am I in some kind of trouble?"

He ignored everything but my last question. "You are not in trouble, but I'm afraid your debriefing can't wait. Please sit down."

The Anna Bowman who joined the FBI in 2016 would have already been sitting down, saving this stern authority figure the trouble of repeating himself. I, however, was a bit less agreeable.

I planted my feet shoulder width apart, crossed my arms, and said, "It's a meat locker in here. If you want to debrief me, turn up the heat or get me a sweater."

I waited until one woman had gotten up from her seat, adjusted the thermostat, and sat back down before I unwound my arms and headed for the empty chair—the hot seat.

The same woman turned on a recording device in the center of the table, leaned toward it, and said, "Please state your full name."

"Anna Claire Bowman."

"Okay, Anna. Let's go back to twenty twenty-one."

9 798991 630832